Lg. read - good

W. Co.
SH

TELL ME MORE

"Talk to me, Tanner."

"It's too late for talk, Callie."

"No. There are things I need to say." Hardly able to speak, Callie whispered in a shaky voice, "You weren't what I expected when I first saw you. I was surprised. The town. . .everybody says you're wild. . .crazy. . .that it'd be hard to know what you're going to do next. I didn't believe it until I saw what you did to Billy Joe."

"I don't want to talk about it."

"Tanner. . .please."

"What do you want to hear, Callie?" Tanner's breathing was labored. "Do you want me to tell you that the first time I saw you when you came running out of the Roundup, something twisted tight inside me? Do you want to hear that even though the last thing I needed was another complication in my life, I couldn't let you walk away?"

"Yes." Callie's voice was a frantic whisper. "Tell me—"

"More?" Tanner's short laugh was caustic. "I'll tell you that I know better than this. . .better than to let something like this happen when I should be concentrating on finding a way to fix everything that's gone wrong from the first day I came back to the Circle M. But instead, I'm looking into your eyes and trying to make myself believe that you came all the way out here just because you couldn't stay away from me."

SECRET FIRES

The Wild One

Elaine Barbieri

LEISURE BOOKS NEW YORK CITY

To Mike and Diane and the new life you've begun together.
Much love to you both always.

A LEISURE BOOK®

February 2001

Published by

Dorchester Publishing Co., Inc.
276 Fifth Avenue
New York, NY 10001

ISBN 0-8439-4826-4

SECRET FIRES

The Wild One

(Book I)
The Wild One

Prologue

1881

"You want me, Tanner." Clare clung to him, her voice quaking with passion. "You want me as much as I want you."

Beautiful Clare. The shadows of the dimly lit hallway did not conceal the hunger in her eyes as she pressed herself against him. Her flawless skin was flushed and her lips were parted. Her unbound hair streamed onto the shoulders of her robe, a golden halo that illuminated small, perfect features. The bedroom door was ajar behind her, revealing a rumpled bed that seemed to beckon. It would be so easy . . .

Beautiful Clare, with the face of an angel *and the soul of a devil*.

Tanner grated, "You're wasting your time."

"Don't be a fool, Tanner!" Clinging tenaciously as Tanner attempted to dislodge the arms she had clasped around his neck, Clare whispered, "I wanted you the first moment I saw you. You felt the same way. I knew it then, and I know it now. It'll be good between us . . . better than good. It'll be—"

"You'd like that, wouldn't you . . . *Ma?*"

"I'm not your ma!"

"No, you're my *stepmother*." Jerking himself free of Clare's embrace, Tanner took a backward step. "Pa kept a lot of women behind my ma's back over the years—young women, beautiful women. We all knew about them, but we pretended we didn't, for Ma's sake. We figured that you weren't any different from the rest of them at first, but you were different, all right. None of those other women had Pa wrapped so tight around her finger that she could've talked Pa into marrying her and bringing her back to live at the Circle M *a week* after my ma died."

"That doesn't have anything to do with us, Tanner."

"Doesn't it?"

"Your pa got what he wanted, that's all. Now it's time for me to get what I want."

"What do you really want, Clare?"

"I want you, Tanner." A steely determination flashed in Clare's gaze, contrasting sharply with her delicate beauty as she said, "I can make you happy. I can make you happier than you've ever been in your life. I want to show you how good I can make you feel." She pressed herself more tightly against him, her voice husky. "Let me show you."

Clare lifted her mouth to his, and Tanner pushed her away with disgust. He reached out too late to steady her as she staggered backward unexpectedly and struck her head against the wall with a harsh crack.

"Bastard!" Fury replacing the passion in her pale eyes, Clare jerked herself free of Tanner's stabilizing grip and hissed, "You'll be sorry for that!"

Hearing familiar footsteps in the hallway below, Clare glared at him with true malice, then cried out unexpectedly, "Tanner, leave me alone! Tanner, please, let me go!"

The heavy footsteps pounded up the stairs. Tall and well-muscled despite his age, Tom McBride stepped up onto the landing. Breathing hard, he demanded, "What's going on here?"

He seemed to swell with rage at the sight of his young wife's tear-stained cheeks, her disheveled state, and the hand she clutched to a bump on the side of her head; McBride did not wait for a response. He rounded on Tanner without a word and connected squarely with a blow to his son's jaw that sent him sprawling. Standing over him, he then rasped, "You didn't expect me to come back from town so soon, did you? You figured you had all the time you needed for your little games—but you were wrong!"

Shuddering with wrath, McBride leaned toward him to continue in a hiss, "I should've expected you to try something like this. You've been nothing but trouble since the day you were born. Your ma spoiled you—always standing up for you no matter what you did—but she's not here to protect you now, and this time you're going to get what's coming to you." McBride took a shaky breath. "Listen to me, Tanner, and listen good. You've gone too far this time. As far as I'm concerned, you're not my son anymore. You're a stranger—an unwanted stranger. I want you off this ranch tonight! If you show your face around here again, I'll come after you with my gun!"

McBride straightened up and turned back to his sobbing bride. Gathering her tenderly into his arms, he drew her toward their room.

Tanner's stomach twisted with nausea as the

door closed behind them. Tender . . . his pa was tender with a scheming whore when he had never given his loyal wife of twenty-five years anything but grief! Tender . . . yet he hadn't blinked when serving his dead wife the final insult of bringing a lying witch home to take her place on the Texas ranch she had loved.

His jaw throbbing and his contempt boundless, Tanner stood up and started toward his room.

"Don't leave me here alone, Tanner!" Lauren McBride's fiery hair was in marked contrast with the sudden blanching of her freckled cheeks as she stared at her brother in alarm. She had returned home to find Tanner packing to leave the Circle M forever, while Stone McBride stood nearby in disapproving silence. But it didn't matter to her what Stone thought. Her older brother always disapproved of everything Tanner did, just as he always disapproved of her because she stood up for Tanner. He couldn't seem to understand that Tanner wasn't only a brother. He was her best friend.

Panicking when Tanner continued to stuff his belongings into a sack without responding, Lauren pleaded again, "You can't leave. You promised you wouldn't. You promised you'd never leave me by myself to face that woman Pa brought home!"

"Let him go, Lauren." Stone McBride's face was expressionless, but his tone was harsh with rebuke as he addressed his sister stiffly. "You should've learned by now that what Tanner says and what he actually does are two different things."

Looking up at his brother, Tanner snapped, "You and Pa . . . you look alike, and you think alike."

"I may look like Pa, but I don't think like him. And I'm *nothing* like him."

"Aren't you?"

"You'd like to believe that, wouldn't you?" Uncharacteristic anger flashed in Stone's eyes as he took an aggressive step. "Then you'd feel better about what happened to Ma—but I'm not going to let you salve your conscience at my expense."

"What happened to Ma wasn't my fault!"

"Wasn't it?"

Tanner's sun-darkened skin paled. "Yeah, you're like Pa, all right."

Stepping between her brothers, Lauren turned on Stone and commanded, "Stop it! Just because you're the oldest, you think you have special rights in this family, but you don't. I'm sick and tired of seeing you and Pa blame everything that goes wrong around here on Tanner."

"And I'm sick and tired of seeing you believe every damned lie Tanner tells you. Well, I'm going to make sure he tells you the truth this time." Turning to Tanner, Stone commanded, "Tell her, Tanner. Tell her why Pa ordered you off the ranch. Tell her that you couldn't keep your hands off that blond whore Pa married, even though you know what she is."

"Tanner wouldn't do that. He wouldn't go near that woman!" Facing Tanner, Lauren demanded, "Tell Stone it isn't true. Tell him you'd never have anything to do with Clare because you hate her as much as I do!"

"He wouldn't believe a word I say. He's already made up his mind what he wants to believe."

"*I* believe you, Tanner." Lauren's youthful face grew pained. "I don't care what Stone says, or what anybody else says. I'll always believe you."

"And he'll disappoint you every time—just like he's going to disappoint you now."

"Don't listen to Stone!" Lauren gripped Tanner's arm. "I know you won't go away and leave me behind."

"Lauren, honey . . ." The lump of pain inside Tanner squeezed tight. "I can't take you with me. You're only fourteen years old, and I don't even know where I'm going from here."

15

"You have to take me with you!" Tears suddenly falling, Lauren begged, "Please, Tanner. I can't stay here. Pa doesn't care about me. Stone doesn't like me any more than he likes you—and Clare *hates* me! You're all I have left!"

"I can't take you with me, Lauren."

"Listen to what Tanner's really saying, Lauren." Stone's strong features tightened. "He's being truthful with you for the first time in his life. He's saying that he's leaving here without you, and none of the promises he ever made to you are worth a damn."

"No, he isn't!" Sobbing, Lauren shook Tanner's arm. "You're not saying that, are you, Tanner?"

Aching at his sister's torment, Tanner rasped, "You're a bastard, Stone. Just like Pa."

"Tanner . . . please."

Sliding his arm around Lauren's shoulders, Stone growled, "Get out of here, Tanner. Get out while the getting's good. I'll take care of Lauren." Frowning when his sister shrugged off his touch, he continued, "Lauren won't let herself believe what I'm saying, but the truth is, none of this would've happened if it wasn't for you. Ma would still be alive, that blond witch wouldn't be sitting in her place, and Lauren wouldn't be crying her heart out because she's learning the hard

way that all you're ever good for is empty promises."

"That's not true!"

"Isn't it?"

"Bastard—"

"Tell her the truth once and for all, Tanner,
and put her out of her misery."

Standing eye-to-eye with his older brother,
Tanner spat, "You're determined to make Lauren hate me, aren't you?"

"I'm determined to make her face the truth."

Turning back to his sobbing sister, Tanner
whispered, "The truth is that I'm leaving, Lauren. If I don't go now, something bad's going to
happen here."

"If you leave without me, Tanner, I'll never
forgive you."

"I'll write to you."

"No!"

"Lauren, honey—"

Lauren's pale face went suddenly still. "So it's
true, after all. You're not taking me with you."

"I can't."

"I hate you, Tanner." Lauren's voice became a
hoarse whisper. "I hate you more than I ever
loved you, and I never want to see you again."

Tanner was motionless as Lauren walked
stiffly from the room; then he looked back at

Stone to say with bitter finality, "Yeah . . . you're just like Pa."

Throwing his bag across the saddle minutes later, Tanner mounted. As he spurred his horse into motion, he was deaf to the voices of the past and blind to all but a sworn determination to leave the Circle M forever behind him.

"What are you looking at, Clare?"

Tom McBride's callused hand closed on Clare's shoulder. Releasing the lace curtain she had pulled aside for a clearer view of the yard and the departing horseman, Clare turned to face her husband. The master bedroom where Tom McBride had spent the last hour attempting to quiet her tears was shadowy in the failing light of day. Well aware of the picture she presented—smooth skin pale, eyelids red, the delicate planes of her cheeks stained by tears that still fell intermittently—she gave a shuddering sigh.

"Tanner's leaving, Tom."

"Good riddance to him!" McBride's lined face tightened. "I always knew this would happen one day. I'm just sorry that you had to suffer because of it."

"I'm so sorry, Tom." Clare stepped into McBride's arms. She laid her head against his chest as his arms closed around her and whispered, "I . . . I tried to hide what was happening from you. I didn't want you to know."

Holding her away from him abruptly, Mc-Bride stared down into Clare's face. "What are you saying?"

"Tanner . . . he was after me almost from the first day I came to the ranch. I tried to hold him off, but he started getting rough. I didn't know what to do."

"Son of a—"

"Please, Tom, I don't want you to get excited." Clare's smooth face creased with distress. "I wouldn't be telling you this even now, except . . . well, I didn't want you to feel guilty."

"Guilty? Let me tell you something, Clare." Drawing her closer so that his mouth was only inches from hers, Tom rasped, "There was never a day in my life that I felt guilty for anything I needed to do. I've lived my life one way—*my* way. I work hard and I play hard. I know what I want, and I get it. And I don't make any excuses. I've never wanted a woman as much as I want you, and I won't let anybody or anything stand in my way. I never had a jealous bone in my body until I met you, because I never cared enough. But I care about you, Clare. I'm going to take care of you, too, and it doesn't matter a damn to me who suffers if he gets in the way."

"But Tanner's your son."

"No, he isn't. Not anymore."

"I'm sorry." Clare stepped back into his arms, and McBride clasped her tightly to him. His breath was warm against her ear as he whispered, "Nobody means more to me than you do, Clare. Nobody."

Turning toward those words, Clare offered him her lips. She slid her arms around his neck when he crushed her mouth with his. She felt his probing tongue and allowed him access to her mouth. She withheld a grimace of revulsion as his kiss drove deeper, as he scooped her up into his arms and carried her to the bed. She gasped as his body moved hotly against hers. She gave a practiced ecstatic cry when he entered her and drove himself home. His grunting sounds of mating deepened, and she closed her eyes, clutching him tight, feigning her passion as her thoughts raged with his rhythmic thrusts.

Tanner should be lying with her now.

Tanner, not this old man!

Tanner, who had complicated her plans.

Tanner, whom she was determined to have.

Tanner, who—

A grunt. A shudder. Completion. McBride raised himself above her in the stillness that followed. He cupped her cheek with his palm, then whispered, "I love you, Clare. I . . . I've never said that to a woman before."

Clare's attempted response was muted by his kiss and she wound her arms around McBride's neck. Indulging him as his passionate forays continued, she remained silently resolved.

Tanner—who would not escape her.

Legacy: Tanner

Chapter One

1886

Tanner McBride opened his eyes to the semi-darkness of the jail cell. He squinted out at the brightly lit sheriff's office through a connecting door left partly ajar. He muttered a low, scoffing sound at the sight of the man seated at the desk, studying a pile of Wanted notices with determined intensity.

The tin star on Sheriff Glennan's chest glinted in the light, and Tanner turned away with a bitter smile. The sheriff was wasting his time if he expected to find his picture on a Wanted poster. As for the bank robbery for which he had been arrested, well, the sheriff would find out the truth about that sooner or later.

Tanner slid an unsteady hand through the thick, dark hair that brushed his shoulders, then rubbed his hand against his heavily-bearded cheek. It occurred to him that he would probably be unrecognizable as the man he once was if not for the McBride-blue eyes that somehow appeared even more piercing in contrast with his unshaven state. But those arresting, silver-blue eyes that so clearly declared his paternal parentage were presently bloodshot and burning; his strong features, hardly discernable underneath his ragged beard, were drawn into a frown; and the smile that had once melted many a feminine heart was nowhere in evidence.

Tanner adjusted his lank, tightly muscled frame against the hard cot beneath him in an attempt to ease his discomfort, but the effort was useless. The cot was as hard as a rock, his head was pounding, and every bone in his body ached.

Visions of an empty bottle of red-eye, and of his own, shaky hand raising that last drink to his lips flashed before his eyes, and Tanner's stomach did a nauseating flip-flop. He had little memory of the previous evening, except for his determination to forget the letter he had received that afternoon and all the harsh memories it evoked. Unfortunately, like too many similar efforts in the past, it had failed.

Despite himself, Tanner reached into his pants pocket and withdrew the sheet of crumpled paper.

Despite himself, Tanner read the letter again.

Dear Mr. McBride:

In accordance with instructions contained in the last will and testament of Thomas J. McBride, dictated to me and dutifully signed and witnessed on this date, the fifth of March, in the year of our Lord 1886, I am forwarding this letter to all potential heirs to his estate so they may be informed of the conditions for inheritance prescribed in the above legal document.

It is the intention of your father, Thomas J. McBride, to bequeath equal shares of the Circle M Ranch and all his remaining assets to each of his progeny, and to his wife, Clare Brown McBride. Mr. McBride has stipulated, however, that in order to be eligible for this bequest, his progeny must present themselves at the Circle M Ranch no later than nine months from the date of this letter; to remain there pending the arrival of the other heirs, at which time the details of the inheritance will be specified. Those of his progeny who do not appear within that period will forfeit their shares of the estate. The forfeited shares will then be added to the award of Clare Brown McBride.

Thomas McBride has made it clear that no exceptions will be made to the conditions he has outlined.

The official business of this letter concluded, I feel it is my duty as solicitor to the estate and longstanding friend of the McBride family, to include the information that Thomas McBride is gravely ill, that his condition has been pronounced terminal, and that he is not expected to live out the year.

Hoping to see this matter drawn to a conclusion that is satisfactory to all, I remain,

Yours most sincerely,
William Benton Hanes, Esq.

Tanner stared at the neatly drafted sheet in his hand.

Gravely ill. Not expected to live out the year.

The old bastard was dying and wanted him to come home.

Forcing himself to consider that thought for a

long, silent moment, Tanner then crushed the letter in a savage fist and tossed it across the cell. He watched as it settled in a dusty corner, and then spoke aloud a response that came from the bottom of his heart.

"Not a chance."

"All right, McBride, you're free to go, but you're not out of this by a long shot." Sheriff Glennan's thick handlebar mustache twitched with agitation as he slapped Tanner's gunbelt down on the desk and spat, "You're as guilty as the rest of those fellas that shot up the bank, even if you were too drunk to get away like they did."

"I didn't have anything to do with that robbery, Sheriff."

"You were in on the planning the night before the robbery. You were holding the horses in the alley while the others were in the bank."

"Sheriff—"

"Everybody in town heard you and that Terry Malone in the saloon the night before the robbery, joking about how rich you were going be real soon."

"Sure."

"And Barney Martin saw you holding those horses' reins while Malone and the other two fellas were shooting up the bank."

"Whatever you say, Sheriff."

Sheriff Glennan poked his jowled face forward and spat, "Matt Logan was a good man! He was working hard to get his ranch back on its feet, and I don't intend to let his killers go free!"

Tanner did not respond.

"You're a cold-hearted bastard, aren't you, McBride?"

"I didn't have anything to do with that bank robbery."

Sheriff Glennan's face grew apoplectic. "You think you're smart. You think the law can't do anything to you because you weren't *in* the bank during the robbery. Well, maybe I can't keep you in jail now, but when I catch Malone and the two others, and when they get done talking, I'll be putting you right back in that cell with them, where you belong."

"Whatever you say."

"So keep looking over your shoulder, McBride, because one of these days, you'll see me coming after you."

Not bothering to respond, Tanner buckled on his gunbelt and left Sheriff Glennan behind him.

Tanner kept his mount to a steady pace along the trail. The sun was setting in glorious shades of yellow and gold, yet the heat of the spring day lingered. He had been riding for hours in the direct sun, which had only increased the physical discomfort in which he had awakened that morning. He was hot, sweaty, and intensely aware that he needed a bath. He hadn't taken the time to bathe before leaving Sheriff Glennan and the town far behind him. His stomach was rumbling loudly, and he realized he hadn't taken the time to eat, either.

Frowning, Tanner glanced again at the sky and at the sun, which was dropping rapidly into the horizon. He had gotten as far away as he could from the mess that he had left behind him. If he didn't stop soon, he'd be making camp in the dark.

Dismounting minutes later, he walked to the nearby stream and kneeled beside the rippling water. He leaned toward it and grunted when the throbbing in his head began again. Damn that Terry Malone! Terry had been the worst possible person to show up so unexpectedly in that saloon, at a time when he was sitting with his pa's last will and testament in his pocket, and with the weight of unwanted memories on his mind.

Terry Malone, big, brawny and always ready for trouble, had been just the traveling partner

Tanner was looking for that first year after he left the Circle M and made the decision to leave Texas far behind him. They had headed west, and the trouble they had stirred up wherever they went, and the laughter that followed, had been the perfect medicine to help him forget the events of that last day at the Circle M. They had been two peas in a pod, Terry and him—until the day when he had stepped back and gotten a clear look at Terry, and an even clearer look at himself. That was the day when the laughter had stopped, when he had tipped his hat to Terry, and had gone his own way. In the aimless years since, he had had no regrets in making that decision.

But the truth was that despite his denials to the sheriff, he wasn't really sure what happened after Terry sat down at his table and helped him polish off that first bottle of red-eye. He remembered that at one point during the evening, he had pulled the letter from William Benton Hanes, Esq. out of his pocket and shoved it in Terry's face, and he remembered that Terry had laughed and said he'd be happy to go back to the Circle M with him so they could both be rich.

Strangely, he didn't remember much else after finding himself standing in the narrow alleyway beside the bank, with shots ringing out only moments before Terry and two others came running toward him, moneybags in hand. He remembered that Terry had laughed at his startled expression before he and the two others jumped on their horses and rode off. Within seconds, Tanner was mounted and following behind them, but it was already too late.

Terry and the other two got away. He didn't.

Tanner frowned as he glimpsed his reflection in the stream. Plunging his head down into the ripples with disgust, he held it there until his lungs were bursting, then sat back on his heels, gasping for breath. Still dripping, he reached again into his pocket for the letter he had retrieved from the dusty corner of his cell. It was too dark to read the words, but that didn't matter. He had the letter memorized.

Gravely ill. Not expected to live out the year.

The old bastard.

The forfeited shares will then be added to the award of Clare Brown McBride.

To the award of beautiful, vicious Clare . . .

Chapter Two

The day was unusually hot and getting hotter. Tanner lifted his hat from his head and wiped the perspiration from his forehead with the back of his arm as his mount moved steadily forward. He raked his fingers through freshly cut hair that adhered wetly to his scalp, his expression solemn as he perused the surrounding terrain. There was nothing quite like the look of the Texas prairie in spring, when the range was green with new grass, when leaf buds on the post oaks and blackjacks were swelled to bursting, and the lacy foliage of the mesquite fluttered in the breeze.

A fleeting smile touched Tanner's lips when he remembered Ma's pride in the land. Ma, so slight, with red hair that curled with a life of its own, with pale skin that freckled in the sun, and with a love that never faltered in her brown eyes. Her love was never clearer nor her smile brighter than when her children were young and she would halt the wagon midway to town, at a point where McBride land extended as far as the eye could see, so she could point out the brilliant blues and yellows of the bluebonnets and wild mustard that dotted the hillsides, and the scattering of white prickly poppy and scarlet Indian paintbrush in between. He recalled the tremor in her voice when she said that her heart always came to life with the bluebonnets in the spring, and that her greatest joy was in knowing that long after she was gone, the land she loved would belong to her children.

As he grew older, the blooming of wildflowers meant to him that spring roundup would again begin with the call of the meadowlark at dawn, and end with the evening whistle of the whippoorwill as the cattle bedded down for the night. He remembered that he had paid little attention to the colors of the hillside, which were muted by clouds of dust while driving a herd, and which were obscured by wavering shadows on long night watches while he sang off-key to restless beeves. Yet it was suddenly clear to him that those colors, scents, and sounds, those long days and endless nights, were a part of him that years of absence could never erase.

Other, equally vivid memories returned, and Tanner's smile vanished. He saw Ma's hand trembling as another day waned and Pa again failed to return home for the night. He remembered that on those many occasions, she continued her work, serving the ranch hands their evening meal with a smile that was unnaturally bright. He recalled Stone's tight expression when he was still too young to understand the reason for the brief, heated flare-ups between Ma and Pa that followed Pa's unexplained absences—arguments which inevitably ended with his father turning his back on his mother while she held back tears. He had often worn the same expression as Stone when he grew older, and his smile became as forced as Ma's when Lauren started looking up at him with a question in her eyes as well.

Tanner's roaming gaze halted on a lone tree in the distance, a solitary sentinel that jutted upward toward the cloudless blue sky. He had felt as alone as that tree when childhood ended. With Stone growing more remote with every passing year, he tried to spare his ma and Lauren by pretending nothing was wrong, but he knew in his heart that Tom McBride hardly cared they existed. Resentful and rebellious, unwilling to accept a situation over which he had little control, Tanner had challenged his pa at every turn—and the war between them had begun. Pa had been right that last day when he'd said that Ma always stood up for him. He suspected that those times when she faced Pa down on his behalf had allowed her the only true satisfaction she ever received when confronting her husband—but those clashes resulted in another problem. Stone had disapproved of the conflict Tanner caused, and the friction between them had heightened.

A brief breeze cooled Tanner's brow, returning him to the present. His reflection in the stream that day had been sobering. In it, he had seen the face of a man he had never expected to be—a man who had allowed circumstances to shape him into someone he no longer recognized—or respected. That man had been aimless too long.

In that moment of sudden clarity, the last of Tanner's youthful rebellion had faded. In its place had risen a mature resolve that grew stronger and clearer with each mile he now traveled.

Yes. He was going home.

"A ticket to Sidewinder, Texas, please."

"Where did you say you wanted to go, ma'am?"

"Sidewinder, Texas."

"Are you sure about that?"

The afternoon sun beat with unrelenting heat on the narrow, rutted street beyond the otherwise deserted stage depot where Callie stood. Behind a high, official-looking desk, a thin, balding clerk stared at her over small glasses perched at the end of a large nose. His eyebrows jumped upward almost comically as she replied without a smile, "I'm sure."

"Got friends there, ma'am?"

Callie's gaze grew frigid. She had been traveling for days. Impatient, tired, and soot-stained, she had stepped down from a railroad car that had left no part of her unbruised, in a town that was little more than a bump along an endless stretch of rails, with the knowledge that her journey was far from its end. She was in no mood for the speculative stare of an inquisitive stranger.

The clerk's gaze narrowed when she did not respond. Eyeing her from head to toe, he assessed the straight, brown brows over her unfriendly, honey-colored eyes; the clear, sun-tinted skin drawn smoothly over her high cheek-bones; the brown hair streaked with gold that she wore tied simply at the nape of her neck. He appeared to note with particular approval the womanly curves under the plain traveling clothes she wore. He commented abruptly, "You don't look like a fancy woman to me."

A fancy woman . . .

"Them's the only kind of woman that travels alone to Sidewinder nowadays." When Callie remained silent, he continued, "Sidewinder was a quiet enough town years back, but it's changed of late. Women from the outlying ranches still come in to do their shopping during the day, and to go to church on Sunday, but for the most part, there ain't much more there than a long line of saloons that cater to wranglers out to have a good time. A pretty young woman like you wouldn't be safe in a place like that all alone."

"I can take care of myself."

"That ain't the point. People are going to think—"

Slapping a handful of coins on the desk with a sound that reverberated loudly, Callie snapped, "I asked for a ticket to Sidewinder, Texas, not a lecture."

"Yes, ma'am, a ticket to Sidewinder it is!" A revealing flush tinted his face as he pushed a ticket in her direction. "The stage leaves in an hour—and it don't wait for nobody!"

Frowning, Callie picked up her case and walked out onto the street. She paused in contemplation. So Sidewinder, Texas, was a town with a reputation. She had expected as much, but what she hadn't expected was that her appearance would cause outright speculation as to her reason for going there. The nosy clerk had done her a service.

An hour. She didn't have much time.

Walking briskly back toward the stage depot an hour later, Callie ignored the gulping cough of the clerk who observed her approach from the office doorway. She forced her rouged lips into a coy smile when a buckskin-clad passenger stepped down from the stage, extended his hand to her with an elaborate flourish, and said, "The clerk said I was going to have a lady passenger for company on this trip, but I got to say that I wasn't expecting nothing as pretty as you. It's a pleasure and a privilege to offer you a hand up, ma'am."

Running her palm over the upward sweep of her hair, on top of which a small hat with an elaborate plume was perched, Callie handed him her case. She scooped up the hem of her yellow satin gown, allowing the grinning fellow a glimpse of the generous bosom exposed by the neckline, and replied with a flutter of heavily kohled eyes, "That's what I do best, you know."

"What you do best, ma'am?"

"What I do best—giving fine-looking gentlemen like you pleasure, of course."

The wrangler's grin widened, and Callie accepted his hand, ignoring another round of choking coughs from the doorway behind her. When she was seated in the coach at last, her eyes were cold but her smile was fixed as the conveyance rumbled into motion.

Tanner drew his mount to a halt a few feet from the boundary of McBride land. He stared at the weathered wooden sign bearing the brand of the Circle M, recalling the day when his pa had sent the hands out with those signs to mark the perimeter of the ranch. Stone had been stiff-faced while working with the men, as he always was on the day following one of his father's belated returns. The sight of his ma's forced smile at breakfast, and his father's cold remorselessness at her distress, had firmed Tanner's own decision to make certain his pa didn't get off easily. The morning had gone rapidly downhill from there.

Tanner glanced toward an area in the distance where the road to town wound through uneven terrain, remembering a particular arroyo where the land dropped from a sharp overhang to a dry riverbed below. His heart began a slow hammering as he recalled racing toward that arroyo, unmindful of the pounding hooves behind him. He remembered the moment when he'd spotted the remains of the wagon lying on its side in the dry riverbed, a rear wheel still spinning while the hub of a missing right front wheel screamed a silent accusation.

He remembered the panic and the shouting—the incredulity that overwhelmed his senses when he saw Ma lying there. He recalled his devastating sense of loss when he touched her lifeless hand.

And he remembered the accusations that followed.

Tanner spurred his mount into a sharp jump forward, attempting to ignore a nagging thought that had haunted him ever since. A familiar ache returned as he mused about what night have been, but now could never be. A sense of anticipation mounted as the trail wound through terrain he had traveled countless times. His pace slowed to a gradual halt when the impressive Circle M ranch buildings came into view: the

ranch house, large, with the luxury of a second
floor that most ranch houses in the area could
not boast; well-tended outbuildings with a barn
nearby; horses moving in the corral beside the
barn; and a few chickens wandering aimlessly
between; all against a backdrop of the sprawling
Texas prairie where distant hills were colored
with purple and pink shed by the setting sun.
No, nothing much appeared to have changed.

A slender female figure emerged from the
house unexpectedly, gold hair glinting in the
fragmented rays of the sun. She halted to stare
in his direction. The growing shadows could not
disguise her distinctive, fragile proportions, nor
the determined set of her narrow shoulders. He
felt the moment of recognition that shook her
before she went suddenly still, then remained
waiting—a bold, challenge that went unspoken.

No, nothing much appeared to have changed
at all.

"My name's Callie . . . Winslow, and I want a
job."

The sounds of clinking glasses and loud music
from the piano in the corner of the Roundup
Saloon filled the brief pause as Callie waited for
a reply from the well-dressed proprietor to
whom she had been directed. Ace Bellany's gaze

was frankly assessing, sweeping her from the top of her elaborately plumed hat—lingering briefly on the abundance exposed by her revealing neckline—to the toes of her dusty, black satin shoes. Callie returned his appraisal just as boldly, noting that he was good-looking, despite a complexion that obviously saw little sun and a soft build that bespoke too many nights spent exercising little more than a quick mind and nimble fingers. She noted the darkly fringed eyes and high cheekbones that hinted at a mixed heritage, and the shiny black hair and small mustache that were meticulously groomed. His solemn black jacket and matching trousers were offset by a spotless white shirt and an elaborately brocaded waistcoat, all obviously tailored to his measurements. He was slick and sharp in appearance, the epitome of a professional gambler; but, strangely, she liked what she saw. Ace said, "We've got enough girls working the bar right now. Can you do anything special, besides looking good, sweetheart?"

Forced to think fast, Callie responded with a smile, "Other than being able to hold my liquor as well as any man, I'm a woman of many talents. I'm lucky at cards, and I'm a damned good entertainer." She paused. "By entertaining I mean fancy dancing, or singing beside a piano—not the kind of entertaining that gives a lady calluses where the sun don't shine."

"Prefer to make your living standing on your feet, do you? Too bad." But his smile said otherwise as he continued, "So you're a regular Lillie Langtry."

"I haven't had any complaints."

Obviously intrigued, Ace said unexpectedly, "Charlie over there at the piano can play anything you can sing. Let's see what you can do."

Callie paused, caught red-handed in her exaggeration of her singing talent. The details she had neglected to mention included the fact that her audiences had been mostly uneasy cattle incapable of negative comment, and the only accompaniment she was accustomed to having for her serenades was the call of an occasional night bird, the sound of creaking leather, and the howls of lonely coyotes.

Ace waited.

It was now or never.

Callie walked toward the piano with a provocative sway and more bravado than she felt. She leaned toward the whiskered fellow who looked up at her inquiringly, her voice dropping a husky note as she whispered, "My name's Callie, Charlie. I need a job and I just told Ace Bellamy over there that my singing's second only to Lillie Langty. If you can play "Beautiful Dreamer," I'm about to fake it to the finish and see what happens."

"Darlin' "—Charlie's whiskered face pulled into an appreciative grin—"there ain't nothin' you'd have to prove to me, but if it's 'Beautiful Dreamer' you want, that's what you'll get."

Turning toward the curious stares aimed in her direction as Charlie's enthusiastic introduction captured the attention of all, Callie crossed her fingers, then opened her mouth to sing.

"Beautiful dreamer, wake unto me . . ."

To Callie's incredulity, rowdy cheers and thunderous applause were still ringing when Ace Bellamy reached her side at the conclusion of her song. Appearing somehow amused, he stretched out his hand and said, "Looks like you're hired. You can start tonight."

Almost weak with relief, Callie replied, "Tomorrow would be better. I just got into town. I don't have a place to stay yet."

Observing her too closely for comfort, Ace replied, "Annabelle Chapin's boardinghouse is at the end of the street. Turn right when you walk out the door. You can't miss it. She isn't too friendly, but her place is clean and the food's good. You can stay there until you find a place that suits you better." Ace paused, the interest in his gaze apparent. "Something tells me that I'm going to enjoy having you at the Roundup, Callie."

"Something tells me I'm going to enjoy being here, too, Mr. Bellamy."

"We're going to be friends . . . good friends. Call me Ace."

Callie's smile faded when she emerged onto the street. Her parting statement to Ace had been a lie, like many others she had spoken since she had packed her bag and set out on her journey. Her intention in coming to Sidewinder had nothing to do with enjoyment. It had nothing to do with looking for a job, either, entertaining or otherwise.

Callie glanced back at the brightly lit establishment behind her. The Roundup Saloon—the biggest and best saloon in Sidewinder, Texas. What better place to find *him*?

The rider approached, wrapped in the shades of a brilliant sunset, but all faded into insignificance in Clare's mind as the figure drew nearer. She had known this day would come.

Clare fixed a smile on her lips as satisfaction soared. Five years had passed since Tanner had turned his back on her and the Circle M, but that last day was still as fresh in her mind as if it were yesterday. She had relived that scene countless times, cursing the moment when she had allowed the situation to slip from her control. She had been furious with Tanner for rejecting her. She had been determined to make him suffer. Tom's arrival at the house had been unexpected and inopportune, because it had allowed her a momentary satisfaction that had turned as bitter as gall.

Five years had passed, and she was still angry, with herself and with Tanner, who had managed, for the second time since she had arrived at the Circle M, to compromise her well-laid plans.

Tanner drew nearer, and Clare's smile wavered. His hat was pulled down low on his brow, but she could see him looking at her with that same steady gaze that raised an inexplicable excitement inside her. She could see that he was broader in the shoulder, and that his rangy frame had become more heavily muscled. He had grown older, harder. It had always pleased her that he wasn't handsome in the way his father was; that unlike his brother, he bore Tom McBride no resemblance at all aside from the striking blue eyes that so easily identified each member of the McBride clan. But, in truth, Tanner's greatest appeal hadn't been related to his physical characteristics. He had backbone. The way Tanner faced his father down excited her. He was smart, intense, bold, fearless in his challenge. He had been a challenge to her as well, one that she had been unable to ignore, one that had stirred in her an inner heat unlike any she had ever experienced. His resistance to her charms had angered her, and she had become determined to break Tanner's will as his father never could. She had looked forward to that day as a victory that would be second only to the moment when Tanner became a willing servant to her every whim—just like the father he despised.

That was what she had started out wanting five years ago. In the end, she had been unable to think past wanting *him*. Despite the five years that had passed, it had taken only one glimpse of Tanner to realize that she wanted him still.

"Senora Clare . . ."

Clare turned sharply toward the raspy, heavily accented voice that interrupted her thoughts. Annoyed at the graying servant who had appeared silently beside her, she snapped, "What do you want, Manuelo?"

Manuelo's pointed glance toward Tanner's approach heightened her anger. "I'm not blind! I

can see that it's Tanner! I can handle him. Go
away. I don't need a nursemaid."

When Manuelo glanced again toward Tanner,
Clare hissed, "Go away, damn it! If you mess up
this moment for Tanner and me, I'll make you
sorry!"

Paying no heed to the old servant's frown as
he slipped from sight, Clare returned her attention to the approaching rider. Yes, he was older,
harder. He was a man, now.

Tanner drew up nearby and dismounted, then
walked to within a few feet of her. Always just
beyond her grasp . . .

Clare broke the silence between them.

"I've missed you, Tanner. Welcome home."

Callie counted the first week's rent out onto a
dining room table that shone from wax and elbow grease. She had unconsciously noted that
similar attention had obviously been paid to the
sideboard where dishes awaited the morning
meal in neat stacks that were arranged with a
symmetry and order that appeared to carry over
to all quarters of Annabelle Chapin's boardinghouse. Ace had been correct in describing the
place. It wasn't fancy. The furniture was old and
well preserved, and the space was limited. It
didn't take more than a glance to see that private

space had been rearranged to accommodate the house's present function, most likely due to necessity, if she were to judge from its owner.

Her bag in hand, Callie turned to follow the tall, slender Annabelle Chapin up the staircase to the second floor. Of course, Callie could only assume that the woman had turned her home into a boardinghouse because of necessity, but it was a reasonable guess. It certainly couldn't be because the woman enjoyed meeting people. Callie had never seen colder brown eyes than Annabelle Chapin's when the woman had opened the street door and saw her standing there. With no pretense at small talk after Callie introduced herself, Annabelle had assessed her from head to toe. The conversation between them had been short and to the point.

"I charge by the week. Lodging includes breakfast at six and dinner at six, and those who don't get to the table on time go without. I expect a week's payment in advance, and payment every following Friday. I allow no fraternizing in the rooms, and occasional visitors in the parlor if I'm notified in advance." Annabelle's gaze had swept her again. "And at the first hint of scandal, you're out on your ear."

To which Callie had merely nodded.

It was her passing thought as Annabelle had

reached for a key on the wall rack that with hair the color of ripe wheat, features that might be considered pleasant, and a well-turned backside still shapely enough to attract the attention of a healthy male, the woman might still be in the running for a man. It was her guess that Annabelle was not yet thirty, yet she had *spinster* written in every aspect of her demeanor, including the rigid set of her shoulders as she led the way upstairs. She unlocked the door to the room and handed Callie the key in cold silence.

Annabelle headed back down the hallway, and Callie entered her room and pushed the door closed behind her. She swept the interior with a cursory glance. She had seen better. The wallpaper was faded, the dresser, table, and chair were a little the worse for wear, and the rug had obviously served its purpose for more years than it ought. Yet the bed looked comfortable, clean, and inviting, the lamp on the nightstand was free of stain and freshly filled, and the linens on the washstand in the corner appeared clean. Callie sniffed cautiously. The pleasant smell bespoke careful airing of a room that had obviously seen more traffic than the Pacific Express.

Nothing fancy, but clean. As for Annabelle Chapin's lack of conversation, nothing could suit her better.

Walking the few steps to a window that over-looked the street, Callie frowned as the din of evening grew louder. Drawing down the shade, she shut out the outside world, pulled the foolish hat from her head, shook her hair down onto her shoulders with a sigh of relief, and proceeded to remove her gaudy gown. Her fingers still fumbling, she was momentarily amused in recalling her own audacity after the ticket clerk's illuminating comments about her appearance. She had walked boldly into the nearest saloon and offered to buy the gold satin gown right off the back of the first saloon girl she saw. Iris, as the woman's name turned out to be, had been amused at her offer and had entered the game with true spirit. For a reasonable price, she had provided the needed accessories for the masquerade, going as far as to apply the face paint needed to properly transform her.

Halting at a glimpse of herself in the washstand mirror, Callie frowned. With her hair lying in riotous disarray on her bared shoulders, with her full breasts daringly exposed in a lace chemise that revealed more than it concealed, and with her gold gown pooled around her feet while she stood wearing only black stockings secured with lace garters, she had shed all traces of her former self.

Callie frowned at the irony of her transformation. The female attributes now so blatantly exposed—always a hindrance that had attracted the wrong kind of attention from men—were now her greatest asset. She would use them well, but the transformation was only on the outside.

Kicking her feet free of the heavy satin, Callie unlatched her case and burrowed through it until her hand closed on the cold, smooth handle of the derringer she had bought a few days previously. A sissy gun. That's what she might have called it at one time, but it would now serve her purpose—because a bullet was a bullet, after all.

"Where is everybody?"

The words were a harsh question that rebounded in the silence of the living room as Tanner awaited Clare's response.

"We're shorthanded. The ranch hands have been working longer hours to make up for it. Tiny hasn't been too happy with them coming home late every night."

"Who's Tiny?"

"The cook."

The cook, of course. Clare had been "too delicate" to handle cooking for the hands. They'd had a steady parade of cooks after Ma died. Clare had found an excuse to fire every one of them that was female.

Tanner glanced around him. Nothing at all had been changed in that small, silent room. The furniture was the same—Ma's furniture. The same pictures hung on the wall. His mother's precious music box still lay in a place of honor on the corner table, carefully framed family daguerreotypes that his ma had cherished still held a place of honor on the mantel, and a bouquet of bluebonnets filled the small crystal vase that had been a wedding present his ma had particularly fancied.

Bluebonnets.

An inexplicable anger rose inside Tanner. "Where's Pa? I want to see him."

"He had a bad day today and he's in his room, sleeping. I think you should wait until morning to visit him. He's not doing well, you know."

He could see it was breaking her heart.

"I told him he should be more careful with his health, but he wouldn't listen to me."

Of course.

"Doc Pierce said his sickness has something to do with his lungs. I was devastated."

She hadn't changed a bit.

Clare took a step closer. "I'm glad you decided to come back, Tanner. I've had so many regrets about the way we parted. I thought about you often, wishing I could make it up to you somehow."

And she was still trying to make him believe her lies.

"You're the first one back, you know."

"What do you mean, the first one?"

"Oh, didn't you know? Your sister was miserably unhappy after you left. She cried every day, ranting and raving about how you had left her, saying she hated you and everybody else on this ranch. She was quite impossible. She *begged* Tom and me to send her away from this place. We finally relented and sent her to a finishing school in Savannah. She decided to stay there with her aunt when she was done with her schooling."

"That was convenient for you, wasn't it?"

"You always think the worst of me, Tanner."

He wondered why.

"Stone didn't stay too long after Lauren left. We haven't heard from him since."

"So Stone was the last to leave."

"I don't know why he left. Tom never told me."

Tanner's expression said it all.

"We have a lot of things to talk about, Tanner."

Tanner's lips twisted with distaste. The strain of a dying husband hadn't seemed to affect Clare unfavorably. She was well rested, her looks had only improved, and her confidence was at an all-time high. His pa must really be close to the end.

Tanner turned toward the staircase.

"Where are you going?"

Not sparing her a backward glance, Tanner took the stairs two at a time and strode toward the door to his father's bedroom. He had been traveling for more time then he cared to remember to a place where he had sworn he would never return, and he'd be damned if he'd wait another minute and take the chance that the old bastard would die before he could say what he wanted to say.

At the doorway with his hand on the knob, Tanner halted, unexpectedly hesitant until he heard a familiar voice from within.

"What're you waiting for, Tanner? Afraid to come in?"

That damned old man.

Tanner pushed the door open. His angry advance into the room halted abruptly beside the bed of a person he hardly recognized.

"What's the matter? Surprised at what you see?"

He was. More than surprised. He was numbed.

"What did you expect? Bill Hanes wrote in that letter that I was dying, didn't he?"

Tanner continued to stare. The strong, hard, vigorous cattleman that he remembered had virtually disappeared. The figure outlined underneath Tom McBride's light coverlet was almost skeletal. The full head of gray hair that lay against the pillow stood up awkwardly on his shrunken skull, and his blue eyes were bright spots of color above cheeks that were hollowed to the bone.

"Don't waste your time pitying me, Tanner. That's not what I brought you back for."

"You didn't bring me back. I came back because I chose to."

"Five years, and you didn't *choose* to waste a minute's thought on the Circle M before you got Bill Hanes's letter, so don't go giving me any of that damned nonsense! You came back because you didn't want to miss out on what you figured you had coming."

"Still the same old bastard—"

"And I'm thinking you're still the same troublemaker."

"A troublemaker because I saw you for the man you were."

"What kind of man was that?"

"Do I need to tell you?"

"Whatever kind of man I was, I took care of you kids and your ma. You had a roof over your head, food in your stomach, and clothes on your back."

"Which we earned from the minute we were old enough to know how, while you spent all your spare time with your *ladies*."

"I built up this place into the one of the biggest and best ranches in this part of Texas!"

"With Ma right by your side, but you never gave her credit for that, either. And when Ma was gone—"

"I wouldn't head that way if I were you."

"You wouldn't, huh?"

Tom McBride's skeletal frame began shuddering. "All right, if that's the way you want it, I told you to fix the wheel on that wagon, but you didn't do it. You didn't do it because *I* was the one who told you to! It didn't make any difference to you that your ma was going to take that wagon to town the next day."

"I fixed that wheel."

"Sure, and that's why it came off when it did! That's why your ma ended up on the bottom of that arroyo!"

Bile surged to Tanner's throat as he rasped, "Convenient how I managed that, wasn't it, Pa, so's you could put a ring on the finger of your pretty young whore not even a week later."

"Watch your mouth, Tanner."

"So you could bring her back here to sully Ma's memory!"

"Seems to me your ma was the last thing on your mind that day in the hallway when you were forcing yourself on Clare."

"That's right . . . forcing myself on poor, innocent Clare."

"She stuck by me! None of my own flesh and blood did!"

"She stuck by you? I bet she did, until your back was turned."

"Damn you, Tanner! I'm going—" Tom McBride gasped, his angry response cut short as his eyes widened and he struggled to catch his breath. Struck motionless by the sight of his father's frenetic breathing and the harsh, wheezing sounds emanating from his wasted body, Tanner was brushed roughly aside by a short, squat fellow who rushed to his father's aid. Still rooted to the spot, he felt a light touch on his arm drawing him backward.

"Tiny can take care of him." Clare's voice was startlingly calm, her expression emotionless as she pulled him into the hallway and closed the door behind them. "This has happened before. It'll pass."

"What's that fella doing in there with Pa?"

"He's taking care of him like Doc Pierce told him to. Don't worry about it."

Frantic gulping sounds still echoed from behind the closed bedroom door, and Tanner grated, "He needs a doctor."

"There's nothing the doctor can do for him right now."

"So you say."

"Your pa doesn't have much longer. Nothing you say or do will change that. And nothing you can say will change what he feels for me. Do you know why that is, Tanner? It's because I made your pa feel things he never felt with any other woman. I'm good at that, you know."

Yeah, he knew.

"If you play your cards right—"

Dismissing her with a growl of contempt, Tanner didn't bother to wait for Clare to finish speaking. Hitting the staircase at a run, he was in the yard and mounted when he saw the weary group of ranch hands returning. A familiar voice called out as his mount approached them at a gallop.

"Tanner, boy . . . is that you?"

Drawing up sharply beside them, Tanner accepted the hand Jeb Riggs extended in welcome. Unconsciously noting that the slim, leathery faced foreman was the only man in the group that he recognized, he said, "I'm going for the doctor, Jeb."

Jeb's smile fell. "The boss is havin' trouble breathin' again, is he?"

"Yeah."

"Clare don't like botherin' Doc Pierce. She says Tiny can handle things well enough."

"Yeah? Well, we'll see."

Tanner turned his mount toward town. He frowned when Jeb grasped his reins unexpectedly. His expression sober, Jeb said, "The boss is dyin'. You know that, right?"

"There's no way I could miss it." Tanner glowered. "It's just like that damned old bastard to get me back here so's he can try putting the guilts on me by dying the day I return. Well, I'm not going to give him the last laugh if there's anything I can do about it."

Ignoring Jeb's frown, Tanner jerked his reins free and spurred his mount into motion.

"How are you feeling, Tom?" Clare brushed the heavy gray hair from McBride's damp forehead, then grasped the skeletal hand that trembled on the covers. She waited for the weak twitch of his fingers that signified he had heard her although his eyes remained closed.

Tiny stood a few steps behind her, and Clare motioned him backward with annoyance. The fact that the man was a mute and incapable of gossip had been the deciding factor when she had hired him as a cook a year earlier, but the fellow now disgusted her. She hated the way he hovered over the bed when she was in the room, his shoulders rounded and his stocky body alert, his small, dark eyes watching her every move. If she didn't know that it would be impossible to find someone else to handle the sickening, everyday duties involved in Tom's care, she would have ordered him off the Circle M. She had already decided that as soon as Tom died, she would do just that. But in the meantime . . .

Forcing herself to ignore Tiny's presence, Clare whispered again, "Tom, can you hear me?" She waited for another twitch of his fingers before continuing, "I'm so sorry, dear. I asked Tanner to wait until tomorrow to see you. I wanted to prepare you for his return, and . . . and to try to convince him not to cause the same old hostility to start all over again. But he wouldn't listen. Tom . . ." Clare leaned closer. The slight tremble in her voice was exactly the note she was looking for. "It was a mistake having those letters sent, Tom. Tanner hasn't changed. It's obvious that the only reason he came back was to try to take advantage of you while you're at your weakest. I couldn't bear that. Please, let me tell him you want him to go . . . for your sake."

McBride's eyes opened into narrow slits. "No."

"Then let me do it for *my* sake."

"No."

"Tom—"

Tom released her hand and turned his head away from her, and Clare's jaw clamped tight. She stood up abruptly. The bastard had dismissed her!

Glancing up at Tiny, she saw that the fellow's vigilant gaze had not missed a single detail of their brief conversation, and she forced a smile. "He's tired. He should sleep."

Her anger under tenuous control, Clare left the room.

A full moon unchallenged by a single cloud illuminated the Texas prairie with the light of day—but Tanner's ride to town had seemed endless. The frivolity of evening was in full swing when Sidewinder's main street came into view, and Tanner took a moment's pause as he entered town, frowning at the change that five years had wrought. Bawdy music and shouts of laughter echoed on the night air, while wranglers milled on board walks lined with swinging doors that were seldom still. Freight wagons were parked haphazardly, narrowing the brightly lit street. Mounted riders came and went, swaying pedestrians negotiated wavering paths to their next stop, and women of questionable character lingered along the way. He scanned the storefronts, startled to see that the general store, the gun shop, the saddlery, the town eatery—all had been squeezed out of prominence by the startling number of saloons that had sprung up in his absence.

The rasping sound of his father's labored breathing returned to mind, and Tanner drew back on his mount's reins, his gaze searching for the building where Doc Pierce's office had formerly been situated. In its place was a dress shop, where one glance at the garish gown sharing equal space with a more sedate garment in the window further defined the change that Sidewinder had undergone.

Tanner nudged his mount forward. His jaw twitched with satisfaction when he spotted a storefront at the far end of the street with the familiar medical symbol that Doc Pierce was so fond of. Tanner kicked his horse into a sharp jump forward.

A shriek of laughter below her window jolted Callie awake. A round of raucous male laughter followed as she rolled onto her back and stared up at the shadowed ceiling of her room. She could not count the number of times she had been awakened in the same manner since she had fallen into bed with exhaustion that evening, and she was getting damned tired of it!

Callie threw back the coverlet and stood up abruptly. Stomping to the window, she drew back the shade to glare down into the street below. She gave an annoyed snort as a brightly clad woman slipped through the doors of a saloon, with two grinning cowboys following close behind. A thought returned to agitate her—one that had crossed her mind several times as she had attempted to sleep. It was apparent that the room she now occupied had not been the only one available in the rooming house. It also became more obvious with every passing hour that Annabelle had not just *happened* to give her this particular room facing the street. She had become convinced that either Annabelle believed a "woman like her" wouldn't be bothered by the noise, or that a "woman like her" would become a part of the rowdy scene too soon for it to really matter. Annabelle doubtless figured she'd be better off saving the quieter rooms for more respectable boarders. The fact that frigid Annabelle was half right only served to irritate her more.

Callie's attention was diverted by an approaching rider who spurred his mount into a sudden, dangerous leap forward on the crowded street below. She gasped aloud when a tipsy wrangler stepped out unexpectedly into his path, and the rider reined back sharply to avoid the fellow, then fought to control his rearing horse. Leaping from the animal's back as soon as it had quieted, the rider confronted the man who had stumbled in front of him.

Callie observed the brief argument that followed with disgust. Two fools. They deserved each other.

The rider remained staring after the drunken cowboy as the fellow wove his way toward the next set of swinging doors. Anger was evident in the set of his broad shoulders. He turned and walked toward the darkened storefront across the street. She noted the symbol on the window. A doctor's office.

The rider pounded on the door, then squinted at a small, handwritten sign in the window. He turned toward her abruptly. Callie took an unconscious step backward as he scanned the street, mouthed a curse, and remounted. His bearing stiff, he started back down the street.

Callie followed the rider with her gaze. The fellow was obviously in good health. The emergency that had brought him to town in such haste at this time of night couldn't be for himself. She had imagined him a fool who had no more on his mind than an evening's pleasure, when in reality he might be on an errand of life and death—

But . . . wait a moment.

Still watching, Callie saw the rider glance at the Roundup as he rode past. Her sympathy changed to disdain when he drew back on the reins abruptly, then negotiated a place at the crowded hitching post. Dismounting, he strode resolutely toward the wide, swinging doors.

She had been right about the man all along! Whatever medical emergency had brought him into town, he had already managed to dismiss it in favor of the beckoning lights of the Roundup Saloon—while some poor, sick fool awaited his return.

Callie released the shade and returned to bed. Yes, she knew that fellow's kind. He'd be drunk before the hour was out.

The heat and din of the Roundup Saloon assaulted Tanner as he thrust open the swinging doors and stepped inside. He scanned the room. The sign in Doc Pierce's window had said that he was out on a call and was uncertain when he would return. Unless the doc was a changed man, he would stop to wet his whistle as soon as he came back. All Tanner needed to find him was a bit of luck.

"Tanner! That is you, isn't it?"

Tanner turned toward William Hanes as the slight, balding solicitor shouldered his way through the crowd. Tanner realized belatedly that he should also have recalled that Sidewinder's best and only lawyer was never more articulate than during the hours when he relaxed with a few glasses of red-eye at his favorite saloon each night. It was just Tanner's luck to have run into him in this particular saloon when he had no desire for the conversation that was obviously about to begin.

Tanner accepted the hand extended to him in greeting. "Hello, Mr. Hanes."

"I'm glad to see you, Tanner!" Hanes slapped his shoulder with a smile. "I had my doubts that any one of you McBrides would respond to my letter, but I surely hoped you all would. You're the first to get here, you know."

"I know." Tanner did not return his smile. Bill Hanes had been his pa's lawyer for as long as he could remember. Hanes had shared his pa's confidences as even his ma never had. Tanner had resented that, although his ma never seemed to have taken offense, and he had never said much more to the man than he needed to. This time was no different. "I'm looking for Doc Pierce," Tanner said.

Hanes was immediately alert. "Why? Has Tom taken a turn for the worse?"

Impatient, Tanner shrugged. "He doesn't look too good. That's why I came to get the doc."

"Clare isn't inclined to call Doc Pierce in too often. I've tried to talk to her about that, but—"

His patience almost nil as he was jostled by a bearded fellow making his way to the street, Tanner interrupted brusquely, "The sign on Doc's door says he doesn't know when he's getting back."

"He's delivering a baby at one of the outlying ranches."

"Do you know which one?"

"No."

Tanner's frustration soared. He had expected this. He had expected that Clare wouldn't have changed; and she hadn't. He had expected that his pa wouldn't welcome him with open arms, and he didn't. He had expected that the Circle M might look the same but that inevitable changes would have occurred to which he would object, and that was also true. But he had not expected that the sight of his father's illness would affect him to such a degree, or that the compassion it stirred would disappear the moment his pa started to speak. And he had not expected so driving a desire to prove that the days when he could be manipulated by his pa or Clare's intrigues were over. Yet the situation was again slipping out of his control. The trip to town was proving to be a waste of time, and he had almost ended up running down a drunken cowpoke in the process. No, he didn't like the way things were going at all.

"Let me buy you a drink." Hanes ushered him to the bar and signaled the bartender, then turned to look at him over his spectacles. "Don't expect a miracle, Tanner." he said. "It isn't going to happen."

Tanner tensed. "Meaning?"

"When did you get back? Yesterday? Today?"

"Today."

"It's going to take time to settle things with your pa."

"Pa doesn't have time."

"You know what I think of your pa."

Tanner's gaze intensified as he spat, "No, I don't."

"I'll tell you, then." Bill Hanes's gaze was direct. "I think Tom McBride is a strong man who is dedicated to his land. I respect him for that." Tanner's lip curled contemptuously, but Hanes continued, "He's also a man whose character is severely flawed in many ways, not the least of which he demonstrated in the way he treated your mother. Emily was a good woman. She didn't deserve what Tom did to her, but she was unable to change him. If she couldn't change him over twenty-five years of marriage, you can't expect to come back and change things in a day."

"I didn't come back to change things. And I didn't come to Sidewinder for any other reason than to get the doc."

Studying Tanner intently for another moment, Hanes added, "I know your pa gave the decision to send those letters a lot of thought. He has a definite reason for trying to get his children back on the Circle M before he dies."

"It certainly wasn't to make peace, that's for sure."

"Your meeting with him went that badly, did it?"

Tanner did not reply.

"There's time yet. The others will arrive before the deadline."

"You think so, huh?"

"You came, didn't you?"

Silence.

"Be patient. Don't expect miracles—and stay away from Clare."

Tanner rasped, "I'd tell you to keep your advice to yourself if I thought it would do any good."

Refusing to take offense, Hanes smiled. "I didn't say it would be easy to avoid Clare, if you know what I mean."

Tanner's gaze narrowed.

"I'm not as blind about Clare as your pa chooses to be." Hanes said. "But I'm your pa's attorney, so I think I've said enough for now." Raising the drink that had been placed in front of him, Hanes emptied the glass in a gulp, slapped it back down on the bar, and continued without blinking, "And since I've already had my limit, I'll also say good night." Turning back, he added, "You know where I am if I'm needed in any way."

Not bothering to watch the graying attorney's departure as he wove his way across the crowded floor, Tanner had only one response to the advice so freely given. Signaling the bartender, he said, "Leave the bottle."

Chapter Three

"Did he come back last night? Where is he?"

Openly agitated, Clare stood in the upstairs hallway, her fair hair loose on her shoulders, her silk wrapper hanging open to reveal a sheer strip of lace and silk underneath. Manuelo stood silent beside her, intent on her disturbed expression as she continued to quiz him sharply.

"Do you know where he is? Damn it, Manuelo, you're not deaf and dumb! Answer me!"

"Senor Tanner came home last night, without bringing the doctor. He slept in the bunkhouse."

"In the bunkhouse?" Clare laughed aloud. She had watched Tanner's departure the previous evening and had heard from the returning ranch hands that he had gone to town to get the doctor.

She had spent the remainder of the night lying awake, alternating between wishing that Tanner were dead and wishing that he were lying beside her. She had gone directly to his room upon awakening. When he wasn't there, her agitation had increased.

So Tanner had slept in the bunkhouse.

"He's afraid of me, Manuelo." Clare laughed. "He's afraid of me because he knows he's weakening. I'll get him yet."

"You desire him, Senora Clare . . ." Manuelo's small, dark eyes were disapproving. He had met Clare's mother, Mary Raines, at the lowest point in his life, when he was ill and destitute. In a lifetime filled with bitterness and want, Mary Raines had been the only person who had ever spared the ugly, ignorant fellow a moment's thought. He had worshiped her. When he was again well, he became the devoted servant of both mother and daughter, with no task too menial for him to perform. Since then he had shared their fluctuating circumstances with no goal in mind beyond gratifying their every wish. He silently claimed them as his family, although he knew that to speak that thought aloud would repel them. Upon Mary Raines's death, his slavish devotion to Clare had deepened.

Manuelo continued softly, ". . . but Senor Tanner is not worthy of you."

"You speak like an imbecile!" Her fair skin flushing hot, Clare rasped, "No man is worthy of me in your eyes. Even if you were right, what difference does it make if I want him? What both you and Tanner don't seem to realize is that each time Tanner rejects me, I become more determined. I'll have Tanner at my beck and call, Manuelo, sooner or later, and then the fun will begin."

Manuelo eyed Clare more closely. He did not like the heat in her cheeks. He did not like her agitation. He had seen her like this before and knew that she often acted impetuously when in this state. They had worked and waited for the end that was rapidly approaching. He would not have her risk it all.

"The ranch hands are at breakfast, aren't they?" Clare made a visible attempt at control. "Is Tanner with them?"

"*Sí*. I heard him say he will be riding out with the men today."

"Tell him I want to see him."

Manuelo hesitated.

"What are you waiting for?"

"I would not have you act imprudently."

"Just tell Tanner I want to see him! No, tell him *Tom* wants to see him. I'll stop him before he gets that far."

"Senora Clare—"

"Do what I say, damn it!"

With a growing sense of dread, Manuelo turned to do Clare's bidding.

Callie pulled the heavy gold satin away from her damp skin as she walked along Sidewinder's main street. The heat of the morning sun had already caused trickles of perspiration to begin traveling down the valley between her breasts, and she knew her underarms would soon be ringed with sweat. Two steps out onto the street, she had made the abrupt decision that she would not spend a minute longer than necessary sweltering in the oppressive garment. Two more steps and she had decided to forgo breakfast in favor of a swift visit to the nearest dress shop.

Callie's stomach rumbled aloud. She had risen too late for a boardinghouse breakfast after her sleepless night. It occurred to her that since she would begin working in the Roundup that evening, she would seldom awaken in time to eat breakfast in the boardinghouse—to Annabelle Chapin's pleasure, she was sure. She could not help wondering what had happened to sour Annabelle's disposition so early in life. And then she wondered why she cared.

"Howdy, Miss Callie!"

Turning toward the enthusiastic greeting, Callie looked at the smiling cowboy whose sundried skin, bowed legs, and roughly cut gray hair proclaimed a life spent in the saddle as clearly as did his scuffed, hand-tooled boots. The manner in which he eyed her outlandish appearance also indicated that he was a man deprived of female company for too long. He knew her name. She stared at him a moment longer. She had never seen the man before in her life.

"You don't remember me, do you?" His whiskered chin bobbed with a laugh. "But I remember you, and I got to tell you that hearin' you sing in the Roundup yesterday was just about the sweetest thing these old ears of mine have heard in a month of Sundays. Ace said you'd be back tonight, and I'm here to say that I'm going be there, sittin' right by Charlie's piano so's I don't miss a single word that comes out of them pretty lips of yours."

Callie fluttered her kohl-darkened lashes, then purred, "Thank you. What's your name, cowboy?"

"My name's Digby Jones, ma'am. And I'm mightily pleased to meet you."

Callie accepted his hand. "It was my pleasure singing for you Digby. I'll be looking for you tonight."

Callie unconsciously shook her head as she continued down the street. Her voice was the sweetest thing his old ears had heard in a month of Sundays? The poor fellow had to be tone deaf.

Callie halted abruptly before a window displaying a lightweight gown in a gaudy red color so bright it made her eyes water, and a simple blue cotton that made her long for home. She went inside.

Pausing as her eyes became accustomed to the darker interior of the store, Callie turned toward the busy tittering of a cluster of sedately dressed women nearby. An older woman sporting more poundage than appeared healthy glanced in her direction before continuing, "He came into town just as bold as could be, I tell you! Can you imagine the nerve of him, standing right there at the Roundup bar, drinking as if nobody would remember what happened five years ago because of him?"

A pale, slender woman with graying hair replied, "You aren't being fair, Tessie. You're only repeating hearsay. Nobody knows for sure that he was really responsible. After all, it was his ma."

"Well, I'm as sure as I'll ever be that everything said about him is true. He always was the wild one of the family—good for nothing but stirring up trouble! His pa was always after him!"

"His pa." The third woman gave a disapproving snort. "If that man was my husband, I'd have set him straight, right off—that, or I would've taken a six-shooter to him."

"His pa was a hard worker!"

"His pa was a womanizer!"

"Think what you like. All I can say is, his pa might've had an eye for the ladies, but at least his pa wasn't the one responsible for killing his own ma."

"Tess!"

"Emily McBride was a good woman! She didn't deserve what Tanner did!"

Callie froze.

Tanner McBride . . . the only member of a gang of murdering bank robbers who had been too drunk from the previous night's revelry to escape the sheriff.

Tanner McBride . . . whom the sheriff had released from jail with only a warning.

Suddenly aware that she was shaking, Callie turned toward the rack of gaudy dresses. She closed her eyes, straining for control. McBride had returned to his hometown sooner than she had expected. He had come to the Roundup the previous night, while she lay asleep in the boardinghouse just down the street.

The heated discussion between the matrons continued as Callie struggled to control her emotions. Moving her trembling hand through the dresses on the rack, she told herself that she needn't be upset. All she had lost was a little time. A bottle of red-eye and the bright lights of a saloon were as necessary to a man like McBride as breathing. He'd be back. She had committed his description to memory. He was tall, broad-shouldered, with a rangy build. He had light blue eyes and long, dark, ill-kept hair, and was heavily bearded. He was also sullen and unfriendly, and apt to drink alone. She'd recognize him the minute he walked through the door.

Callie forced up her chin. She had missed an opportunity last night, but she'd get another. And when she did, she'd be ready. And waiting.

"No, don't knock on your pa's door. He's sleeping."

Tanner turned toward Clare as she stepped out of the shadows of the upstairs hallway. He had returned from his frustrating trip to town the previous evening and had slept poorly. He had awakened that morning with only one clear thought: to ride out with Jeb and the ranch hands. The breakfast table had been unnaturally quiet. He had suffered the inquisitive stares of the men in silence, grateful that Clare had not yet risen. He had come upstairs when summoned to his father's bedside—only to have Clare step out into view the moment he reached the second floor.

Clare approached, her lustrous hair lying against narrow shoulders clad in a revealing robe. She halted enticingly close and turned her matchless features up to him with a smile. The scene was all too familiar. It was one that had played over and over again in his mind during his long years of absence from the Circle M— and he had no desire to repeat it.

Tanner's reply was gruff. "Manuelo said my pa wanted to see me."

"Your pa's sleeping, just like I said."

"*You* sent Manuelo. I should've known."

Ignoring his reply, Clare prompted, "What happened last night, Tanner? You went to town for the doctor but you came back without him." Tanner did not reply, allowing her to guess, "Doc was too busy . . . or not in town, is that it? And your pa lived through the attack, just like I said. I'm so sorry, Tanner. You didn't get the opportunity to play the hero by fetching the doctor and showing up your evil stepmother, did you?

Tanner's lip curled with contempt.

"And when you came home, you decided to

81

sleep in the bunkhouse. Tanner, Tanner . . ."
Clare shook her head. "Are you so afraid of me
that you wouldn't even chance sleeping in the
house that you grew up in, just because I'm
here?"

"Afraid of you?"

"Afraid you're weakening."

"My pa's the only man in this house who's
weakening, Clare."

"You're not feeling even a little twinge, Tanner?" Clare's warmth radiated out to him. "Not
even a little nudge of desire? You haven't started
wondering in the back of your mind what it
might really be like to hold me close . . . how it
would taste to kiss my mouth?"

"Clare—"

"I'll tell you how it would taste, Tanner. It
would taste good—better than any woman's kiss
you've ever known. You've never felt skin that's
smoother under your lips than mine, or known
a body more willing. No woman would ever give
to you the way I would give, and no other
woman would ever take you inside her the way
I would. It would be so easy, Tanner . . . and so
good."

Yes, it would be so easy. He remembered that
thought.

Tanner took a backward step. He halted his

retreat as Clare pressed, "Scared of me, Tanner?"

"I could think of a better word to use."

"Really?" Clare's pale brows rose delicately upward as her hand moved unexpectedly to the revealing bulge in his crotch. "But the truth is, Tanner, darling, you're harder than a banker's heart."

Tanner thrust away her hand and glanced toward McBride's bedroom door.

"Don't worry. He's sleeping. He can't hear us."

"Would it make any difference to you if he did?"

"I suppose . . . but I'd find a way to explain things. And Tom would believe me, because he wants to believe me."

"That's what Pa wants, but what do you want, Clare? You never did tell me."

"I did tell you. I want you."

"No, I want to know what you *really* want."

"I don't know why you refuse to believe me."

"Don't you?"

Her expression suddenly intense, Clare whispered, "I don't sleep with him anymore, Tanner. I haven't slept with him since he got sick months ago. We have separate rooms now, because the doc said it would be easier for him that way. I took the room at the end of the hall—the far end.

We'd have all the privacy in the world there. Nobody'd know."

"No, nobody'd know."

"Don't be so noble! Your pa wouldn't have hesitated a minute."

"I'm not my pa."

"That's what I'm counting on, Tanner."

Tanner perused Clare's expression, his gaze narrowing. "What's the matter, Clare? You don't want to share the inheritance, is that it? You didn't expect me to come back, but now that I'm here, you're hoping to turn Pa against me again so he'll drive me out."

"Tanner—"

"What've you got planned for Stone if he comes back? More of the same? What about Lauren?"

"I've never given either of those two a second thought."

"No, just me."

"Only you, Tanner."

"Me . . . and my pa."

"Tanner—"

"I hate to repeat myself, but you might as well give it up. You're wasting your time."

"No . . ." Clare's cheeks were suddenly bright. "I'm not wasting my time, because if I were, you wouldn't be afraid to sleep in the same house with me."

"I'm not afraid."

"You're either afraid of what people will say, or afraid of me. Which is it?"

"Neither."

"You're going be here a long time—a few months, at least, until the deadline passes. Are you going to keep sleeping in the bunkhouse like a hired hand, or are you going to take your place in the main house like a McBride?"

When Tanner remained silent, Clare hissed, "Afraid of me, Tanner . . . or afraid of yourself?"

The McBride blue of Tanner's eyes went suddenly frigid. "I'll move my things in later."

Flushed with triumph, still standing in the hallway where Tanner had left her, Clare walked toward the far end of the corridor and said, "You can come out now, Manuelo."

Manuelo emerged from the shadows in answer to her summons, and Clare smiled triumphantly. "I heard you sneaking up the rear staircase to spy on me. Well, what did you think of the show? A few more days, and he's mine."

Manuelo shook his head.

Clare's smile faded. "He's mine, I'm telling you! I felt his heat in my hand. He won't be able to fight himself too much longer."

"Senor Tanner is a difficult man."

"So's his father."

"No. He is not like his father."

Clare's delicate features drew into a sneer. "That's right, he isn't. And if he was like his pa, I wouldn't want him."

"Senor Tanner's resolve will be difficult to overcome."

"And the victory will be even sweeter."

"You wish to control him."

"I *will* control him."

"But you must take care that he does not succeed in controlling you."

Recoiling from Manuelo's response as if she had been struck, Clare grated, "That was a stupid thing to say. Get out of my sight!"

Turning her back on the silent servant, Clare walked stiffly down the hall. She paused briefly in front of her husband's bedroom door and adjusted the neckline of her gown to expose a tempting view of the firm, white flesh beneath. She then pushed the door open. Advancing quietly to his bedside, she leaned over him to whisper, "Tom, are you awake?"

McBride's eyes opened into weak slits.

"I hardly slept all night, darling. I was so worried about you." Clare stroked his clammy brow. "You have to get well, Tom. I just don't know what I'd do if I lost you."

* * *

Fresh beads of sweat trailed from Tanner's temple as he strained to hold the fencepost steady. He had been working with the ranch hands since early morning as they restrung fencing on the west pasture that had been trampled during a recent thunderstorm. He had driven himself hard, speaking little to the men who worked beside him. As their inquisitive stares continued, he had mentally rebuked himself for the scene that had transpired in the upstairs hallway earlier.

He remembered climbing the stairs with both dread and expectation after his pa's summons. But it hadn't been his pa who had sent for him. In hindsight, he wondered if he was the only man at the breakfast table who had truly believed it was.

"Hold that post steady!"

Tanner looked up at Jeb, frowning. He restrained a sharp response, his grip tightening as other ranch hands wound the wire, and he wondered, not for the first time that morning, at the wisdom of returning home.

Tanner considered the thought again. He had been well aware that coming home wouldn't be easy, hadn't he? Bill Hanes's letter had made it clear that Clare was still in his pa's favor, and he had known that he was the last person either one of them had expected to return. He had prepared himself for any difficulty that would ensue, or so he had thought.

Be careful. Stay away from Clare.

His meeting with Bill Hanes had been unexpected. Left standing at the bar with the solicitor's warning echoing in his mind, he had picked up the bottle in front of him and refilled his glass, but he had gotten the glass only halfway to his lips before common sense returned. He had then waited at the bar, drinking little and speaking only to those who spoke to him, in the hope that Doc Pierce would return. He had waited in vain. He had finally left a message for Doc with the bartender, and had ridden back to the Circle M by the light of the moon, and with a sense of uncertainty as to what he would find waiting for him when he arrived.

Tanner gave a low snort. As it turned out, he shouldn't have worried. According to the report Jeb had gotten with great difficulty from the speechless cook, his pa was no better or worse for the attack, and was sleeping peacefully. Exhausted, unwilling to face another confrontation, Tanner had carried his saddlebags into the bunkhouse and fallen onto the nearest empty bed. But in retrospect . . .

The Wild One

Afraid of me, Tanner?

Was he?

"Tanner, damn it! Hold that post steady!" Jeb's impatient reprimand brought him back to the present. About to reply just as sharply to the foreman, he saw Jeb's expression flicker as he said, "Never mind. We're all tired and hungry. Let's stop and eat somethin'."

Keeping to himself, Tanner sat down a distance from the hands who had gathered in a group to eat and talk. He had nothing to say to the others at present. They were strangers, and he was in no mood to satisfy curious questions. He unwrapped his lunch. Bread and smoked ham, prepared by the enigmatic Tiny. It did not miss his notice that an extra sack had been readied for him.

"I figured you'd be ridin' out with me and the men today, so I told Tiny to make somethin' up for you, too."

Tanner looked up as Jeb sat beside him. Sweat still streamed from the foreman's brow, and his craggy face was flushed from the sun. The look of him was warmly familiar, almost prompting a smile. Of a similar age to his pa, Jeb had been with the Circle M as long as Tanner could remember; but unlike his pa, Jeb had changed little. His brown hair was a little more streaked with gray, and his leathery skin a little more lined, but he was still thin and wiry, with a look in his eyes that was direct and honest. Tanner remembered that Ma had relied on Jeb in ways that she had never been able to rely on his pa. He had sensed a mutual respect between them, which had raised Jeb even further in his esteem. Jeb was a hard worker and a good man—those words, straight from his ma's mouth, were great praise that she had spoken with true warmth. But Tom McBride had never given Jeb an inch, or a word of approval or appreciation.

Tanner spoke abruptly. "I never could figure why you stayed at the Circle M when I was a kid. Pa never gave you the time of day, other than when he was barking orders. All you needed to do was say the word, and any ranch around here would've taken you on as foreman. You probably would've been paid better, and I know you would've been more appreciated. If I was you, I'd have been long gone from the Circle M."

"I sometimes wonder myself why I stayed." Jeb hastened to add, "But your pa was a fair boss, you know, and the money was good."

"Come on, Jeb . . ."

Jeb sighed. "I won't lie to you. It was damned hard workin' for that man, especially watchin' what was going on. I don't think there was a day when I didn't ask myself what your pa was lookin' for when he strayed like he did, spendin' time with all them other women when he had a woman like your ma at home. Hell, your ma was a real lady! She was better-lookin' than most of them others, too, and there wasn't one of them who could hold a candle to her when it came to heart."

"It wasn't their hearts that my pa was interested in."

"Guess not. It got under my skin the way he treated you boys, too. Stone never worked long enough or hard enough, or took on enough responsibility to suit your pa. All Stone ever got from him was criticism for settin' a bad example for you."

"Stone . . . set a bad example for me?"

Jeb nodded. "Hell, and I knew it ate you up the way your pa treated all of you, especially your ma. You was determined to pay him back in your own way. I knew all them wild things you did, like gettin' drunk and carryin' on the way you did, was just to spite your pa. Just like I knew there was a lot more going on in that head of yours than you ever let on. The only person you ever back-talked was your pa . . . and you was good to your ma. That said it all for me. As for Lauren . . ."

91

A familiar pain twinged inside Tanner.

"Well, your pa never did hold with havin' a daughter. Seems to me he just didn't have time for her." Jeb shook his head. "The man had everythin', and he threw it away. Sometimes when your ma and me talked . . ." Jeb's voice thickened. "Your ma was true blue to him, right up to the end. It was her dream . . . she kept hopin', right until that last day, that your pa would straighten out, that he'd come to her and say he was sorry for all the bad things he done, and for the way he treated her and you kids over the years. She would've forgiven him, Tanner."

"I know."

"She wanted that dream to come true. She wanted the family to be whole again. She wanted to see you all workin' side by side on the land she loved, so that when she died . . ."

Jeb's voice faded and he swallowed hard.

"I did fix that wheel, Jeb."

"I never believed you didn't, boy."

Feeling his own throat construct as well, Tanner said, "But Ma's gone, and you're still here."

"Your ma's not really gone from this place, you know."

"As far as Pa's concerned, she is."

"But not as far as I'm concerned. That fair-haired honey your pa took to his bed ain't never going to push your ma's memory off this land."

"Not for you and me, maybe."

"Not for your pa, neither, I'm thinkin'."

Tanner was suddenly angry. "Pa never gave Ma a minute's thought while she was alive. What makes you think he's sparing her any time now that she's dead?"

Jeb's gaze was direct. "He sent for you and the others, didn't he?"

"He has a reason for that. I don't know what it is yet, but he does."

"Yeah, he's got a reason, all right. Your pa's a complicated man."

"He's a bastard."

"He's that, too." Jeb paused. "But you came back. It's what your ma would've wanted."

"Ma would've wanted it, but it's what I wanted, too. Pa ran me off this place five years back, and I just kept on running. But I'm not running anymore. I came back to face everything that happened, to face what people are thinking and saying about it and me, and to find out if this is the place where I really belong. And I'm not leaving until everything's settled."

"Everythin'?"

"Meaning I'm not letting anybody chase me off the Circle M again, until I'm ready to go."

"Did you tell your pa that yesterday?"

"My pa wasn't listening."

"Maybe he's waitin' for Stone and Lauren to come back."

Tanner paused, then spoke aloud the thought that still gnawed at him. "Clare said Lauren begged them to send her away."

"I've got my doubts about that. I can't see your sister beggin' *them* for nothin'."

"Clare also said she doesn't know why Stone left."

"Outside of your pa, she's probably the only one who does."

"I've been thinking. Does Clare know about—"

"I don't think so."

Tanner nodded, then glanced at the men conversing softly a distance away. "There's not a single hand on this ranch who was here when Ma was alive. What happened to them all?"

"Butch, Slim, Manny, Nate, Larry, Tim—they all left, one by one. Things wasn't the same after you boys and Lauren cleared out. I'm thinkin' they couldn't stomach it no longer."

"What do these men know about what went on back then?"

"Rumors, I guess. I expect they all heard about your ma's accident at one time or another, and I'm thinkin' they're about to hear a lot more about it once the talk starts all over again. But nobody had to explain to them about the kind of man your pa is, because he just kept gettin' harder and harder to work for until the day he was flat on his back. And when it came to Clare, nobody had to tell those boys the kind of woman she is, either. Seems the only man who was ever blind about that, is your pa."

Tanner hesitated, then questioned bluntly, "Did Clare try turning you around to her way of thinking after Pa got sick? By that I mean—"

"I know what you mean." His eyes suddenly as hard as flint, Jeb grated, "That woman damned well better not have tried! She's the boss's wife and I give her the respect the name warrants, but I don't give her nothin' more. She ain't fit to shine your ma's shoes. She wants this ranch, all right. I figure that was her aim from the beginnin' when she took up with your pa, but she don't want it because her heart's in the land, like it was with your ma." Jeb paused to take a breath. "So if you're askin' me outright if I ever had anythin' to do with that woman, the answer is no."

Standing up abruptly, Jeb muttered, "No, she ain't good enough to shine your ma's shoes."

Tanner watched as Jeb walked back to his horse to get his lunch. Jeb's shoulders were stiff and his jaw was clenched tight. He was angry to have had Emily's name mentioned in the same breath with Clare's.

Tanner watched Jeb a moment longer. He wasn't sure when he had first realized that Jeb had loved Ma. He knew that Jeb had never told Ma how he felt about her. Now, in retrospect, he sometimes wished Jeb had.

Tanner raised the sandwich to his mouth and took a bite. Yes, he sometimes wished Jeb had.

Chapter Four

The sun was preparing to set as Callie began the long walk down the street toward the Roundup Saloon. The conversation she had overheard that morning in the boutique had stunned her. Finally gathering her wits about her, she had pretended an interest only in shopping and had listened intently until the women stopped talking. She had then made her way around town to discover that Tanner McBride was the topic of conversation wherever she went. What she had consequently learned only served to confirm what she already knew about him. Wild in his youth, he had been reckless, unpredictable, and irresponsible, so much so that his irresponsibility had caused his own mother's death in an accident that could have been prevented. He had then demonstrated the depth of his regret and sorrow by forcing his attentions on the young wife his father brought back to the ranch only a week after his mother's death. That last act of Tanner's was the last straw for a father who was apparently not much better than his son, and Tom McBride had then run his son off the ranch.

Callie's lips tightened. Now, five years later and five years the worse for wear, Tanner McBride was responsible for another death. The only difference, this time, was that she was going to see that he didn't get away with it.

With that thought foremost in her mind, she had marked time until evening approached. Finally slipping on the lightweight garment she had purchased that morning, she had swept up her hair, painted her face, and slid into her high-heeled shoes. She had then stood back to appraise herself critically in the washstand mirror. She had noted with cold satisfaction that her upswept hair caught the light, drawing the eye while accenting streaks of gold within the darker mass; that kohled lashes made her eyes appear the shade of deep, mellow honey; that a swipe of color had ripened her lips to a luscious, tempting red; and that the startling crimson of

loons gleamed ever brighter and the music from within grew louder. Looking through the doorways as she passed, she saw brightly clad woman lounging by the entrances in obvious expectation of arriving customers, and she restrained a frown. Her new profession was the last one she would have chosen, if not for the circumstances which had brought her to Sidewinder, but she had no intention of allowing her reticence to show. Focusing her eyes on the Roundup as she neared, she told herself she couldn't expect Tanner McBride to show up at the Roundup again tonight, and that it was just as well if he didn't. She needed time to settle in. She couldn't afford any costly mistakes.

That thought in mind, Callie did not miss a step as she pushed open the broad, swinging doors of the Roundup and walked inside. The overwhelming odors of tobacco smoke, liquor, sweat, and heady perfume assaulted her in a rush, and she paused, struggling against the inclination to frown. Scanning the room, she saw that the bar was already lined with cowpokes of every age and size, that the card tables were in full play . . . and that the brightly dressed ladies of the establishment were looking at her in a way that did not appear at all friendly. Seated at a table in the corner, Ace Bellamy stood up when he saw her. At the same moment a familiar, gravelly voice addressed her warmly.

"Howdy, Miss Callie! I've been waitin' for you." His whiskered face beaming as she turned toward him, Digby Jones continued, "I've been thinkin' about hearin' you sing all day long. There ain't a fellow at the bar that ain't been waitin' as anxiously as me, too. Charlie over there at the piano is ready any time you are."

Callie groaned inwardly, but her smile was bright as she responded, "You sure make a lady feel welcome, Digby, but I haven't talked to Charlie yet about what songs I'll be singing."

Digby paused, his expression wistful. "I was kinda hopin' you'd sing 'Beautiful Dreamer' again. I've been tellin' folks all around town how you sing just like an angel." Digby flushed. "If you don't mind, ma'am."

Callie glanced back at Ace. He was seated again, appearing amused as he looked in their direction. Turning back to Digby, she cooed, "How could I refuse?"

The bunkhouse was deafeningly silent as Tanner packed his bag. He wasn't smiling. He had spent a long day working with the men, and he had been dead tired by the time the Circle M ranch house was again in sight. He had gone imme-

diately to the house upon arriving, hoping to talk
to his pa, only to find him asleep. Disturbed that
another day was ending before he was able to
clear things up between them, he had sat down
to eat with the men, but his appetite had fled the
moment Clare took her place at the head of the
table. All conversation had ceased at her appearance, and it was clear that Jeb's assessment
of the ranch hands' feelings about the boss's wife
was correct.

Appearing to feel no uneasiness, Clare had
eaten leisurely, addressing the men in a manner
devised to emphasize her position as the boss's
wife. In marked contrast, her attitude toward
Tanner had been familiar and accompanied by
lavish smiles that had raised eyebrows among
the silent hands. The silence had deepened when
she asked him with calculated deliberation,
"Will you be moving back into the main house
tonight, Tanner?"

Witch! With that single question, Clare had
succeeded in planting a suspicion that was
bound to bear fruit in the minds of every man
present. Already marked for one misdeed he
hadn't committed, he could see that Clare intended for him to be marked with another.

Clare had awaited his answer. So had the
men. He had left them waiting.

Despite Clare's obvious attempt to manipulate him, however, one truth had emerged clearly. He needed to take his place in the main house, where he belonged.

Leaving the bunkhouse without looking back, Tanner entered the main house to the reverberating ring of clanging pots coming from the direction of the kitchen. Tiny was washing up after supper, and Clare was apparently with him. He could hear her talking to the cook in a tone more suited to addressing someone who was deaf, rather than mute. He heard her voice flare with irritation. Tiny had obviously managed to convey a contrary response despite his inability to speak, a response which Clare did not intend to accept. Tanner was almost amused. His exposure to Tiny had been limited, but he sensed that the wily mute had found a satisfying way to deal with the lady of the house that was unavailable to other men.

Grateful for the opportunity to enter unobserved, Tanner moved quickly up the stairs. He paused at his pa's door, then pushed it slowly open. The room was dark and silent except for the sounds of steady breathing coming from the emaciated man in the bed.

Cursing the wave of sadness assaulting him, Tanner pulled the door closed. Pa was dying, but with each rasping word he had demonstrated that he was still the same bastard he had always been.

Tanner walked toward the door to his room. He glanced at the closed bedroom door beside it. Stone's room. The sadness within Tanner deepened. Three years older than he, Stone had been his idol while he was a boy. Stone had shown more patience with him than their father ever did, and he had silently hoped he'd one day be like Stone in every way. He was uncertain when Stone began to change, when he became silent and withdrawn, spending more and more time away from the ranch. Neither could Tanner pinpoint when things started going wrong between them, when Stone started looking at him with the same disapproval as their pa. He now suspected that the time coincided with the day when Pa started blaming Stone for the actions of his "wild and undependable" brother.

Tanner's gaze strayed toward the doorway farther down the hall, and his heart squeezed tight. Lauren's room. He had been six years old when Lauren was born. He remembered his amazement in seeing the small, doll-like baby with red fuzz covering her head—red fuzz that perfectly matched his ma's fiery hair. The years passed, and he recalled the hurt and the puzzlement in Lauren's eyes when Pa ignored her. When Stone could no longer find time for her either, Tanner had tried to compensate for their neglect by serving as both father and older brother—while all the while, Ma had strained to hold the family together.

He remembered Lauren's tears that last day. He had written to her, long letters in which he had tried to explain why he had been unable to take her with him, but his letters had gone unanswered.

Refusing to indulge the painful memories any longer, Tanner pushed open the door to his room, then halted abruptly. Everything was just as it had always been; nothing in the house appeared to have been moved or changed since his ma died. Yet in reality, everything was different.

Suddenly angry, Tanner tossed his bag on the bed. He was halfway down the stairs when Clare stepped into view below. He halted briefly when she asked, "Where're you going, Tanner?"

He strode past her without responding and heard her add, "Running away again?"

Leaving that question unanswered, he walked out the door.

The applause was deafening. Taking a demure bow, Callie smiled at the grinning piano player and whispered over the din, "I owe you, Charlie."

"Miss Callie . . ." Digby was beside her in a wink. "The boys and me want to buy you a drink."

"Wait a minute, Digby," Ace interrupted, appearing unexpectedly at her elbow. "This lady has some things to straighten out with the boss first."

"Aw, Ace, have a heart."

Ignoring the old cowboy's protests, Ace steered Callie toward his table and seated her with a flourish, saying, "Ma'am, you're the toast of the Roundup Saloon."

Raising her brows at his elaborate salute, Callie questioned, "Why do I have the feeling you're not as impressed with my singing as some of the other boys seem to be?"

"Sweetheart—" Ace sat beside her and took her hand. He looked deeply into her eyes. "You're no Lillie Langtry."

Callie laughed aloud. "Finally, a fellow who isn't tone deaf."

His smile broadening, Ace leaned closer. She could smell the sweet scent of his breath, and the even sweeter smell of his cologne. And she could see his eyes dancing when he said, "But even if you don't have much of a voice, you sure have something that knocks these fellas for a loop." He paused. "It could be that red dress, I suppose, and then again, it could be the way you fill it out."

Unable to resist joining in the play, Callie leaned toward him, allowing him a glimpse of the firm, white flesh spilling over the daring neckline of her gown as she whispered, "I just want to know one thing, boss. Am I supposed to be flattered or insulted by what you just said?"

"I suppose you should be flattered, because I'm going to tell Charlie I want you to be singing at regular intervals through the evening."

"Like a cuckoo striking the hour, huh?"

Ace's smile stretched wider. "I like you, Callie Winslow. I can see I wasn't wrong when I said we're going to be friends."

"Friends . . ." Callie looked pointedly at the sullen brunette who had been staring at them from the moment Ace took her arm. "Is that lady in blue over there by the bar a 'friend' of yours, too?"

"That's Angie. You haven't met the rest of the girls yet. I'll have Angie introduce you to them."

"Angie is . . . ?"

"She's my woman, sweetheart."

Admiring his honesty, Callie extended her hand. "Friends it is. Anything else you want to tell me?"

"Just keep the songs light and the fellas laughing, and your pay will be waiting for you at the end of the week. And one other thing."

Callie waited.

Suddenly deadly serious, Ace continued, "Unless I miss my guess, you're new to this game. I've been wondering what brought somebody like you to this saloon, but whatever it was, I have one last thing to say. You look great in that dress, Callie Winslow. Like the rest of the men in this saloon, I'm salivating. If you're as smart as I think you are, you'll keep them salivating and won't believe a word any one of them tells you, because odds are that they'll be talking to you with a part of them that has no connection to the heart. And the truth is, a young woman can grow old real fast around here if she's not careful, and I wouldn't like to see that happen to a friend."

Ace was still holding her hand. Suddenly as serious as he, Callie replied, "I may not be the innocent you think I am, Ace."

His dark eyes studied her.

Instantly regretting that small disclosure, Callie withdrew her hand from his and smiled brightly. "And that's all I'm tellin' you. Thanks for the advice."

Standing, Callie took a deep breath and strode toward the bar.

*   *   *

"Tanner moved his clothes into his room. He said he was 'taking his place as a McBride.' Then he walked past your door and down the stairs without looking back." A hint of tears in her eyes, Clare whispered, "I'm sorry, Tom. I wish Tanner wasn't such a disappointment to you. I know you were hoping that he had changed, but it looks like . . . well . . ." She shook her head, as though unwilling to go on.

Tom McBride nodded, and Clare gripped his hand tighter. His hand was bony, like the rest of his body, but the eyes that returned her gaze were acutely clear. Damn the man! He had recuperated from the attack—again.

Tom responded in a voice that belied his fragile appearance, "Where did Tanner go? Tell him I want to talk to him."

"I don't know where he went. He left the ranch and wouldn't say where he was going."

"Jeb probably knows."

"If he does know, he won't tell me. You know Jeb doesn't like me." Clare leaned closer. "Tom, darling, I don't want you to expect too much from Tanner. You know how he is. The way he looks at me . . ." Appearing to regret that disclosure, she continued hastily, "I . . . I just don't think he's changed very much."

"Have Jeb tell Tanner that I want to see him when he comes back."

Clare nodded, then began hesitantly, "You know how much I want you to get well, Tom." Her smile wobbled artfully as she continued, "And you know what happened the last time you tried to talk to Tanner. Those letters you asked Bill Hanes to send . . . I wish I had known about them ahead of time. I would've tried to talk you out of it. You're not up to what you've let yourself in for."

"It's now or never, Clare."

"Don't say that!" Clare buried her face in his shoulder. Her voice was muffled when she said, "You will get well." She drew back abruptly, her cheeks damp. "But I don't think you should talk to Tanner yet, for the sake of your health."

His gaze never clearer, Tom responded, "There's only one person who can set Tanner straight, and that's me. Tell him I want to see him tomorrow morning."

"Tom—"

"I'm tired now. I want to rest."

Pulling the bedroom door closed behind her, Clare stood stock still. The bastard had dismissed her again!

Clare remained motionless for an endless moment as she struggled to control her frustration. How much longer would she have to wait?

111

*   *   *

The bright lights and loud music of Sidewinder's main street called to him like an old friend, but Tanner nudged his mount on. An endless parade of thoughts had moved across his mind on the long ride to town. The only conclusion that had emerged with any clarity was his need to talk to Doc Pierce, so he could learn firsthand what his pa's condition really was. He didn't want to chance causing another episode like the one the previous day, but he had the feeling that time was running out.

Riding resolutely past the bright lights and swinging doors, Tanner ignored the bawdy music and raucous laughter echoing from within. He remembered earlier times when he had deliberately ignored his duties at the ranch, favoring wild races through town, long evenings spent in his favorite saloon, and even longer nights with willing ladies whose names he couldn't remember. That strategy had earned him the satisfaction of infuriating his pa, but it had also earned him a reputation that had eventually turned against him.

Halting in front of Doc Pierce's storefront at the end of the street, Tanner drew back on his reins with frustration. The sign was still in the window and Doc's living quarters in the rear were dark.

Damn.

Bill Hanes's bespectacled image came to mind, and Tanner scowled. He didn't really want to talk to his father's solicitor again. Hanes had made it clear that he had said all he was able to say to him for the time being; yet he had no choice.

Tanner turned his mount in the direction of the Roundup.

The din inside the Roundup was growing deafening.

Unaccustomed to the quantity of hard liquor she had consumed, Callie excused herself from her avid admirers with a mumbled excuse and a wink, then turned toward the rear of the saloon. Her thoughts had started reeling, and she was acutely aware of the danger of that. She needed a few minutes to clear her head.

Changing direction abruptly, Callie headed for the far corner of the bar. Ace's warning had been right on the mark. Whether it was the red dress or her "fine" singing, she had become the toast of the Roundup for the night. She had been deluged with requests for songs, had had her glass filled more times than was prudent, and had also become the object of the amorous intentions of every lonesome cowboy who had walked through the doors—too many of whom had obviously taken her red dress and husky tone to mean far more than she intended.

Callie attempted to stabilize her thoughts. The bartender turned toward her when she tapped the bar, his thick, black mustache curling like outrageous handlebars above his upper lip. Wiping his hands against the white apron spanning his sizable girth, he questioned, "What'll you have, Callie?"

"Water, Barney . . . please."

A flicker of amusement twitched the fellow's jowled cheeks. Slapping a filled glass down on the counter, he leaned toward her and whispered in a confidential tone, "You're settin' a bad example for the customers, you know."

"There isn't a fellow in this place who can see past the glass in front of him right now, Barney, and you know it."

"I wouldn't say that's true. It looks to me like there's plenty here tonight who can't take their eyes off you."

"Like Digby and Billy Joe."

"Like the boss."

Callie glanced toward Ace's table to see that Angie had assumed a proprietary stance behind him, and that her hand rested easily on Ace's shoulder as he dealt another round. Angie had introduced her to the rest of the girls as Ace instructed, and the truth was that once the sullen expression had been erased from her face, the outspoken brunette had been downright likable. Strangely, Callie felt that the liking was mutual—which could not be said for Marcy, Lola, Rita, Candy, or Maria, who still watched the attention she was getting with open resentment.

If they only knew.

Aware that Barney awaited her reply, Callie raised her shoulder in a casual shrug. "I saw the boss watching me, too. I'll tell you a secret, Barney. He's trying to figure me out, but I think doing that's going be harder than he thought it would be."

A familiar introduction from the piano behind her was met with cheers, and Callie forced a smile. After walking toward the piano with all the stability she could muster, she leaned down to whisper into Charlie's sympathetic ear, "I've sung just about every song I can think of and my mind's gone blank. Got any suggestions?"

" 'Camptown Ladies' might be nice." Charlie leaned toward her with a toothless grin. "Seems like the fellas here are feelin' real good tonight. You might even be able to coax some of them into singin' along with you."

At her nod, Charlie started playing. Taking her

cue, Callie began, "Camptown ladies sing this song . . ."

Startling her, a robust chorus shouted back, "DOODAH, DOODAH!"

The noise within was calamitous.

Scowling, Tanner glanced inside the Roundup. With the exception of the card tables where the players continued their games unaffected, it appeared that every man in the house was singing at the top of his lungs. He hesitated. He was in no mood for this. If he didn't need to talk to Bill Hanes . . . if time wasn't slipping away from him faster than he wanted to acknowledge . . .

His mood darkening by the moment, Tanner pushed open the doors and walked inside.

A woman in a red dress was singing as Tanner worked his way to the bar. The deafening response from the crowd blasted louder as he signaled to Barney Doyle for a drink. He emptied the glass in a gulp, then turned to survey the room more closely. His gaze lingered briefly on the singer. She was young, pretty, and well endowed, but he gave her no more than a moment's thought as he continued his sweep of the room. Bill Hanes wasn't there. Irritated, he turned back toward the bar and motioned to the bartender.

Barney moved closer and leaned toward him with his hand cupping his ear as Tanner asked, "Has Bill Hanes been here yet tonight?"

"No, he's late. He should be arrivin' any time now."

Just his luck.

Tanner tapped the bar for a refill. He downed the second drink and grimaced as the liquor burned a blazing path to his stomach. He was about to signal for another refill when he realized where his present mood was taking him.

Making an abrupt decision, Tanner slapped his coin down on the bar and walked back out through the wide swinging doors.

Echoes of applause were still ringing as Callie made her way through the crowded room. She acknowledged the compliments with a nod and a smile in passing, and restrained a frown as pats on the shoulder slipped lower than they ought. The smoke . . . the noise . . . Her head was pounding and her stomach was churning. She needed a breath of fresh air.

Ahead of her, Digby and Billy Joe waited for her at the bar, but Callie halted abruptly. With a jolt of panic, she felt a sudden lurching in her stomach.

Reaching the street with a speed born of desperation, Callie dashed toward the narrow alleyway between the Roundup and the building next door. She reached it just in time to empty her stomach into a discarded pail lying in the shadows.

I can hold my liquor as well as any man.

Her boast came back to haunt her as Callie lowered herself to her knees. Ace had been right again. She needed to be careful. She had allowed overconfidence to affect her judgment, and she was now paying the consequences. Inhaling deeply, she was suddenly grateful that this rude awakening had occurred before it might have compromised her plans.

Callie sat back on her heels and inhaled again, but her head was still swimming.

"Are you all right?"

Startled at the sound of the deep voice, Callie turned toward the male outline visible at the entrance of the alley. She squinted in an attempt to identify the voice.

"Can you get up?"

Damn it! Who was he? This was all she needed—a witness to describe her embarrassment so the scene could be retold over and over again at the bar until she became the town joke!

"Do you need some help?"

"I'm fine." The wobble in her voice belying her

words, Callie fortified herself for another effort to stand.

The fellow walked toward her and reached down to take her arm, but she jerked it away. "I said I'm fine!"

"You don't look fine."

"Just leave me alone."

"All right, if that's the way you want it."

The fellow stepped into a shaft of light as he turned to leave, exposing the same hard features and strong jaw that had been visible from across the street in the semidarkness of the previous evening. She blurted, "Oh, it's you!"

Tanner stopped in his tracks and looked at the woman in the red dress. He waited until she stammered, "The doc's office . . . it's under my window. I saw you knocking on his door last night before you rode up the street to the Roundup."

Tanner maintained a deliberate silence. He didn't know what had made him follow this woman into the alleyway. He had been waiting near the doors for Bill Hanes to arrive and had only glimpsed her face when she emerged onto the street, but something had jerked tight inside him at that instant. Now looking down at her where she sat back on her heels, the lush femininity unconsciously exposed in her outrageous red dress more distracting than he chose to admit, he knew he had made a mistake. She remembered seeing him on the street the previous night. She had watched him go to the doc's office, and from there to the Roundup. He didn't like being watched. Nor did he like the accusation he had sensed in her voice.

She was struggling to stand. Despite himself, he gripped her arm and raised her to her feet.

"I said I don't need any help."

"That's not all you said."

The woman shrugged off his hand, her expression stiff. He knew the look. Her head was reeling and she was having trouble putting her thoughts together. Taller than he had expected, she still reached only a little past his chin. However, the curves that filled out the folds of her red dress were potent indeed, and when her honey-colored eyes regarded him in obstinate challenge . . .

Tanner frowned and halted his straying thoughts. He had no time for the reaction this feisty little tart aroused in him.

"How's your friend?" she asked abruptly.

"My friend?"

"Your friend, whoever it was who needed a doctor last night. You rode to the doc's office like the devil was chasing you, but it was easy to see that you weren't the one who was sick."

No, he didn't like being watched.

Shrugging when he didn't respond, the woman adjusted the ridiculous red plume that had almost worked loose from her hair, then leaned over and raised her skirt to brush the dirt from her knees, carelessly exposing a glimpse of long, slender legs. Noting his attention as her neckline gapped provocatively, she jerked it back into place with a narrowed gaze and said, "I have to get back to work. The boss'll be looking for me."

He didn't doubt that.

Surprising himself, he said, "I'll buy you a drink."

She searched his expression briefly, then took his arm with a caustic, "I might just as well."

Almost amused by her response, Tanner frowned at the shouted greetings that began the moment the swinging doors thumped closed behind them.

"Hey, Callie, where you been with that fellow?"

"Will you go for a walk with me, too, Callie?"

"Going to sing another song for us, darlin'?"

"Hell, she don't have to sing. Just lookin' at her's good enough for me!"

"Come over here, Callie!" A bearded wrangler

beckoned with a toothless leer. "Come sit on my lap!"

Responding to that last with a lift of her brow that stimulated shouts of laughter, Callie turned back to Tanner. Her smile was deliberate as she drew him toward the bar.

Suspecting that the flirtatious smile Callie flashed up at him was for the benefit of the dark-haired proprietor of the saloon, who was watching them intently, Tanner heard the husky quality she introduced to her voice as she said, "You know my name by now, fella, but I don't know yours."

He paused. "It's Tanner. Tanner McBride."

Tanner felt the jolt that shook her. She was no longer smiling.

"You know the name?"

Appearing momentarily speechless, she said, "I'd have to be deaf not to. You're the talk of the town."

"I always have been, one way or another." A familiar resentment darkened his expression. "And you know something? I don't give a damn."

Tanner heard a subtle change in her voice as she responded, "You know something? I don't give a damn, either."

Surprising him, she leaned warmly against him. Her voice dropped a husky note lower.

"And I don't mind saying I'm looking forward to gettin' to know you."

The evening shadows had lengthened into darkness. Aware that the rest of the hands had retired to the bunkhouse for the night, Jeb walked across the yard, mentally checking off the few chores remaining before he would be free to join them.

His stomach made a vocal complaint, and Jeb unconsciously rubbed the tightly muscled expanse. Supper had not set well with him. The lavish attention Clare had showered on Tanner at the supper table had disturbed him. He had almost been able to hear the other men's minds working when she asked Tanner if he was moving into the main house that evening.

Jeb scowled. Clare had known that Tanner belonged in the main house and would eventually move into his old room, but she had made sure the men would question his reason for doing it. Talk was bound to start, just as Clare had planned. And if he didn't miss his guess, she'd be only too happy to provide a firm basis for the talk if Tanner was agreeable.

He had never known a more conniving woman.

"Jeb . . . wait a minute."

Halting at the entrance to the barn, Jeb turned toward the familiar voice. Clare approached him, her pale beauty visible even in the deep shadows of the yard—but hers was a surface beauty that left him cold.

"Tanner rode off without saying where he was going. Tom wondered where he went."

Tom . . . and Clare.

"Tom said you'd probably know where he was headed."

As if he'd tell her.

"Well?" She was getting impatient. "Do you know where Tanner went or don't you?"

"No."

"What do you mean, no?"

"I don't know. I didn't figure it was my business to ask."

Jeb saw the look she shot him. It said, *You don't like me and I don't like you.* It said, *When I get control of this ranch, you'll be the first one tossed out.* He was accustomed to those looks.

"Are you trying to tell me something, Jeb?" Clare took an aggressive step. "Are you saying it's none of my husband's business where Tanner went?"

Jeb restrained a reply.

"Or are you trying to tell me that it's none of *my* business?"

"Ma'am, you said the words. I didn't."

Clare's lips tightened. "You think you're indispensable on the Circle M, don't you, Jeb?"

Jeb maintained his silence. His amazement that Tom McBride could have preferred this woman to Emily had never been stronger. This woman's beauty was hard and calculated, while Emily's had been natural and warm. Emily's beauty had glowed like the sun. He remembered that had been his thought when he rode onto the Circle M and saw Emily for the first time. Emily had been pregnant with Stone, and she had been so radiant that the sight of her had stolen his breath. It had been only a short leap from there to the eventual realization that he loved her. His love for her had grown stronger with every year that passed, but he had not fooled himself into thinking that Emily would ever love him as anything more than a friend. There had been only one man for her.

Growing more angry by the moment, Clare continued, "You think the place will fall into ruin without you, but you're wrong! Just so you understand, I'm telling you now that the time is coming when I'll prove that the Circle M doesn't really need you at all."

No, she didn't hold a candle to Emily.

"Are you listening, Jeb?"

She didn't even come close.

"Jeb! Did you hear me?"

"Ma'am." Jeb held Clare's gaze without blinking. "I haven't missed a word."

Her face flushing, Clare turned back toward the house. Jeb scowled as he watched her cross the yard. The love of his life had belonged to another man—another man who still had no idea of the wealth he had squandered by turning away from her. Jeb had done his best to conceal Tom McBride's many infidelities from Emily. He had kept his silence during a particularly delicate time when he had known that to do otherwise might have broken her spirit. He respected that silence still.

Clare disappeared into the house. She slammed the door behind her, darkening Jeb's scowl.

Emily's image flashed before his mind. Emily of the fiery hair and sparkling eyes; of the dimpled smile and soft, kind words; of the heart filled to bursting with love; and of the heart that was torn and bleeding.

Jeb took a choked breath. He had tried to lessen the pain Tom McBride had caused her. He had failed, but he would not fail Emily again this time. That was his vow.

*   *   *

Callie forced a smile as she approached the bar on the arm of Tanner McBride.

Tanner McBride . . .

Her sheer incredulity at the moment when he said his name had almost overwhelmed her. She had been caught off guard, expecting that she would recognize him the moment she saw him, but he was not the drunken degenerate she had envisioned. He was taller and more tightly muscled than she had anticipated, with a rangy build more suited to a man who spent long hours working in the saddle than to a fellow who passed his time eluding the law. Nor was he coarse, bearded, and ill-kempt as she had expected. His clean-shaven features were too strong and hard to be considered handsome, but they somehow enhanced the unsettling masculine appeal that rang in his deep voice. Most disturbing of all, however, were the clear, arrestingly blue eyes that had regarded her so intently. Her heart had skipped a beat at the fleeting thought that those startling eyes might be capable of seeing through the deceit she practiced, to the cold intentions beneath. She knew she could not allow that to happen, at any cost.

Someone called her name, interrupting her thoughts, and Callie turned toward the sound.

"Hey, Callie, give us another song!"

"Yeah, how about 'Oh Susanna'?"

"You sure do look pretty when you sing, Callie!"

"You look damned pretty just standin' there, darlin'!"

"Come on, Callie."

Nearing the bar, Callie answered the shouted encouragements with a smile that faded abruptly at the sight of Billy Joe's tight expression and belligerent stance. She knew instinctively what it meant.

"Callie, honey . . ." Raising his voice so it might be heard above the noise, Billy Joe addressed her as she neared, "I don't know where you latched onto that fella whose arm you're holdin', but you're makin' a big mistake if you think he's going to give you a good time tonight. You'd do best to come right over here by me, where you belong."

Tanner's muscular arm tightened revealingly under her palm. Gripping harder, Callie responded lightly, "This fellow said he's going to buy me a drink, Billy Joe, and I'm holding him to it."

"You know who he is, don't you?" A chill moved down Callie's spine as Tanner stopped in his tracks, squaring his stance. Billy Joe continued, "His name's Tanner McBride. You don't want to go wastin' your time on a fellow who killed his own ma."

In a flash of movement too quick for Callie to fully comprehend, Tanner pinned Billy Joe against the bar. Twisting his shirt up against his neck in a grip so tight that Billy Joe gasped for air, Tanner held him helpless as he spat, "If I were you, I wouldn't say another word."

Callie stared at Tanner McBride. His features contorted into a mask of menacing rage, he was almost unrecognizable as the man he had been moments earlier. She saw the power he held under tenuous restraint as he glared down into Billy Joe's white face, and she saw the deadly intent that shone in his blue eyes.

Callie's heart seemed to stop.

Deadly intent.

She heard Ace's voice beside them say, "Let him go, McBride. He's drunk."

Tanner's fist twisted tighter and Billy Joe gasped again.

His soft tone clearly audible in the sudden silence of the saloon, Ace urged, "You don't need trouble right now, McBride, any more than I want trouble here. Let him go."

Quaking with wrath, Tanner grated, "Billy Joe's got something to say to me first . . . isn't that right, Billy Joe?"

Billy Joe made a choked attempt to speak.

"Spit it out!"

"I . . . I made a mistake. I talked out of turn."

Tanner's fist twisted tighter still.

"I'm sorry." Billy Joe strained for breath. "I'm sorry!"

Releasing him so abruptly that Billy Joe almost fell to his knees, Tanner watched as the other man pulled himself erect, then walked unsteadily toward the door.

Callie could not look away from Tanner McBride. His fury was written in every line of his face.

Callie's heart pounded. This person was the true Tanner McBride. She would not let him get away.

Damn him! Where was he?

Clare twisted restlessly in her bed. Turning angrily onto her back, she stared at the shaft of moonlight spilling through her bedroom window. Her jaw was tight with frustration. She had already visited Tanner's room twice since retiring, with the thought that he might have returned while she dozed. She had come back to her bed each time angrier than before.

Clare fought to control her escalating emotions. Tanner had entered her thoughts often during the long years while she had waited for him to return to the Circle M. His face had been especially clear while she had endured Tom McBride's intimate forays. Tanner, with strong, hard features that were transformed by a smile that could be teasing and warm. Tanner, whose taut, sun-darkened skin she longed to smooth with her palms. Tanner, whose lean, rangy power she had dreamed of bringing to life under her stroking touch.

A shadow passed over the moon. The room darkened and Clare's expression grew grim. She was anxious. She needed relief.

Closing her eyes, Clare slid her hand down to the warmth between her thighs and touched herself intimately. Deluding herself, she told herself it was Tanner's hand caressing her. Indulging herself, she pretended it was Tanner's hand seeking the nub of her passion . . . Tanner's hand stroking her with growing intensity. She saw Tanner's face as vividly as if he were beside her. She smelled his masculine scent. She felt his breath on her face. She saw his lips move into a smile—a smile just for her.

Tanner's touch moved deeper, with greater urgency. He was raising her higher. He was satiating her with growing heat, leading her to fruition. Her climax came suddenly and fiercely, as her body pulsed with sharp, jerking spasms and she called Tanner's name out aloud.

Her heart pounding, Clare opened her eyes to the darkness of her room. Her hand was moist. Her body was still quaking. She had allowed herself temporary relief, but in doing so, she had only whetted her appetite for the time when Tanner would truly be lying beside her.

Clare walked to the washstand and poured fresh water into the bowl. She bathed herself leisurely, pretending it was Tanner's hand that smoothed the scented soap against her body, that it was Tanner's hand that caressed her breasts, that it was Tanner's hand that found the intimate crevice between her thighs and slid again inside.

Clare groaned aloud. Tanner's hand. Tanner's touch. Tanner. She was ready for him, and she was waiting.

The raucous sounds of merriment resumed at full volume as Tanner leaned against the bar, drink in hand, but the sting of Billy Joe's taunt lingered. The realization that Billy Joe had merely been too drunk to hold back what everyone else in Sidewinder believed to be true gnawed relentlessly at his innards.

Tanner glanced at Callie. He had been poor

company since the episode with Billy Joe. It was a mystery to him why she had remained at his side when every man in the saloon was calling her name. Neither his silence nor the incident with Billy Joe seemed to have put her off.

Callie was talking to him, her glance sultry and her voice husky. She had attempted to draw him out, telling him that she had arrived in town the previous day, that she had taken a room in Annabelle Chapin's boardinghouse, and that she intended to stay in Sidewinder until she tired of the town.

Tanner stared at Callie without responding. Common sense told him that this seductive little witch was the last thing he needed to complicate his present situation. But common sense did not prevail when she raised those honey-colored eyes toward him.

Tanner's glance slipped to Callie's lips as she spoke again. They were full and colored a delectable red. Somehow he knew that underneath that paint, they were pink and warm, and sweeter than any he had ever tasted. He saw flashes of white teeth as she continued talking. Her tongue darted out to moisten her lips, and his stomach clenched tight.

Tanner resisted the urge to draw Callie closer. If the time and place were different . . .

Forcing himself to draw away from her, Tanner reached into his pocket for his watch. The warm gold caressed his palm, and he frowned. Ma had given the watch to him. It had been her father's, and there had been tears in her eyes when she placed it in his hand.

Shaking off his somber thoughts, Tanner realized that an hour had passed since he had walked back through the Roundup's door—and Bill Hanes still hadn't shown up. Observing his frown, Callie started to speak, only to be interrupted by loud introductory chords from the piano in the corner. He felt her stiffen when the crowd around them erupted in a cheer.

"It's time to sing, Callie!"

"Charlie's waitin' for you at the piano!"

"You've got the voice of an angel, Callie!"

The voice of an angel . . . Tanner's mouth twisted wryly. He had heard Callie sing. It wasn't her voice that these fellows were cheering.

The piano player pounded another chord and Callie turned toward Tanner. A strange intensity was in her gaze when she whispered, "Wait for me."

Cheers sounded again as Callie started toward the piano. She responded with a wiggle and a wink, and the roar rang louder. Turning back toward him when she reached the piano, Callie flashed a look meant for him alone, and his throat went dry.

The saloon doors pushed open as Callie started singing. The short, slender fellow who entered and began working his way toward the bar drove Callie's performance from Tanner's mind. He waited until the man drew within a few feet of him, then stepped into sight.

"Hello, Doc."

Doc Pierce looked up over his wire-rimmed glasses as Tanner extended his hand. Doc accepted it and shook it firmly. "I've been waiting for you to get back to town," Tanner said.

Doc stepped up to the bar and signaled for a drink while Tanner scrutinized him more closely. Weary downward lines marked the doctor's face with shadows. He was older and grayer than Tanner remembered. He was also thinner, his shoulders more stooped, and the sadness in his eyes more profound. Downing his drink, Doc signaled for another, then turned toward Tanner.

"I've been out at the Carson ranch. Betty Carson's baby died. I stayed until they buried it. It was a girl."

Tanner had no response.

"When did you get back to town, boy?" Doc Pierce's gaze was devoid of accusation as he continued, "I was wondering if you'd come."

"You knew about the letters my pa sent?"

"Sure I did. I was with him when he asked Bill Hanes to send them. Clare wasn't there. She was in town."

A cheer sounded as Callie finished her first chorus, and Doc glanced around him with a frown. "It's noisy in here tonight. Let's go outside. I'm thinking there're some things you've got on your mind that you want cleared up."

Downing his drink as soon as Barney placed it on the bar, Doc made his way toward the entrance with a shuffling gait. He sighed as the doors flapped shut behind them and looked up. "I'm tired, Tanner. I've been up day and night for four days, so this conversation's going to be short. Come on and walk with me."

His expression grew pensive as Tanner fell into step beside him. "You want to know what's happening with your pa, is that it?"

Tanner nodded. "He looks bad."

"He's dying, but you knew that. It's his heart."

"I thought it was his lungs."

"Heart . . . lungs . . . they're related, you know. One starts failin' and the other fills up. His attacks have been getting closer and more severe. Sooner or later he isn't going to make it through one of them."

"He had some kind of an attack the first day I got here. I rode into town to get you, but you were already gone."

"I couldn't have done too much more for your pa than Tiny probably did. He's a find, that Tiny." Doc shrugged. "Clare don't like him much, though."

Tanner searched Doc's expression in the dim light. He spoke frankly. "There are some things I need to say to my pa before he dies, Doc—things that have waited too long already. What I don't want is for the same thing to happen again that happened the last time I tried to talk to him."

"If you're looking for me to give you some assurances, I'm going to disappoint you."

"So you're saying . . ."

"What I'm saying is that I can't be certain what will happen if something you say excites him. The only thing I can tell you for sure is that if you don't say what's on your mind soon, you may lose your chance."

"But—"

Doc halted at his doorway. Regarding Tanner intently, he continued, "Look, Tanner, I heard all the rumors making the rounds when your ma was killed. I heard all the rumors circulating when you left the Circle M five years ago, too. As far as I'm concerned, none of it's my business, but for the record, there's no doubt in my mind that you'd never do anything that might risk your ma's life. As for Clare, well, I'm thinking a good woman like your ma would never raise a son fool enough to fall for the games that woman plays."

"It's too bad my pa doesn't agree with you."

"Your pa hasn't used too much common sense in dealing with his family up until now, or he wouldn't be in the predicament he's in. Your pa asked me, and I obliged him by giving him a time limit on how long he can expect to be around. Nine months—but that ain't no guarantee. The truth is, he might not make it that long."

Doc paused, seeming to reconsider that thought. "Then again, knowing the kind of man your pa is, he might just be ornery enough to last the nine months out."

Doc paused with his hand on the doorknob. "I'll ride out to see your pa when I'm rested up, if that's what you want, but I doubt if I'll be telling you anything different than I'm telling you now."

Doc asked unexpectedly, "Do you think the others will come when they get your pa's letter?"

"I don't know."

"I saw Stone before he left. He said he wasn't ever coming back, and you know how Stone is once he puts his mind to something."

"Yes, I know."

"As for Lauren . . . I think her heart was broke. She went back to Savannah where your ma came from, and I don't think she had in her mind ever seeing the Circle M again."

A familiar ache tightened inside Tanner.

"Sorry, Tanner. I wish I could say something that would make you feel better." Doc shook his head. "Hell, I hate to say it, but it looks like everything's going Clare's way."

Clare.

Tanner's jaw hardened. "No, not everything's going her way."

A smile picked at Doc's lips. "Glad to hear you say that, boy."

Staring at the closed door long minutes after Doc had disappeared inside, Tanner turned back toward the Roundup. Applause was still ringing when he paused at the entrance and looked inside. Callie had just finished singing.

Suddenly having no stomach for any of it, Tanner walked abruptly toward the hitching post and untied his horse's reins. Mounted moments later, he turned his horse back toward the Circle M.

Callie . . . sweet as honey. He'd never know for sure.

Callie worked her way through the crowded room, her gaze intent on the bar where she had left Tanner McBride. Struggling to control her panic, she ignored the slurred words of praise rained upon her by a swaying cowboy nearby and motioned for Barney's attention.

"He's gone." Responding to her unspoken question, Barney continued, "He left with Doc. I saw him standin' outside the door when you were finishin' your song, but he walked away."

Callie's heartbeat rose to thunder in her ears as she demanded, "Did he say he was leaving town?"

"Don't know. It'll be a shame if he don't come back here, though."

"A shame?"

Barney reached under the bar and withdrew a gold pocket watch. "He left his watch on the bar."

Barney held the pocket watch by its gold chain. Staring at it for a silent second, Callie snatched it from his hand and dropped it into the neckline of her gown.

"Hey!" Barney stared helplessly at the firm, white flesh of her generous cleavage. "What am I supposed to say if Tanner comes back lookin' for that watch?"

"Don't worry. I'm going to make sure Tanner gets this . . . and everything else that's due him."

Her smile hard and her mind resolute, Callie touched her fingers to her forehead in a jaunty salute, then started back through the crowd.

Chapter Five

"Clare! Is that you?"

Morning sunlight filtered into the hallway beyond Tom McBride's bedroom. Clare halted impatiently at the sound of his voice. She turned toward the closed door with a frown.

"Clare . . ."

Damn the man! She had no time for him now.

"Clare, are you out there?"

Teeth clenched, Clare reached for the doorknob, then paused with cold deliberation. Her delicate jaw still tight, she tossed back her hair and straightened her shoulders. Let him wait. She had waited five years to get what *she* wanted, hadn't she?

Clare took a calming breath. She was in a

mood, and she knew it. She hadn't liked what she'd seen in the mirror that morning. A restless night had left dark shadows under her eyes and tight lines of frustration around her mouth. She didn't like appearing at less than her best, and she didn't like the idea that Tanner had thwarted her.

Clare remembered awakening a short time earlier to see daylight creeping through her bedroom window—and to realize that the night had slipped away from her. Throwing on her robe, she had moved quietly down the hallway to Tanner's room. Her frustration had multiplied when she pushed open the door to see that Tanner's bed had indeed been slept in, but that he was already gone.

The smell of bacon and the sound of male voices coming from the dining room below had sent her anger soaring. She had rushed back to her room to dress, with the thought of joining Tanner and the men for breakfast, and she had not been more than a few steps from the staircase when—

"Clare . . ."

Affixing a smile on her lips, Clare pushed open the bedroom door and moved quickly to Tom's bedside. She took his hand.

"Tom, dear, what's wrong? Hasn't Manuelo or

Tiny come up to tend to you yet this morning? You sound upset."

She didn't like the way Tom's eyes searched her face. "I want to talk to Tanner."

"I was just on my way downstairs." She hesitated. "He didn't come home until late last night. I was asleep and I didn't get a chance to tell him you wanted to speak to him." She paused again, adding as if unwillingly, "I'm afraid he's slipping into his old ways."

Tom's gaze stared deeper. Somehow uncomfortable under its intensity, Clare laid her head against his shoulder. She steeled herself against the repulsive deterioration of his body as she whispered, "I'd do anything to spare you this aggravation, Tom. It must be terrible to have your son disappoint you over and over again. Please don't hold yourself responsible for his faults."

"He's my son, Clare."

"Tom—"

"Tell him I want to see him . . . now."

Startled at the underlying strength in his voice, Clare straightened up and looked down into Tom's face. His eyes were clear. His color had improved. He appeared somehow . . . stronger.

Sudden panic sent a flush of heat to Clare's face. No, he couldn't possibly get well!

"Clare . . ." Tom's voice gentled. He reached for her hand. "Don't upset yourself. Just tell Tanner to come up here."

Sliding her hand out of his with feigned reluctance, Clare stood up, then nodded. She drew the door closed behind her and stood motionless, her expression tight. Tom McBride. Still lucid. Still dangerous.

Then raising her delicate chin, she smiled. But no . . . he'd never get well.

"Let me help you, ma'am."

Her hands resting on her mount's saddle, Callie turned toward the bearded fellow standing a few feet away. She squinted as a beam of brilliant morning sunlight caught her eye, then blinked away the momentary blindness.

She had arrived at the livery stable a short time earlier to discover that the proprietor was Dan White, whose heart she had obviously captured forever the moment she had sung his favorite song the previous night. She had almost been amused at the way his eyes widened at first sight of her this morning. She had purchased her new riding outfit with great care earlier that morning, aware that the split skirt hugged her small waist and hips too tightly, and that the white shirtwaist, deliberately purchased a size too small, did little to disguise the ample female proportions underneath. She had seen him swallow with particular difficulty as his gaze dipped to the cord of her hat, which had settled in the cleavage artfully exposed by a shirtwaist button she had neglected to secure. It appeared the message she meant to convey was very clear, but in Dan's case, it had only made him frown.

Responding to his offer of help, she said, "That's all right, Dan. I can mount by myself."

"Ma'am . . ." The bewhiskered fellow shook his head. "I just don't feel right about seein' you ride off alone . . . a young, pretty woman like yourself. It just ain't safe."

"I can take care of myself. Don't worry."

"You might run into somethin' you ain't ex-pectin'. Then what would you do?"

Her smile softening her words, Callie replied, "A young, pretty woman like me would handle it, just like she always has." Anxious to end the conversation and be on her way, Callie turned back to her horse and mounted with a quick, fluid movement that startled Dan into silence.

Regretting her brusqueness, Callie repeated more softly than before, "Don't worry. I'll be all right."

Not allowing Dan time for a response, she guided her mount out onto the street.

Relieved when Sidewinder slipped into the distance behind her, Callie glanced up at the cloudless sky and breathed deeply as a soft breeze fanned her. The land sprawling out on either side of her was scented by wildflowers and was resplendent with brilliant red, yellow, and blue as far as the eye could see. The scents evoked sweet memories that had recently become painful, and her throat grew tight. She was intensely aware that if things were as they should have been at that moment, she would be riding on the land she and Matt shared, and Matt would be riding beside her. Shouting brief commands to the men, his eyes ever watchful as they searched out strays, her brother would be keeping the cattle moving and the ranch hands working with the skill and good humor that was so much a part of his personality.

Callie's throat squeezed tighter. She remembered the day Matt surprised her with a ticket to St. Louis to visit their mother's sister—a birthday present. She remembered the flicker of sadness in his eyes when he said he wished it could've been easier for her growing up. He said he had done his best for her, but he wished he could've done more. He wished she'd had the time to do all the things other girls did, instead of having to work alongside him.

Callie smiled unconsciously. Matt had been so protective of the sister ten years his junior who had been left in his care when their parents died. He hadn't seemed to realize that he had unwittingly provided her with an education far broader than most young women were afforded. Somehow it hadn't occurred to him that casual conversations between the ranch hands, while she poured over her lessons beside the campfire, had taught her far more than she could ever have learned in books.

Callie remembered how Matt's face had brightened when he put the ticket in her hand and said that since the ranch was getting on its feet, he could finally afford to do something special for her birthday. She hadn't had the heart to tell him that she would rather have stayed home so she'd be able go the bank with him when he went to make the final payment on the loan they had worked so hard to repay. Instead, she had accepted the ticket with thanks, and when the time came, she had boarded the train and said good-bye.

That was the last word she had spoken to her brother. She was in St. Louis, at a frivolous party thrown by a silly, immature young woman who had never done a real day's work in her life, when Matt walked into the bank to pay off the loan. He did not come out alive.

She had taken the first train home when the news finally reached her. She could not recall too much that happened in the days full of sorrow that followed, but burned indelibly into her mind was the moment when she stood alone over her brother's grave, with a single name drumming in her mind.

Tanner McBride, who had been part of the murderous gang that killed her brother.

Tanner McBride, who had been released from jail the day before she returned home.

Tanner McBride, whom she had vowed to find.

Tanner McBride, who would lead her to the rest of the gang so that justice could finally be done—justice, one way or another.

Callie ran her hand over the smooth leather of her saddlebag and stroked it lightly. Yes, Matt would have called it a sissy gun—but a bullet was a bullet, after all.

"You wanted to see me, Pa?"

Tanner stood stiffly at the foot of his father's bed. Having slept poorly after returning from town the previous night, he had risen early with the thought that a good breakfast might alleviate the throbbing in his head. Clare's unexpected appearance at the breakfast table had had the reverse effect. The announcement that his father wanted to see him could not have been more inopportune.

He had entered his father's airless quarters, where the windows were closed tight against any draft. The room was overly bright and hot. The stagnant atmosphere added an aura of unreality to the scene when the wasted man in bed responded to his question in a voice unexpectedly strong and strident, "That's right, I wanted to see you. We need to finish the conversation we started a few days ago."

Tanner frowned, his talk with Doc the previous night flashing to mind.

"Don't look at me that way." McBride's voice was antagonistic. "I'm not dead yet. And I'm still the boss around here, so there're some things I want you to get straight."

His concern vanishing, Tanner replied, "I've got some things to say, too."

McBride's faint smile was caustic. "Same old Tanner."

"No . . . I'm not."

McBride's eyes said otherwise before he spat, "The last time you stood where you're standing now, you said my letter didn't bring you back, that you came back because you chose to come back."

"That's right."

"Why?"

"Because you're dying." Tanner's voice was cold. "Because I need to know some things before you do."

McBride's blue eyes were mocking. "Looking to drag old skeletons out of the closet?"

"Maybe."

"Say what you got to say and be done with it, then!"

Tanner withheld a sneer. "You said I'm the 'same old Tanner,' but I'm not. The *old* Tanner who left this ranch five years ago didn't leave because you threw him off, like you thought. He left because he couldn't bear to know the truth. The *new* Tanner won't leave until he hears it."

"What are you talking about, damn it?"

"I fixed that wheel, Pa."

"And you say you aren't the same old Tanner!"

A slow fury increased the pounding in his head, and Tanner took an aggressive step. His pa would never change. He was still the same arrogant, self-centered bastard he had always been.

Tanner locked his pa's gaze with his. "I said . . . I fixed the wheel on ma's wagon, yet it fell off."

"You're talking like a fool! Say what you mean right out instead of beating around the bush! If you want me to—" McBride abruptly stopped speaking. His eyes widened. "Are you saying you think I had something to do with that wheel coming off . . . that I had something to do with your ma's accident?"

"Did you?"

Tom McBride was suddenly breathing hard. His face whitening, he spat, "I'd tell you to get out of this room and never come back, but I've got some things to say to you first." His hollowed chest heaved with strain. "I sent that letter to all of you because I wanted you all back here at the same time."

Increasingly breathless, McBride struggled to continue. Unwilling to see a repeat of the previous episode between them, Tanner made a move toward the door.

"Don't you leave yet, damn it!" McBride's eyes were bulging. "Listen to me! I want you to stay here . . . on this ranch . . . until the others come. But I want you to stay away from Clare!"

Momentarily stunned, Tanner laughed aloud.

"You laugh . . ." McBride managed a stiff nod. "Just stay away from her!"

Tanner stopped laughing.

"I don't need to see you again, either—not until the others come—so stay out of this room, too!"

Tanner stiffened.

"And if you think I'm going to give you the satisfaction of an answer to your question . . . you're wrong! Get out! I've got nothing else to say to you until the others get here."

"That might be never."

"You'd better hope . . ." McBride wheezed. "You'd better hope it's not."

Tanner stared at the pathetic shell of a man who glared at him.

"Get out, I said!"

Disregarding the venom in McBride's gaze, Tanner repeated, "I fixed that wheel."

"You didn't!"

"I fixed it."

"Bastard!"

Tanner's response was aborted when he was unexpectedly thrust aside by Tiny's powerful hand. Turning angrily toward Tiny as the short, squat fellow rushed past him, he heard the hollow rattling of McBride's breath, and took a step back.

Strangely numb as he walked out into the hallway, Tanner felt neither pity nor concern.

Instead, frustration twisted deep by the time he reached the yard where the ranch hands were mounting up. Pa had won again. Frail and weak as he was, he had still managed to put off responding to the gnawing question that had gone so long unanswered.

"Tanner . . ."

Tanner looked at Clare as she walked up behind him. Not bothering to respond, he mounted his horse and rode out with the men, leaving her glaring after him.

Callie glanced up at the position of the sun in the cloudless sky, then nudged her mount to a faster pace. The pleasant morning was turning hot. There was little shade, and unlike the comfortable clothes she was accustomed to wearing on the trail, the close-fitting attire she had purchased that morning was beginning to adhere to her like a second skin.

Consoling herself that it wouldn't be much farther, Callie mused at the ease with which she had gotten directions to the Circle M Ranch. Hiram Wiggins at the general store had welcomed her warmly when she entered early that morning to make her purchases. She had realized when his smile seldom faltered that the balding, middle-aged storekeeper probably greeted everyone with the same good humor. She had momentarily envied him, remembering a time when her smile was seldom forced and her heart was light.

It had not been difficult to direct their conversation toward Tanner McBride as she busied herself among Hiram Wiggins's wares. His expression sobering, Hiram had rambled on, needing little encouragement. She had emerged a short time later with her purchases and directions to the Circle M.

Callie scrutinized the surrounding terrain with a practiced eye. She had been on the trail for well over an hour. According to Hiram's directions, the wooded patch she had just passed signaled that she would soon be on McBride land. She should be able to see the first Circle M marker when she rode over the next rise.

Matt's image flashed unexpectedly before her mind, and Callie's throat choked tight. Matt wouldn't have approved of what she intended to do. He had kept a close eye on the ranch hands, and on every man who so much as glanced in her direction. If he could see her now . . .

Callie's expression hardened. But Matt wasn't with her now, and he never would be with her again—because someone had made the split-second decision that her brother's life was worth no more than the price of a single bullet. Tanner McBride had been a part of it. She would not rest until she had proved to him and all involved that they were wrong.

Her jaw tight, Callie urged her mount over the rise ahead. The marker with the Circle M brand came into view. No, it wouldn't be much longer.

"Tanner. Tanner!"

Tanner turned, abruptly aware that Jeb was shouting his name.

"Over there by you, that heifer's runnin' off!"

Wheeling his mount with a practiced hand, Tanner leaned low over the saddle as he raced to catch the fleeing animal. He cursed as the heifer eluded him and stumbled into a bramble thicket that held it fast. The heifer was bawling loudly when he reached its side. Working to free it with minimal damage, Tanner watched as it scrambled back toward the herd long minutes later. Much the worse for wear, he cursed again at the sight of his ripped shirt and the deep gouges in his arm.

"You keep this up and you're going to end up killin' yourself."

Tanner glanced up into Jeb's scowl as the foreman reined up beside him.

"Damn it, Tanner, what's the matter with you today? You're endin' up to be more trouble than you're worth this mornin'!"

Tanner's jaw clenched. "So the damned critter almost got away from me! I caught her, didn't I? And I got her out of trouble."

"Yeah . . . sure." Glancing behind him to see the ranch hands observing their exchange, Jeb dismounted. "Look at yourself, Tanner," he continued in a softer tone. "You're a mess. Your shirt's torn and you're scratched to hell. You look like you've been in a fight."

"I'll live."

"Think so?" Jeb shook his head. "I'm not so sure. Not if you keep up the way you've been going this mornin'. You're an accident waitin' to happen. Look—" Jeb took a step closer—"I know you had words with your pa this mornin' and you got things on your mind. I'm not askin' what he said to you that's got you so riled up. All I'm sayin' is that your mind ain't on what you're doin' and you're no help here. Do yourself a favor and quit for the day. You can go back to the ranch and—"

"No."

"Then go to town and find some woman who'll help you work off some of that frustration you've got stored up inside you. Hell, there should be some of your old lady friends left in Sidewinder! Even if there ain't, you shouldn't have too much trouble findin' a woman to oblige you."

Silence.

"Tanner, listen to me. You're a distraction here, and we've got a lot of work to accomplish before we start brandin'. We can't afford to fall behind. Do what I say . . . give yourself a chance to cool off."

Tanner's silence lengthened.

"Tanner . . ."

"All right!" Tanner turned toward his horse.

"Tanner . . ."

Tanner looked back and met Jeb's eye. "You're right. I'm not doing anybody any good here. I'll see you tonight."

Tanner was mounted and on his way before Jeb could reply.

There it was, just where Hiram Wiggins had said it would be.

Callie looked at the sparkling stream that wound its way through the distant countryside. Picture perfect, it followed a rambling path that appeared to originate beyond a wooded glade to the west. If her sense of direction was correct—and she was sure it was—it was due west from that glade to the Circle M ranch house.

Refusing to acknowledge the sudden tightening of her stomach, Callie kicked her mount forward. She maintained her accelerated pace until she reached the trees, then drew back on the reins. The cool shadows of the forested patch were tempting. She was hot and sweaty. She had no doubt her face was unnaturally flushed and that her discomfort was obvious. She was not at her best at a time when she needed full confidence to accomplish her purpose.

Making a sudden decision, Callie turned her mount into the glade at a cautious pace. Out of the sun's beating rays, the air was immediately cooler. The breeze that rustled the trees overhead stirred the air. She urged her mount toward the stream and dismounted, allowing him to drink. Walking upstream, she crouched by the water's edge, removed her hat, and scooped water into her palms to drink. Repeating the process until her thirst was quenched, Callie then rubbed the cool water over her heated face and neck. Partially relieved, she attempted to pick her damp shirtwaist away from her skin. When the effort proved useless, she made a sudden decision.

Standing up, Callie unbuttoned the stifling garment and stripped it off. The air cooled her as she draped the shirtwaist over a low-hanging limb. Disregarding her flimsy lace chemise, she turned back to the stream to splash water liberally on her shoulders and breasts.

She breathed deeply. Better, but not enough.

Pulling off her boots, she tossed them aside, then rolled the bottoms of her split skirt up to mid-thigh before stepping down into the stream to splash the cool water against her legs.

"That looks like it feels good."

Callie jerked erect as the familiar masculine voice broke the silence. Turning abruptly toward it, she struggled to hide the sudden pounding of her heart as she responded, "Tanner . . . it's you."

"That's right, it's me."

Dismounting, Tanner advanced toward Callie slowly, marveling at the sight before him. Incredibly, it was Callie, looking far different from the brightly clothed saloon woman he had met the night before.

He walked closer. Her face was washed clean of the previous night's paint, exposing skin that was fine and smooth. The damp tendrils of hair lining her face somehow emphasized the graceful contours of her cheek while revealing a youthful vulnerability not previously evident. But her honey-colored eyes were the same. They were clear and bright with challenge, except for the flash of an emotion he could not quite identify. She stood boldly, with only a layer of transparent lace between his gaze and the firm, white swells of her breasts. Momentarily mesmerized, he watched a bead of glistening water trickle from her neck in a tantalizing downward path that disappeared between the firm mounds.

Annoyed when his body reacted predictably, Tanner attempted to ignore the dark aureoles pressed against the bodice of Callie's lacy undergarment as he asked, "What are you doing out here on Circle M land, Callie?"

"I came to see you, of course."

"You came to see me. Why?"

"You left the Roundup without saying goodbye. I wondered why."

Tanner's eyes narrowed. "You came all the way out here to ask me that?"

Callie shrugged. "And . . . you left something behind on the bar."

"My watch." He had realized it wasn't in his pocket after he left the house that morning, but he had thought he'd left it in his room. "Where is it?"

"In my saddlebag."

Tanner turned toward her horse.

Callie said, "I'll get it."

Wading onto the bank, Callie approached her nervous mount and unbuckled her saddlebag. He sensed her momentary hesitation when she reached inside. Withdrawing the watch abruptly, she turned back toward him with her hand held behind her back, then said, "What are you going to give me for it?"

Sharp disappointment furrowed Tanner's brow. "I guess I should've expected that."

"Really? Why?"

"You came a long way just to do a favor for somebody you hardly know." He paused, then said, "How much do you think your trip's worth?"

"I asked you what you were going give me. I don't want money."

"Not money . . ."

"No. Telling me what made you leave last night would be better." Callie looked up at him, her gaze direct. "There aren't too many fellas who would've walked out on me like you did . . . especially after I encouraged them to stay." She shrugged. "Truth is, my pride was hurt. Then when I heard you left with Doc, I figured there must've been some kind of an emergency that took you away."

Tanner did not respond.

"Don't want to tell me?" Callie's gold eyes narrowed seductively. "What's the matter, Tanner? Need a little coaxing?"

"Give me the watch."

"Your friend sick again?"

"Give me the watch, Callie."

"It's your pa that's sick, isn't it?"

"I said . . . give me the watch."

161

"Why won't you talk to me?"

"I can take the watch from you without any problem, but I prefer not to. I'd rather you put it into my hand."

Withdrawing her hand from behind her back, Callie dropped the watch into the bodice of her chemise. It glittered tauntingly underneath the lace as she said with sudden earnestness, "I heard a lot of talk about you last night, but I don't believe half of what was said."

"Maybe you should."

"You don't mean that. I saw the look on your face when Billy Joe said what he did. You don't want me or anybody else believing—"

"It's none of your business."

"Isn't it?" Callie's gold eyes were suddenly burning. "I thought we were getting to know each other last night. I saw the way you were looking at me, and I was feeling the same. I know you wouldn't have left like you did if something hadn't happened to upset you."

"Whatever happened was *my* business."

"It was my business, too!" Advancing until she was so close that Tanner could see the fiery sparks in her gaze, Callie murmured huskily, "Talk to me, Tanner."

Startled at her own emotional plea, Callie struggled for control. What had begun as a ploy to encourage Tanner's confidence had become an earnest entreaty that came from somewhere deep inside. "About what Billy Joe said."

"I don't want to talk about what Billy Joe said!"

"Everybody's saying—"

"Give me the watch, damn it!"

"Tanner—"

"All right, if that's the way you want it."

Callie gasped as Tanner reached unexpectedly into the neckline of her chemise and grasped the watch. She caught his hand through the fine lace and held it immobile, her heart thundering as she said, "I won't give the watch up without a fight."

"Let go of my hand."

"No."

"You're making a mistake, Callie."

"Am I?" Callie's breathing grew ragged. "It won't be the first if I am."

"Give me the watch, now, or you may regret it."

"Maybe . . ." Callie responded in a whisper, ". . . and maybe I won't."

He was losing it. Callie's breasts were warm against his hand. The soft flesh tantalized him as she held his hand imprisoned with hers. He twisted his hand in an effort to loosen her grip, an action that was inadvertently caressing, and Callie's eyelids flickered. His body hardened. He moved his hand again, the action more deliberate, and he heard her gasp. The sweet rush of sound shuddered through him with sudden heat.

"Callie . . ."

His voice was hoarse, hardly recognizable as his own. He saw the sensual droop of Callie's eyelids, felt her breasts rising with quickened breathing against his palm. He hadn't intended this.

"Callie, give me the watch and leave, before it's too late."

"I said . . ." Callie's voice faltered. "I won't give it up without a fight."

"Callie . . ."

"I told you—"

"I know what you told me." Cupping Callie's head with his free hand, Tanner lowered his mouth to hers with a grating rasp. "Damn it, I know."

Sweet as honey . . . The words sounded in his mind as Tanner touched his lips to hers.

Sweeter than any he had ever known . . . The sentiment echoed deep inside him as he devoured her mouth with his kiss.

Callie's lips separated under his and his tongue drove deeper, delving to stroke her tongue, teasing it into play. He heard her weak protest when he tore his mouth from hers, then trailed heated kisses down her throat toward the warm swells beneath. Pushing the chemise from her shoulders, he bared the tender flesh fully at last and covered an erect crest with his lips. Pleasure jolted through him at Callie's impassioned grasp, and Tanner suckled her boldly, claiming one rounded breast, then the other, with heated fervor.

She was sweet . . . so sweet. She was hot and giving, and he hungered for her, even as a nagging voice in the back of his mind warned . . .

This was wrong. She hadn't intended things to go so far.

Breathless, hardly capable of coherent thought as Tanner raised his head from her breast to cover her mouth again with his, Callie fought the waves of madness overwhelming her. She was helpless under his touch as his mouth consumed hers.

Struggling for control, Callie rasped, "This is too fast. I need time. I . . . I need you to talk to me. Talk to me, Tanner."

"It's too late for talk, Callie."

"No. There are things I need to say." Hardly able to speak, Callie whispered in a shaky voice, "You weren't what I expected when I first saw you. I was surprised. The town . . . everybody says you're wild . . . crazy . . . that it'd be hard to know what you're going to do next. I didn't believe it until I saw what you did to Billy Joe."

"I don't want to talk about it."

"Tanner . . . please."

"What do you want to hear, Callie?" Tanner's breathing was labored. "Do you want me to tell you that the first time I saw you when you came running out of the Roundup, something twisted tight inside me? Do you want to hear that, even though the last thing I needed was another complication in my life, I couldn't let you walk away?"

"Yes." Callie's voice was a frantic whisper. "Tell me—"

"More?" Tanner's short laughter was caustic. "I'll tell you that I know better than this . . . better than to let something like this happen when I should be concentrating on finding a way to fix everything that's gone wrong from the first day I came back to the Circle M. But instead, I'm looking into your eyes and trying to make myself believe that you came all the way out here just because you couldn't stay away from me."

"I couldn't."

"Callie." Tanner's voice was a tortured plea. "Don't lie to me."

"I'm not."

"Callie . . ."

"Why did you leave me last night, Tanner?"

Silence.

"When you didn't come back, I thought . . ."

"I left because I knew what would happen if I stayed, damn it!" His gaze impassioned, Tanner rasped, "I knew it wouldn't take much before you'd edge yourself down deep inside me, and I didn't want that, especially after I talked with Doc and he . . ."

Halting abruptly, Tanner held her in his scorching gaze. "All right, you wanted the truth, and this is it. You're the last person I want in my arms right now. I knew that last night, and I did my best to avoid it. I would've preferred Marcy, Lola, or Maria, or any other woman I'd be content to use and forget. I knew it wouldn't be that way with you."

Tanner took a hard breath, his gaze gripping hers. "But it's too late for me to back away now. It's . . . too late."

Callie's heart was pounding. She had encouraged Tanner to speak, but she hadn't expected the raw emotion in his words. Nor had she expected his intensity, the yearning that rang in his voice, or the hunger that shone so fiercely in his blue eyes.

"Callie . . ."

He was waiting for her to respond. The husky rasp of his voice, his need, raised a responsive longing within her so deep that she shuddered under its assault.

"Answer me, Callie."

She could not.

"Callie . . ."

Not trusting her voice, knowing she could respond in no other way, Callie raised her lips to his.

Tanner's mouth closed over hers fiercely then. Yielding to his kiss, indulging it, Callie surrendered to the emotions that rose in an overwhelming swell.

Callie protested softly when Tanner withdrew his mouth from hers. The last of her control slipped away as Tanner sank to his knees to devour her breasts with new hunger. She wrapped her arms around him, clutching him closer as he suckled her with growing heat. She was beyond conscious thought as he fumbled with the buttons on her skirt and in a swift movement stripped it away. She gasped when he separated her thighs and nuzzled them to taste her intimately.

Seeing herself as if from a distance, Callie groaned aloud when Tanner caressed the nub of her passion with his tongue. Her knees buckled as wave after wave of spiraling passion left her weak. She felt Tanner's strong arms easing her to the ground, where he returned to the moist crease with sweeping forays.

Conscious thought drained away while Tanner's tender ministrations raised her to a plane of ecstatic oblivion. She felt it coming then, the shuddering within that helplessly shook her, the jerking spasms that racked her with joyous heat as her body pulsed in ecstatic release.

Suddenly aware of the cool ground beneath her, Callie opened her eyes to see Tanner crouched above her. Still breathless as he spread her thighs with his callused hands, she saw only the hot pinpoints of light in his clear eyes as he whispered, "Callie . . . sweet as honey."

The glorious heat resumed as Tanner lowered his mouth to her once more, and Callie closed her eyes. Drawing deeply from her with hungry yearning, Tanner assaulted her with his loving. Helpless against the fervor building within, Callie indulged his intimate journey, glorying until the intensity, no longer bearable, erupted in a flash of white heat that brought her again to climax.

Lying weakly under his touch, Callie did not protest when Tanner raised himself to kiss her breasts. Licking and teasing, he savored the delicate flesh until she was again hot and yearning underneath him. "Tanner . . ." she gasped in a whispered plea. "Not yet," he whispered.

She was no longer capable of protest. Tanner's tongue stroked her with growing heat, and Callie felt a new euphoria rising. Beyond conscious thought, she was hardly aware of his shifting movement as he drew back from her to slip his hand down into the moist crease he had explored so intimately. Opening her eyes, she saw Tanner looking down intently into her face. Her eyes drifted closed as he stroked her, but the urgency in his voice forced them open as he urged, "Look at me, Callie. Don't close your eyes. Let me see how I'm making you feel." His blue eyes burning her, Tanner rasped, "It's time for *you* to talk to *me*, now. Tell me how you feel."

Callie shuddered as he urged again, "Tell me, Callie."

"I feel good . . . so good."

"Tell me."

"I feel . . . I want . . ."

She was looking at him . . . floundering in the heat of Tanner's gaze when her body began a new pulsing. Tanner drew back abruptly, halting her body's quaking spasms as he stripped away his clothes. She gasped when his naked flesh met hers at last. He thrust himself deep inside her, then paused, his eyes unreadable in the endless moment before his hard body erupted with sudden passion.

Replete, motionless beneath him, Callie heard Tanner's ardent whisper.

"It's too late now, Callie . . . because you're mine."

The soft buzzing of an insect aroused Callie from her sleep. Stirring, she opened her eyes slowly to the sway of leafy branches overhead. A warm breeze bathed her naked flesh, soothing her. She mumbled softly, her eyes again closing. A callused palm moved against her breasts, and Callie opened her eyes to see Tanner looking down at her, his expression sober. Scrutinizing her a moment longer, he whispered, "We have to get moving. It's getting late."

The moment somehow unreal, Callie returned Tanner's stare. He lowered his mouth to hers slowly, drinking long and deep.

"Tell me you want to leave," he whispered against her lips.

Callie was somehow unable to respond.

"Callie . . ."

171

Her hands rose to cup Tanner's face as if of their own accord, and Callie drew his mouth back down to hers. Disbelieving her own actions, she opened her mouth under his, encouraging his kiss. She separated her thighs as Tanner pulsed hard and strong against her. Lifting herself to accommodate him, she joined his rhythmic thrusts as he drove deep inside her.

Her need expanding, Callie clutched Tanner close . . . closer still. She was breathless, when his strong body shuddered and she met his passion with an ecstatic cry of fulfillment.

Tanner was lying hot and damp against her warm flesh when reality abruptly returned. Appearing to sense her growing discomfort, he stood up and drew her to her feet beside him. His gaze somehow gentle, he urged her into the water and slowly, meticulously bathed the residue of their loving from her skin. Abruptly frowning, he said, "I don't want you to go back to the Roundup tonight."

"I'll lose my job if I don't."

"Stay with me."

Panic jolted through her, and Callie shook her head. "No."

Drawing Callie close, Tanner eased his body against hers, then slipped himself inside her with a swift, unexpected movement that left her gasping. Stroking gently within her, he rasped, "Stay."

"No."

His voice labored, he pressed, "Callie . . ."

"N . . . no."

Clutching him close as he throbbed within her, Callie joined him in a swift flush of heat that left them again replete.

Callie opened her eyes to the blue heat of Tanner's gaze. "Stay or go . . . " he whispered with sudden ferocity, "you're still mine."

Scowling, Clare walked briskly down the upper hallway toward Tom McBride's room. Tom had called for her. When summoned, she again had to respond like a trained puppy obeying its master.

Clare struggled to stifle her resentment. She was tired of this! She recalled the day Doc Pierce came to the house months earlier to examine Tom after one of his more severe attacks. She remembered her difficulty in controlling her true feelings when Doc pulled her aside for the sober diagnosis that her husband was dying.

Dying! She had been overjoyed! Her endless wait was almost over, and the Circle M would soon be hers. She would then be free, and everything she had planned and worked toward for five interminable years would come to fruition.

So she had thought. Actuality, however, was far different from that dream. Instead of attaining freedom, she had become a slave to Tom's sickness, a drudge forced to watch as he died a little at a time, stringing out the days in long, empty hours while she continued to cater to him.

Clare's expression was a mask of hatred. As for the Circle M becoming hers, she had taken only one day away from Tom's bedside—one day to go to town—and during that single absence, he had arranged to have the letters sent to his sons and daughter, summoning them home.

Damn Tom McBride to hell for that! His eyes had held hers as he awaited her words of understanding when he told her what he had done. Had she had her choice at that moment, she would have gouged those eyes out rather than standing there with a false smile of compassion plastered on her face.

The bastard!

Nobody means more to me than you do, Clare. Nobody.

I'm going take care of you, Clare, and it doesn't matter a damn to me who suffers if he gets in the way.

Promises.

She had always known that Tom McBride was good at breaking promises. What he didn't know, however, was that she had made a promise to herself. She had sworn to that promise years earlier, and she did not intend to break it. Despite the torment of these last, lingering days, she would remain *at* the bedside of Tom McBride in a pose of tender understanding, while taking her pleasure *in* the bed of Tanner McBride.

A smile flickered across Clare's lips. Tanner was weakening. She had seen it in his eyes when he had ridden out that morning. It was just a matter of time.

Clare paused outside Tom's door. She pushed it open quietly to discover that he had finally fallen asleep. She was free, if only for a few hours.

Clare drew the door closed and continued down the hallway toward the staircase. The men would be returning from the range soon, and Tanner would be with them.

Yes, Tanner.

Damn it all, what had she done?

That question reverberated in Callie's mind with no answer immediately forthcoming. Tanner's strong arm encircled her waist. He drew her back more firmly against him, supporting her easily where she sat in front of him, sharing his saddle. Her face flushed as she recollected the disconcerting moment when she left Tanner's ardent embrace to discover that she had forgotten to secure her mount, and the impatient animal had wandered off and was nowhere to be found.

Callie frowned, annoyed at her negligence. She hated to admit that the passion-filled hours had consumed her so completely that she had forgotten to do something as basic as securing her horse. She did not enjoy the embarrassment of being forced to ride to the Circle M to borrow a horse in order to return to town. When she made the decision to pursue Tanner, she had never considered the possibility that she would spend hours on end lying mindlessly in the intimacy of his arms.

Mindlessly—an apt and humiliating description. But she was mindless no longer, and her regrets were unrelenting.

Tanner's broad palm moved to cup her breast. The spontaneous shiver that went down Callie's spine infuriated her. What was wrong with her? The hand now caressing her breast might just as well have held the gun that shot Matt. Those eyes that had devoured her with such heat could have watched Matt die. The mouth that had consumed hers with such passion could have been the same one which had given a joyful hoot while leaving the bank, sparing not a thought for the man who lay dead within.

Callie remained silent, still incredulous at her behavior. She could not account for the way she had responded to Tanner. The look in his eyes when they lay intimately close, the quaking in his voice when passion overwhelmed him, the hunger for her that somehow struck a chord deep inside her.

Tanner moved his hand, shifting to caress the crest of her breast with his fingertips, and Callie struggled against the emotions assaulting her.

What had she done?

Her breathing quickening, Callie whispered, "Tanner . . . please."

"Please what, Callie?" Stroking her more warmly, he murmured against her ear, "Tell me what you want."

"I want you to stop what you're doing." Callie looked back at him. She glimpsed the heat rising in the silver blue of his eyes and forced herself to continue. "You said the Circle M ranch house was over the next rise."

"That's right."

His caress continued, and Callie grasped his hand, holding it motionless as she insisted breathlessly, "I want you to stop."

"Is that what you really want, Callie?"

"No . . . yes . . . I mean . . . I don't know what I want, but I do know that I need to get back to town before nightfall."

"No, you don't."

"I do." Callie took a fortifying breath and clenched his hand tighter. "And I want you to stop."

"All right." Tanner's expression grew cold. His hand dropped away from her body.

"Are you angry?" Noting the hardening of his jaw, Callie responded, "This was just one afternoon. You can't possibly expect it to change my life."

"Can't I?" His gaze dropped again to her lips, and Tanner responded more softly, "It's only one afternoon now, but it won't be the last."

Struggling to restrain the heat rising within her, Callie asked, "How do I know I can believe what you're saying? Everybody in town says—"

"If you believed what everybody in town was saying, you wouldn't be here right now."

"I didn't expect things to happen so fast."

Tanner's gaze burned her. "Neither did I."

"Don't you understand? In some ways you're as much a stranger to me now as you were when I started out this morning."

"You know me well enough."

178

Tanner's tone stiffened Callie's back. "Well enough to lie with you, is that what you mean?" Callie's face flamed. "Oh, I forgot. I work in the Roundup Saloon. I'm probably accustomed to letting men make love to me all afternoon . . . on the ground . . . in a wooded glade . . . wherever they want, is that it?"

"No, I know that isn't true."

"How can you be sure?"

"Because I've been with enough whores to know the difference between them and you."

"Oh, you have?" Tanner's comment somehow enraged her. "Stop this horse and put me down," she commanded.

"What?"

"I said, stop this horse and put me down."

"What are you trying to—"

"Put me down, damn it!"

Drawing back on the reins abruptly, Tanner swung Callie to the ground.

Taking a moment to adjust her clothes, Callie grated, "Give me your canteen."

"Why?"

"I don't need your damned horse, but I do need a canteen if I'm going walk back to town!"

"Walk?"

Dismounting, Tanner stared down at her, his expression grim. "Don't be a fool. You can't walk back to town."

"Can't I?"

Tanner's blue eyes burned her. "Why are you suddenly so angry? Is it because I said I've been with enough whores to know the difference?" His gaze pinned her. "Are you jealous, Callie?"

"Jealous!" Callie laughed aloud.

"Is it because you don't like to think of me lying with those other women?"

"I don't give a damn how many women you've had!"

"Yes, you do."

"I said—"

"I know what you said." Closing his arms around her with a suddenness that stole her breath, Tanner held her so close that their lips were only inches apart. "I know that's how you feel, Callie, because I feel the same way," he whispered. "I don't want you going back to the Roundup tonight, where all those fellas will be fawning over you and hoping they'll be the one lucky enough to end up with more than a wink and a pat on the cheek before the night is out."

"I wouldn't . . ." Callie stopped and tried again. "That isn't what I was hired for at the Roundup."

"No? I've got news for you, darlin'. It may not be what you were hired for, but it's not your voice that's got those fellas cheering."

"What those fellas might be hoping for, and what they're going to get, are two different things."

"Maybe."

"What are you saying?"

"I was one of those fellas last night."

"That's different!"

"Why is it different?"

"Because you're . . ." Caution forced Callie's words to a premature halt.

Silent for a long moment, Tanner whispered, "I'll tell you why it's different for me." His mouth inched closer. "It's different because I recognized you the moment I saw you."

Callie withheld a gasp. "You recognized me?"

"It wasn't hard. That something inside me that knotted tight when I looked at you told me you were different from the rest." Tanner paused. "Tell me you didn't feel the same."

"I can't."

"But you want me to let you go."

Another uncontrollable shiver rolled down Callie's spine. Tanner's eyes were so intent . . . his expression so sober . . . his mouth so close to hers. Struggling to restrain herself as her mouth instinctively sought his, she murmured, "It's just that I need time . . . everything's moving so fast."

"You need time to get to know me."

"Yes."

"And while you're getting to know me?"

Callie's gaze held his. The answer within was clear. Crushing her hard against him, Tanner covered her mouth with his, kissing her long and deep. She was lost in the kiss when he pulled back from her abruptly, his breathing ragged. Turning to mount his horse without a word, he swung her up in front of him. He waited until he had settled her comfortably on the saddle, then said, "I'll take you back to town after we get you a horse, if that's what you really want."

"Yes," Callie forced herself to reply, "it is."

"But just remember . . ." Tanner's voice dropped a notch lower. "You're mine."

"Tiny!" Clare walked through the parlor. She called impatiently again, "Tiny, do you hear me?"

The clanging of pots in the kitchen was her only reply. Clare headed in the direction of the din to find the cook working at the stove. Perspiration beaded his brow as he continued stirring a large pot. He did not look up.

"I called you several times, Tiny!" Clare was livid. She had been looking for the lace bed covering that she had bought shortly after arriving at the Circle M. It was one of the few things she had allowed herself to buy for the house, and she had not used it until taking her own room. But she had returned to her room a few minutes earlier and found it missing. As far as she was concerned, there was only one person who could have taken it.

Maintaining a firm hold on her temper, Clare jerked Tiny around to face her as she said, "Have you seen my lace coverlet?"

She could almost see the mute's mind working before he nodded.

"Where is it?"

Tiny smiled, showing uneven teeth that forced a growl of disgust from Clare's lips. "I said, where is it? It's not in my room where it belongs. Did you do something with it?"

Tiny's broad, flat hands balled into tight fists as he simulated the motion of scrubbing on a washboard.

"Oh, no! You didn't wash it!"

Tiny nodded. His grin widened as he motioned, making dots with his fingers against the table.

"Spots? You're telling me my lace coverlet had spots . . . that it was dirty?"

Tiny nodded.

"It was not!"

Tiny held her gaze, then shrugged.

"Where is it?"

Again the scrubbing motion.

"I know! You washed it! Where is it?"

Tiny pointed to the pot boiling on the stove.

"You're *boiling* it?"

Tiny's air of innocence was too exaggerated to be real.

"You did this on purpose!"

Jerking the stick from his hand, Clare dipped it into the pan in front of her and pulled a section of the shriveled coverlet from the water. Her eyes widening, she shrieked, "It's ruined! You ruined it . . . purposely!"

Tiny shook his head in innocent denial.

"I'm going to take the price of that coverlet out of your pay! You won't get another cent from me until you've satisfied that debt!"

Tiny stared back at her.

"Bastard . . ."

Turning on her heel, Clare headed for the yard. She did not see the smile that stretched Tiny's lips wide as she stormed out of sight.

Clare was still fanning herself, attempting to alleviate the heat of her anger, when she noticed a rider approaching. That huge roan was unmistakable. Tanner. He was coming home early, and he was alone.

The rider drew closer, and Clare's carefully arranged smile of welcome froze on her face. He wasn't alone. Someone was sharing his saddle . . . and it was a woman.

Callie stared at the woman who stood as still as a statue, waiting in front of the ranch house as Tanner and she neared. The woman's hair was so blond that it was almost white. It shimmered in the rays of the afternoon sun. Her small features were finely composed and flawless, and her figure was so delicate that she almost appeared sculpted by an artist's hand. Callie had never seen a more beautiful woman. Nor had she ever seen eyes so cold.

Tanner's arm tightened around her. She felt him stiffen as they reined up beside the woman.

"Hello, Tanner," the woman said with a frozen smile. "I see you've brought home a . . . friend."

"Hello, Clare."

Callie stiffened instinctively. Clare McBride—the woman Tom McBride had married within a week of his first wife's death.

Clare's smile remained stiffly in place as she purred, "Why don't you introduce me to your friend?"

Dismounting, Tanner lifted Callie from the saddle. Sliding an arm around her, he replied, "Callie Winslow, meet my *stepmother*, Clare McBride."

A flood of color transfused Clare's fragile features as she replied with obvious displeasure, "I'm pleased to meet you, Miss Winslow. Or perhaps I should call you Callie?" Clare's gaze flashed over Callie's tousled hair and attire. It lingered a second too long on Tanner's hand where it curled around Callie's waist, his fingers resting just below her breast. She continued with mounting venom, "I suppose formality isn't indicated, since it's apparent that the situation is less than formal between you two."

"That's right, Clare." Tanner's voice was curt. "There's no need for formality, or anything else for that matter. Callie won't be staying long. We just came back to get her a fresh mount."

"Really?" Making no attempt to hide her mocking smile, Clare addressed Callie. "Well, *Callie*, you haven't said a word yet. Don't tell me you're a mute. I've had enough of that for one day."

Astonished at the woman's blatant hostility, Callie was momentarily speechless. Clare McBride was obviously the nasty witch she was purported to be. Callie was suddenly certain that Tanner could never have been young enough or foolish enough to have challenged his father for a woman like her.

Clare prompted, "Cat got your tongue?"

"No, not quite," Callie responded without the pretense of a smile. "I'm not a mute, either—or deaf, but I admit to being careless, which is the reason I need to borrow a horse to get back to town."

"You're welcome to borrow a mount. Tanner will get one for you. He's so good with animals"—Clare glanced at Tanner, her knowing smile sweeping him briefly—"perhaps because he's a bit of an animal himself at times." And at Callie's frown, "That's what I hear, of course. I don't speak from personal experience."

Callie felt the tension of Tanner's constraint as he grated, "We'll leave as soon as possible."

"You're taking her back to town?" Clare's lips tightened. "Is that necessary, Tanner? Surely she can find her way back alone. It might be nice if you spent some time here on the Circle M for a change. Your father *is* dying, you know."

"And you know as well as I do that my father told me to stay away from him until he's ready to talk to me."

Startled by Tanner's response, Callie needed only one look at his expression to see he had spoken a hard truth.

Clare dismissed his reply. "Your father's sick. He doesn't know what he's saying."

"He knows what he's saying, all right." Tanner's fingers tightened on Callie's side as he urged her toward the barn. "Let's go."

"Really . . . taking Callie with you into the barn." Clare's delicate nose wrinkled with distaste. "Surely she can wait here with me while you get her a horse."

"No, I don't think so."

"What's the matter, Tanner? Afraid I might say something that would taint Callie's feelings for you?"

"I'm not afraid of anything you could say." Directing a gaze of pure heat into Callie's eyes, he said, "Callie knows how I feel about her. I've made it very clear, in the most convincing way I know." Turning back to Clare's angry flush, he continued with obvious sarcasm, "Besides, I wouldn't want to keep you away from my pa's room any longer than necessary. I know how devoted you are to him."

"Your father's sleeping."

"Oh? But he won't be sleeping long, and as soon as he opens his eyes, he'll be calling for you—and you'll be running to his side like a trained puppy."

Clare snapped, "Is that the way you see it? Or are you jealous that your father prefers my company to yours?"

"I learned early on what and who my pa considers most important to him."

"Meaning . . ."

"I know what my pa wanted, and you gave it to him."

Clare's smile grew tight. "But you don't know me as well as you had *hoped* to, do you?"

"I know you as well as I ever wanted to."

"You're being rude, Tanner!"

"Am I? Tell my pa. Maybe he'll disinherit me and you'll have one less heir to get rid of."

Clare turned stiffly toward Callie. "Tanner is saying all this for your benefit, when the truth is that I've had to fight off his attentions on more than one occasion—which is the reason his father threw him off the Circle M five years ago." Clare swept him again with her gaze. Her face colored when she lingered a moment too long on the bulge beneath his buckle. She turned back abruptly to Callie and said, "He's a randy beast. You've most likely found that out for yourself by now, but don't worry, he won't tarry with you overly long. There's only one woman he truly wants."

Infused with a startling anger, Callie spat, "And I suppose that woman is you, *Mrs*. McBride."

Clare's sneer was triumphant. "Ask him yourself—the next time you and he are flesh to flesh. Ask him who he's thinking about. I'm telling you now, it won't be you!"

His face pale, Tanner turned Callie away from Clare before Callie could reply. Dragging her toward the barn, his stride so long and rapid that she could hardly keep up with him, he left Clare standing behind them.

He waited until they reached the darkened interior of the barn, then turned toward Callie abruptly. Shuddering with wrath, he grated, "I don't need to defend myself against anything that woman says, but I'm going to say this once. For more reasons than you'll ever know, I never, *ever* touched her, and I never will." His astounding eyes held hers. "I need to know if you believe me, Callie."

Callie's throat was suddenly tight. "I believe you, Tanner."

Tanner nodded. "You're one of the few who do."

"I'm sorry, Tanner."

"Sorry?" Tanner frowned. "Why?"

"I'm sorry about your pa."

"I'm not."

"I'm sorry that woman's making life hell for you."

Tanner drew her close. She felt the emotion that shuddered through his strong body as he said, "Don't be sorry for me, Callie. It isn't sympathy that I want from you."

Releasing her abruptly, Tanner said, "Let's get out of here."

Riding beside Tanner as they emerged from the barn minutes later, Callie glanced around the yard. Clare was nowhere to be seen. She saw Tanner follow her gaze, then saw his eyes narrow as a short, stocky man emerged from the house and ran toward them, a sack in hand.

Tanner mumbled, "It's Tiny."

The fellow neared, motioning toward the bag, then toward his mouth.

Tanner accepted the bag Tiny offered hesitantly. "You packed something for us to eat?"

Obviously a mute, Tiny nodded.

"Did Clare tell you to—"

Not waiting for him to complete his question, the mute shook his head emphatically. Cupping his right hand, he flicked his index finger out from against his thumb in quick motions, then cupped his thumb against his forehead and twisted it out in quick jabs.

"You heard us arguing."

Tiny nodded. He raised a fist over his heart, his thumb pointed downward, then made a sweeping half circle with his hand.

"You were happy. So you don't like her either."

Tiny nodded.

"I don't need to ask why."

Tiny nodded again.

"Why do you stay? Because of Pa?"

A pained expression flashed across the mute's face.

"You feel you owe Pa something . . . that's why you're staying?"

Again Tiny nodded.

"You're telling me my pa did something to earn your loyalty?" Tanner gave an incredulous laugh. "Well, that's a first."

Tiny made a series of quick motions, and Tanner went still. He allowed his gaze to linger on the mute's solemn expression moments longer, then turned toward Callie. "It's getting late. Let's go."

They were riding in silence, the tension of the Circle M far behind them when Callie felt safe to ask, "All those motions—how did you know what Tiny was saying to you?"

Tanner's response was clipped. "He was using Injun sign language."

"Oh." Considering his response for a moment, Callie finally ventured, "What did he say to you just before we left?"

Tanner hesitated briefly. His expression sober, he replied, "Tiny pressed his right hand to the center of his chest with thumb down, mean-

Thrill to the most sensual, adventure-filled Historical Romances on the market today...

FROM  LEISURE BOOKS

As a home subscriber to the Leisure Historical Romance Book Club, you'll enjoy the best in today's BRAND-NEW Historical Romance fiction. For over twenty-five years, Leisure Books has brought you the award-winning, high-quality authors you know and love to read. Each Leisure Historical Romance will sweep you away to a world of high adventure...and intimate romance. Discover for yourself all the passion and excitement millions of readers thrill to each and every month.

SAVE AT LEAST *$5.00* EACH TIME YOU BUY!

Each month, the Leisure Historical Romance Book Club brings you four brand-new titles from Leisure Books, America's foremost publisher of Historical Romances. EACH PACKAGE WILL SAVE YOU AT LEAST $5.00 FROM THE BOOKSTORE PRICE! And you'll never miss a new title with our convenient home delivery service.

Here's how we do it. Each package will carry a 10-DAY EXAMINATION privilege. At the end of that time, if you decide to keep your books, simply pay the low invoice price of $16.96 ($17.75 US in Canada), no shipping or handling charges added*. HOME DELIVERY IS ALWAYS FREE*. With today's top Historical Romance novels selling for $5.99 and higher, our price SAVES YOU AT LEAST $5.00 with each shipment.

AND YOUR FIRST FOUR-BOOK SHIPMENT IS TOTALLY FREE!*

IT'S A BARGAIN YOU CAN'T BEAT! A Super $21.96 Value!

 LEISURE BOOKS A Division of Dorchester Publishing Co., Inc.

GET YOUR 4 FREE* BOOKS NOW—
A $21.96 VALUE!

Mail the Free* Book
Certificate
Today!

4 FREE* BOOKS 📖 A $21.96 VALUE

Free Books Certificate

YES! I want to subscribe to the Leisure Historical Romance Book Club. Please send me my 4 FREE* BOOKS. Then each month I'll receive the four newest Leisure Historical Romance selections to Preview for 10 days. If I decide to keep them, I will pay the Special Member's Only discounted price of just $4.24 each, a total of $16.96 ($17.75 US in Canada). This is a SAVINGS OF AT LEAST $5.00 off the bookstore price. There are no shipping, handling, or other charges*. There is no minimum number of books I must buy and I may cancel the program at any time. In any case, the 4 FREE* BOOKS are mine to keep—A BIG $21.96 Value!

*In Canada, add $5.00 shipping and handling per order for first shipment. For all subsequent shipments to Canada, the cost of membership is $17.75 US, which includes $7.75 shipping and handling per month.[All payments must be made in US dollars]

Name _____

Address _____

City _____

State _____ *Country* _____ *Zip* _____

Telephone _____

Signature _____

If under 18, Parent or Guardian must sign. Terms, prices and conditions subject to change. Subscription subject to acceptance. Leisure Books reserves the right to reject any order or cancel any subscription.

(Tear Here and Mail Your FREE* Book Card Today!)

Get Four Books Totally
F R E E* —
A $21.96 Value!

PLEASE RUSH
MY FOUR FREE*
BOOKS TO ME
RIGHT AWAY!

Leisure Historical Romance Book Club
P.O. Box 6613
Edison, NJ 08818-6613

AFFIX
STAMP
HERE

ing *I*. Then he pointed his right thumb at his chest, meaning *me*. He held his right hand horizontally against his chest and moved it in an outward circle, meaning *all*. Then he put both fists against his chest and moved them a few inches forward like it was an effort. That meant *begin*."

When Callie appeared confused, Tanner explained. "What Tiny said was 'We begin.' "

Chapter Six

To William Benton Hanes, Esq.
Sidewinder, Texas
Dear Sir:

I am in receipt of your letter in which you stipulate the terms and conditions of the last will and testament of my father, Thomas J. McBride, as dictated to you on the fifth of March, this year of our Lord, 1886. Since I have not seen or heard from my father in the four years since I came to Savannah, and since I have, during that time, established a full and busy life apart from the Circle M, I hope you will understand that I have a few questions and comments regarding your communication.

First and foremost is my question about my father's state of health. You mention that he is gravely ill and not expected to live out the year. I hope you will excuse my surprise at that statement. My father was always a physically sound and robust person. The fact that he married a woman twenty-three years his junior, who was not the first of his many paramours, would seem to bear proof of the statement that he had the health and vigor of a man far younger than his forty-six years. Therefore, before undertaking a journey of such a considerable distance, I would appreciate a clearer definition of his illness.

Secondly, it is my understanding that my brother Stone left the ranch after I did, leaving the Circle M to my father and his new bride as my father apparently wished. Remembering Stone's unforgiving nature, and recalling the bitterness with which my brother Tanner departed the Circle M, I find myself sincerely doubting that either of them will respond to your letter. I know I need not tell you that my own departure from the Circle M was under equally unpleasant circumstances. I have not heard from either of my brothers in several years, yet the familial connection remains on my part. For that reason, I beg your indulgence when I ask if you would be kind enough to convey whatever information you might have as to their present situations.

I wish to make clear that you need not include any reference to my father's wife, Clare Brown McBride in whatever response you choose to make to this letter. Due to the complicated history of ill feeling between Clare Brown McBride and myself, I made the decision four years ago that I would no longer allow her to affect my future in any way. For that reason, any information you might relay would be superfluous, as it would have no bearing on whether I will eventually choose to return to the Circle M, or how briefly I will stay.

I hope you will not consider it a conflict of interest as my father's lawyer if I ask you to keep your receipt of this letter from him. I would prefer that my father remain ignorant of this communication until I have made the decision whether or not I will return.

Thank you for your forbearance in the reading of this letter. I hope to receive your prompt reply so I may make the appropriate determination with regard to the stipulation my father has outlined.

> Yours most sincerely,
> I remain,
> Lauren Emily McBride

The colors of late afternoon filtered through his office window in dazzling shafts of pink and gold, but William Benton Hanes, Esq. gave no thought to the brilliant waning of the day. Instead, he remained seated at his desk, staring at the missive in his hand for long minutes after the final word was read. Frowning, he lowered the sheet to his desk, his spirits low.

The letter was cold and impersonal, but it was well composed and written in an elaborate, flowery script that reflected an education far superior to any Lauren had been afforded in Sidewinder's painfully lacking, one-room schoolhouse. It was somehow unbelievable to him that the well-worded communication could have been written by the same red-haired, fiery-tempered tomboy that he remembered. It appeared Lauren had changed drastically during the five years past. Through the well-phrased text of the eloquent communication, however, a familiar message was conveyed. Lauren had put the past and its torments behind her in order to proceed with her life . . . but the pain of the harsh memories remained.

Bill Hanes sighed unconsciously. Emily McBride had been so full of life and love, and so sure that in the end right would win out for those she cherished. How it would have pained her to read Lauren's letter and realize that her daughter's heart was deeply scarred. Emily would doubtless have suffered no less for Stone, who had always succeeded so well in keeping his torment to himself. As for Tanner, whom Emily had loved in a special way, to see him also embittered would most likely have broken her heart.

Where would it all end?

With no answer in sight, Bill Hanes picked up his pen.

Tanner halted his horse in front of Annabelle Chapin's boardinghouse. Silent, Callie reined in her mount beside him. The eventful day had begun fading into evening as they reached the outskirts of town, somehow emphasizing the deep silence that had fallen between them during the last portion of their journey back from the Circle M.

Callie's exhaustion was evident—an exhaustion for which Tanner knew he was partially to blame, but he felt little guilt.

Contrarily, he knew that if he had his choice, he would not hesitate to lift Callie from her horse and carry her up to her room, where he would prove to her all over again the depth of the feelings she aroused in him. But the choice was not his. With her silence, Callie had succeeded in erecting a wall between them, despite the yearning that he read in her gaze each time their eyes met.

It had all happened too fast for her; that was the problem. He had sensed the first moment he saw her that she was not the seasoned saloon girl she pretended to be. The spontaneity and depth of her response to his lovemaking had confirmed that belief, as had Callie's silence in its aftermath. Somehow, the breathtaking scope of emotion that had arisen between them had frightened her. She was wary and uncertain. He needed to be patient at a time when he had little patience in reserve, when the instinctive hunger Callie raised in him rubbed his restraint raw.

The quiet that had reigned during their interminable return to town, however, had allowed him time for consideration of the obscure promise in Tiny's parting words.

We begin.

In the end, he had dismissed it from his mind as a well-intentioned show of support by someone who had no power at all.

Dismounting, Tanner ignored Callie's protest as he lifted her from her horse. He heard the catch in her breath as he slid her down against his body, and the heat within him soared. Unable to restrain himself, he urged again, "Don't go to work at the Roundup tonight. Stay with me."

"I can't." Callie's heart pounded against his chest as she repeated, "I'll lose my job."

"So what if you do?" The words came to Tanner's lips with spontaneous sincerity. "I'll take care of you."

"I can take care of myself!"

"That's right." Tanner sobered at the unexpected sharpness of her reply. "You don't need me and I don't need you—but *wanting* and *needing* are two different things." Tanner tipped up her chin so Callie could not avoid his gaze as he continued, "And you want me as much as I want you."

"N . . . no."

"You're a poor liar, Callie."

Callie's expression flickered before she replied, "I don't want to talk about this anymore, Tanner. I . . . I have to get dressed for work."

"Stay with me, Callie."

"No."

"Callie . . ."

"I have to go!"

Separating herself from him abruptly, Callie turned toward the boardinghouse door. He was a few steps behind her when a familiar female voice ordered, "Stop where you are, Tanner."

Tanner turned toward Annabelle Chapin, who stood on the boardwalk a few feet away.

"That's right." Annabelle's voice was laced with steel despite its softness. She held his gaze without flinching as she continued, "I made the rules of the house very clear to Miss Winslow when she came here. No fraternizing in the rooms—with no exceptions."

"With no exceptions . . ." Tanner scrutinized the stern lines of disapproval that tightened her face. "That doesn't sound like you, Annabelle."

Annabelle's dark eyes grew frigid. "Doesn't it?"

"I used to be able to count on you to be on my side."

"People change."

Tanner did not bother to reply. There had been a time when Annabelle and he had been friendly, when she had seemed to want to believe the best of him, but that situation had reversed itself. He was at a loss to explain it, but causing him his only concern at the present moment was Callie's expression as her gaze darted between Annabelle and him.

Annoyed at himself for wanting to explain away her uncertainty, Tanner said, "Annabelle and I have known each other most of our lives. We were friends once." He shrugged. "Looks like we aren't friends anymore."

Callie responded unexpectedly, "I'm sorry to hear that."

Somehow he believed she was.

The tenderness Callie raised in him never stronger than at that moment, he cupped her head with his palm and drew her mouth to his. The tremor that shook her when his lips touched hers for a lingering kiss was almost more than he could bear. Tanner pulled away from her abruptly.

"Go ahead inside. I'll see you later."

Engrossed in his thoughts as he strode down the board sidewalk, Tanner grunted aloud as a fellow stepped out from a doorway, colliding with him. Righting himself, Tanner swallowed his words of apology as the fellow said without a trace of a smile, "So it's Tanner McBride. I heard you were back in town."

It was Garrett Lassiter, only son of Old Lassiter, his father's sworn enemy. The families had been feuding ever since his pa bought the river property the Lassiters desperately needed out from under them. Truth was, his pa had done it deliberately, hoping to drive "those displaced Southerners with more manners than brains out of country that was meant for real men," but his plan hadn't worked. All it had accomplished was to start a virtual war between neighbors who might otherwise have been friends.

Tom McBride had refused to back down from that stand. He had not allowed anyone on the Circle M to back down either.

Tanner stared at Garret Lassiter a moment longer. Lassiter hadn't changed much. He still had his pa's good looks and easy Southern way, but he was bigger than his pa, standing about eye to eye with Tanner.

Yes, under other circumstances, they might have been friends.

Tanner responded, "That's right, Lassiter. I'm back. Seems like bad news doesn't take long to spread."

"Guess not. You always were a lively topic of conversation around town."

"I know."

"Your pa's illness brought you back?"

"That's right." Tanner gave a wry shrug. "Who would've guessed it?"

"Does that mean Stone and Lauren will be coming back, too?"

"Maybe."

"Stone never did like me." Garrett shook his head. "He threw a fit if I came within ten feet of Circle M land."

"That was Stone, all right."

"Lauren was different." Garret's eyes linked with Tanner's. "Even a blind man could see how lonely she was after you left. I felt bad for her, losing her mother like she did, and with Stone and her always being at odds. Then having to face Clare every day. Everybody knows how that woman is."

Tanner's jaw twitched. "Everybody but my pa."

"I liked Lauren. She had spunk, with all that red hair and freckles. She was growing up to be a real young lady. I wish . . ." Garrett paused, then continued, "Well, Stone did his best to see that I didn't get within ten feet of her, good intentions or not."

"As far as Stone was concerned, every Lassiter was poison."

"That's the truth."

Tanner surprised himself by asking, "How're your ma and pa?"

Appearing equally surprised, Garrett replied, "They're fine. Still going strong. My sister got married and moved back to Virgina."

Tanner nodded. "Well, I guess that's one less Lassiter for my pa to worry about."

Garrett sobered. "Right. Well, I suppose I'll be seeing you around."

With a brief salute, Garrett strode toward his horse. Tanner felt strangely saddened at the thought that his pa had somehow managed to taint every aspect of his life in Sidewinder. Meeting Callie was the one exception.

His expression growing suddenly savage, Tanner grated under his breath, "And I'll be damned before I'll let pa or anyone else change that."

"You're making a mistake, you know."

Callie turned as Annabelle closed the door behind them and addressed her directly. Her heart was still pounding from the warmth of Tanner's kiss, and the realization that if Annabelle hadn't intervened, she didn't know what might have happened.

Damn! What was wrong with her?

Not waiting for Callie's response, Annabelle continued bluntly, "Tanner's trouble. He always was, and he always will be."

Suddenly annoyed, Callie snapped, "What

206

makes you think that's any of your business?"

Annabelle shrugged. "It isn't, but the truth is, your occupation aside, you look like a decent sort. I hate to see you get involved with a McBride. They're not a dependable lot, not any one of them. Tom McBride never gave Tanner's mother a day's peace, womanizing the way he did. And Tanner's no better than his pa, trying to take up with his pa's new bride as soon as they were married."

"You're sure about that story?"

"I have no reason to doubt it."

"What about Stone? Does he get off scot-free, or does somebody have a story to tell about him, too?"

Annabelle raised her chin defensively. "Believe me or not, it's up to you, but I'm telling you for your own good. Ask anybody. The McBride men's heads are easily turned when it comes to women. It's in their blood, and any woman who thinks different is just going to get what she's asking for."

Callie stiffened. She didn't need this. She was weary to the bone and she didn't like defending a man that she knew had blood on his hands.

That last thought struck Callie hard. Yes, Tanner . . . who was no better than a murderer.

"I'm telling you for your own good." Annabelle

was still talking. "Tanner's no good. If you're smart, you'll stay away from him."

If she was smart.

Unable to respond, Callie started abruptly up the stairs.

She couldn't take much more of this.

Clare stepped down onto the first floor. The image of Tanner and the honey-eyed slut walking off to the barn without a backward glance would allow her no peace.

Clare was keenly aware that she had not even glanced toward Tom's door as she passed it. Tiny had gone in there earlier and had not yet emerged—the perfect excuse—and she had accepted it greedily.

Instead, Clare walked toward Manuelo's room at the rear of the house. Her expression tight, she called out, "Manuelo, where are you?"

Manuelo emerged from his room in swift response to her summons. Drawing the door closed behind him, he said, "You called me, Senora Clare?"

"You know I did! Damn you, Manuelo." Clare fought to control her shaking. "I thought I could trust you!"

Manuelo's face darkened at Clare's distress. "What is wrong, Senora?"

"You're supposed to protect me. You promised my mother you would *always* protect me."

"*Sí*, I—"

"Yet you let that offensive mute enter my room when I wasn't present to take one of my precious possessions—my lace coverlet! He ruined it, and it's your fault!"

"Your coverlet—"

"He washed it, and it's ruined!"

Manuelo's expression tightened. "I will see that he pays."

"You will do nothing! Nothing at all, do you hear me?"

"You said, senora—"

"I said the coverlet is ruined. It's too late to do anything about that now." Her control rapidly waning, Clare continued, "But I have a task for you to do by which you may redeem yourself." Clare struggled for composure. "Did you see them—Tanner and that woman?"

"I saw them."

"The woman is a whore. The way he touched her. The way he pretended to protect her from *me!* It was obvious how they had spent the afternoon. It was written all over that woman's face!" Clare shuddered again. "She lorded it over me, Manuelo. She challenged me. It was all I could do not to rip her eyes out on the spot, but

I was too smart to allow her to get the best of me."

"That was wise, senora."

"I warned her. I told her that Tanner would tire of her quickly . . . that *I* was the only woman Tanner truly wanted."

"You said that to this woman?"

"Yes, I did, and Tanner didn't deny it, because it's true!"

"*Sí* . . . it is true."

"I won't stand for it, Manuelo. I won't stand by and allow Tanner to taunt me with his latest whore while I play nursemaid to an old man who is rotting away."

"Senora . . . caution. Senor McBride calls his children around him. There is much to lose if you act unwisely."

"Are you accusing me of being *unwise* again, Manuelo?" Clare's eyes widened. "I told you, I'm not a fool! Tom loves me—only me! He won't believe a word Tanner says."

"You must not allow yourself to become so upset, senora. It will not be much longer."

"It will be an *eternity!*"

Clare sat down abruptly in the nearest chair and covered her face with her hands. Kneeling beside her, Manuelo whispered, "You must not upset yourself, Senora Clare. You have worked long and hard for the rewards that will soon be yours."

Uncovering a face streaked with tears, Clare rasped, "She lorded it over me, Manuelo. She had lain flesh to flesh with Tanner as I never have."

"You will yet have him as your willing slave."

"I know I will, but in the meantime he is with that woman." Clasping Manuelo's callused hand, Clare ordered, "You must go to town, Manuelo. You must find out all you can about Callie Winslow. You must find out her secrets—all of them—and bring them back to me." Clare gave a hoarse laugh. "I'll know what to do with the information you bring me . . . and I'll know what to do with her."

"*Sí*, I will do that."

"Do it now! Go to town tonight, and don't come back until you know everything there is to know about her."

Clare stood up abruptly. Waiting until Manuelo drew himself to his feet beside her, she grated, "I'm depending on you, Manuelo. Bring me what I need and I'll dispense with that woman. Then Tanner will come to me."

"*Sí*, Senora."

Turning toward the sound of Tiny's footsteps on the stairs, Clare brushed the tears from her cheeks and spat, "Go quickly."

Waiting until Manuelo had disappeared through the kitchen doorway, Clare raced up the stairs. She paused outside Tom's doorway to catch her breath, then opened the door and walked inside, her smile stiff.

The stench of the room hit her, and Clare swallowed her repulsion with great effort. She knelt at her husband's side. Overwhelmed by revulsion at his grotesque deterioration, she took his hand.

Tom studied her for a moment, then asked gruffly, "What's wrong, Clare? You've been cryin'."

"No . . . no, I haven't."

"Yes, you have. Tell me the truth."

"It's nothing, Tom."

"Clare . . ."

"It's just . . ." Managing to release a single tear from eyes that were suddenly brimming, Clare shook her head. "I . . . I don't know what to say. It's just that . . . Tanner can be so cruel sometimes."

"Tanner."

"Don't be angry with him, dear. He can't help himself. But . . . but sometimes I don't know where all this is going to end."

Laying her head against her husband's emaciated chest, Clare maintained a victorious silence as Tom stroked her hair and whispered, "Don't worry, Clare. I'll take care of it. I'll see that Tanner gets everything that's coming to him."

The applause thundered on as Callie ended her song and forced a brilliant smile. Her startling red dress and heavy makeup, the smoke, the noise, the sound of clinking glasses and the appreciative whistles from the bar . . . it could have been a reenactment of the previous night at the Roundup.

"Callie, honey, I see you in my dreams!"

"How long are you gonna make us wait for another song?"

"I ain't never seen nothin' prettier than you!"

"Give me a kiss, darlin', and everythin' I have is yours!"

And the shouted response, "Don't listen to him, Callie. You'd lose out in that bargain!"

A sense of unreality swept her as Digby Jones grinned at her from the bar. Yes, the night continued to duplicate the previous one—with one exception. Tanner was not there.

That thought raised conflicting feelings. Taking a stabilizing breath, Callie headed toward the safety of Digby's harmless adulation. Tanner had left her at the boardinghouse door earlier. Exhausted, she had been somehow unwilling to allow herself to dwell on the hours she had spent in Tanner's arms or the promise in his eyes as they parted.

She had been startled to discover that Tanner was nowhere to be seen when she emerged from the boardinghouse a short time later and started down the street toward the Roundup. She had told Tanner she could not afford to lose her job at the Roundup, and she could not, but not for the reasons she had intimated. Her job was her lifeline. Surrounded by the bright lights and noise of the Roundup, she would be able to keep Tanner at a distance. With her mind clear, she would be able to draw him out, to find out where the other members of the gang responsible for her brother's death were located. Then she could end the present farce between them once and for all.

Matt's beloved face flashed unexpectedly before her eyes. Dear Matt . . . whose blood was on Tanner's hands.

"Callie, are you all right?"

Callie turned unsteadily toward Ace as he appeared at her side. The concern in his eyes was belied by his casual tone. He drew her toward his table while replying to inquisitive glances, "This lady's going to spend a few minutes with her boss. Is that all right with you fellas?"

"Hey, it ain't fair for you to pull rank on us, Ace!"

"Watch out, Ace. I'll turn Angie loose on you!"

"Callie or Angie . . . damn, wish I had that quandary!"

Seating her with an exaggerated flourish that satisfied observers, Ace turned toward Callie. Scrutinizing her pale face, he gripped her hands and said, "You're as pale as a ghost underneath all that paint, and your hands are as cold as ice. What's wrong?"

"Nothing." Callie forced a smile. "I'm a little tired, that's all. I . . . I had a busy day."

"I guess you did. The whole town's talking about the way your horse came trotting back to the livery stable without you, and you came riding back hours later with that McBride."

"It caused that much of a stir, huh?"

"Anything that has to do with Tanner McBride starts people buzzing in this town."

Callie did not reply.

"You didn't help it any, you know." Ace frowned. "Half the town saw you and him saying your good-byes outside the boardinghouse."

Callie quipped feebly, "Looks like a woman can't get any privacy in this town."

Ace wasn't smiling. "That's right, she can't."

Suddenly as serious as he, Callie said, "Look, if you're worrying about me—"

"I am."

"I can take care of myself."

"Can you?"

Her temper flaring at his reply, Callie snapped, "I work for you, Ace, but that doesn't give you a right to get mixed up in my personal affairs."

"Maybe not." Ace's dark eyes were intensely sober. "But I know something special when I see it, and I saw it the moment you walked through that door. If it wasn't for Angie, no man, Tanner McBride included, would have stood a chance because I would've swept you off your feet faster than you could blink an eye."

"Ace—"

"Let me finish." Ace's level gaze held hers. "But the fact is, Angie's my woman, and she's going to stay my woman, so that puts me in a different role."

"No, it doesn't. I don't need anybody taking care of me."

"Hell, you sure enough do! Red dress and face paint aside, you're so fresh and clean that every man in the place is looking to be the first to put his brand on you!"

"You're exaggerating. These fellas like my singing, nothing more."

"Like you said, Callie, I'm not tone deaf."

This time Callie did not smile.

"You're making a mistake hooking up with Tanner McBride."

"That's none of your business."

"You saw what he did to Billy Joe last night."

"Billy Joe had it coming."

"Tanner's got a lot of anger stored up inside him that'll be trouble for somebody, and I don't want that somebody to be you."

"You don't even know Tanner!"

"Neither do you."

"She knows me well enough to suit her."

Startled, Callie turned abruptly to see Tanner standing beside them. She was somehow unable to speak as he leaned down, directing his words to Ace in a voice deep with menace. "Let go of her hands."

Ace's gaze was frigid.

"Let her go"—Tanner's jaw jerked spasmodically—"or you'll spend a long time being sorry you didn't."

Callie snatched back her hands, her heart pounding. She stood up and moved to Tanner's side. Looking down at Ace, she said, "I appreciate your concern, Ace, but I'm a big girl. I know what I'm doing. If it's all right with you, I'll do the job I was hired for. If you're not satisfied with that, I'll leave."

Ace stood up slowly, then responded, "As you said, the customers like your singing."

Callie nodded, relieved. Tanner slid his arm around her and she leaned against him as they headed toward the bar.

Music, laughter, bright lights; the sounds of merriment continued, but all was not right within the Roundup Saloon.

The woman was trouble.

Peering through the window where he stood concealed in the shadows beyond the Roundup's swinging doors, Manuelo watched as Senor Tanner reached the bar with the woman at his side. He had seen the confrontation between the saloon's owner and Senor Tanner. He had not needed to hear what was said. Senor Tanner's expression had been enough to chill the blood.

Now standing at the bar with his chest to the woman's back, Senor Tanner dipped his head to whisper something into her ear. The woman glanced up, and Senor Tanner's gaze dropped to her mouth. The din of the saloon echoed out onto the street, but Manuelo heard only the words of his dear Senora Clare's fervent declaration.

I told her that Tanner would tire of her quickly . . . that I was the only woman Tanner wanted.

218

Senora Clare wanted him. She wanted to believe Senor Tanner wanted her, too. It was the woman's fault that he did not.

Burning with hatred, Manuelo watched as Senor Tanner drew the woman closer, so close that his body became a muscular wall against which she leaned while he shielded her from the glances of the other customers. As he watched, Senor Tanner's eyes met hers, and he tightened his arms around her. Senor Tanner was declaring his possession of the woman for all to see, and in his eyes was an open challenge to any and all who might think otherwise.

Manuelo gritted his teeth. It would not be much longer until the goal toward which Senora Clare had diligently striven was realized, yet jealousy consumed her, destroying her contentment.

Manuelo's breathing grew agitated. Senora Clare wanted Senor Tanner. He would see that she got him.

Manuelo's wiry brows met in line over dark eyes as hard as agate. The people of the town gossiped that Senor Tanner and the woman had behaved shamelessly in front of the boardinghouse. The boardinghouse where the woman had taken a room . . .

Yes, he would dispense with the woman, one way or another.

*　　*　　*

"I didn't think you were coming tonight."

Barney placed their drinks on the bar in front of them, but Tanner made no move toward his glass. Instead, he paused in reaction to Callie's comment. He was standing with his chest to her back . . . so close that her firm, rounded buttocks were pressed warmly against a part of his body that left little doubt where his thoughts were residing. A few minutes earlier, jealous beyond rational thought, he had faced Ace Bellamy down in his own saloon because the fellow was holding her hands. He had turned a cold eye on every man who had looked her way since they had arrived at the bar, and he was determined that he would face down a hundred more if necessary to get his message across. Yet Callie had looked up at him with doubt in her eyes.

"What made you think I wouldn't be here?"

Callie shrugged. "You were late showing up. I just thought . . ."

"What did you think?"

Silence . . . then an almost imperceptible shake of her head as Callie replied, "I thought maybe . . . maybe you might've met up with some old friends and forgotten."

"I don't have any 'old friends.' "

"No friends . . ."

"None I care about more than I care about you."

"Not even old traveling partners that you might've met after you left the Circle M?"

"No."

Callie shook her head with a small laugh. "I don't believe that."

Tanner asked abruptly, "Where are all your 'old friends,' Callie?"

"My friends?"

The intense McBride blue of Tanner's eyes held hers. "All those women you grew up with, or worked with after you left home."

"I don't have any women friends."

Tanner's jaw clenched. "Just *male* friends, is that it?"

"A few."

"Where are they now?"

Callie forced a smile. "We had a parting of the ways."

Tanner suppressed his jealousy. Pressing his lips against her cheek, he rasped, "That was their damned fool mistake."

"Tanner, please."

Callie was breathless. He could feel the beat of her heart against the arm he had wrapped around her waist. His own heart was also pounding.

"Let's get out of here, Callie."

"No." Callie shook her head, emphasizing her refusal. "It's early. I'll be singing again soon. Ace said—"

"I don't give a damn what Ace said."

Stubbornly, Callie replied, "You don't want to waste time talking, do you, Tanner? There's only one thing about me that interests you."

"Listen to me, Callie." Tanner's voice deepened. "You feel good in my arms. I can't remember ever feeling about a woman the way I feel about you—and the truth is, I'm not sure whether that's good or bad right now. It just *is*, and that's all I need to know."

"You wouldn't want to know if I was married or not?"

Tanner stiffened. "Are you?"

Callie did not respond. A slow heat spreading through his veins, Tanner grated, "Answer me. Are you?"

"No."

Warm as honey, Callie's eyes held his. "Are you?"

"You know I'm not."

"Do I?"

"Ask anybody in town."

"You've been away from Sidewinder a long time. Things change. Nobody knows anything about what you did with yourself while you were gone."

"It's none of their business."

"Are you telling me it's none of my business, too?"

"Callie . . ." Tanner strove for patience. She was testing him somehow. He didn't like it.

Callie turned suddenly to face him. Their bodies were so close that he caught his breath as she whispered, "You don't want to tell me anything about yourself, do you, Tanner?"

"Damn it, Callie . . ." Tanner took a step backward. "Keep this up, and we won't make it another ten minutes, much less the rest of the evening."

Slipping away from him abruptly, Callie moved a few steps down the bar toward a grinning, whiskered, gray-haired fellow sporting fancy, hand-tooled boots. She slid in next to the seasoned wrangler and said, "I could use a drink, Digby."

The fellow's grin stretched wider. "My pleasure, ma'am."

Tanner emptied his glass, his mind blank. He was not aware of his intent until he closed the distance between them, slapped his empty glass down on the bar, and motioned to the bartender, saying, "Make that three refills here, Barney. I'm buying." And when Callie turned toward him, "Introduce me to your friend, Callie." Towering over the old boy, who did not move an inch, Tanner had to admire the fellow's grit as he addressed Callie again, pressing, "Well?"

Callie's warm honey eyes were suddenly cold. "I didn't think you were in the mood for conversation."

The whiskered cowboy interjected, "I was hopin' to ask Callie to sing another song for us."

"I don't think Callie feels like singing right now."

"I can speak for myself, Tanner."

Tanner grated, "You're pushing too hard, Callie."

Callie blinked. He saw the sudden tears that sprang to her eyes the moment before she turned to the old fellow and smiled brightly. "What would you like to hear? It'll be my pleasure to sing it for you, Digby."

"Miss Callie . . ." The fellow actually blushed. "You know what my favorite song is."

"Take care of my drink." Tanner was acutely aware that Callie was not addressing him when she added, "I'll be back."

Introductory chords from the piano turned everyone's attention in Callie's direction as she approached.

Incredulous at the sudden hush that overtook the crowd when Callie started singing, Tanner ground his teeth. Things weren't going well. Somehow he couldn't seem to make Callie understand—

"Tanner, there you are! I was hoping I'd find you in town tonight."

Tanner turned without enthusiasm toward the familiar voice. "Hello, Mr. Hanes."

Bill Hanes scrutinized him over the wire rims of his glasses, then said, "I thought you'd like to know that I received a letter today."

"A letter . . ."

"From somebody you—"

"SHHHHHH!"

Bill Hanes halted abruptly at the shushing sound from frowning wranglers nearby. Leaning toward Tanner, he continued in a whisper, "Perhaps we should talk outside."

"I'm not much interested in talking right now."

"The letter I received . . ." Bill Hanes paused. "It was from Lauren."

Without a word of response, Tanner led the way toward the door.

The saloon had gone silent, as it did each time she took the floor, and Callie momentarily paused in wonder. She was singing earlier than was scheduled, and she was doing it to irritate Tanner because she was angry. Her attempts to coax Tanner into confiding in her had failed miserably. With each touch, with each glance and word, he had conveyed how much he wanted her, and despite herself, a part of her had responded. But it was painfully clear that whatever intimacy they shared was merely physical.

Callie swallowed against the thickness that rose to her throat. She had cultivated Tanner's interest in order to obtain information about her brother's killers, but the game had become dangerous in ways she had not anticipated. She needed to bring it to an end quickly, before the situation became too complicated to extract herself easily.

Charlie's fingers swept across the keys as she awaited her cue to begin the chorus. At the bar, Tanner had turned to talk with a slight, balding, well-dressed fellow. Her smile froze as their conversation halted abruptly and Tanner headed toward the door.

Callie's heart went still, and tears rose to her eyes again.

You're pushing too hard, Callie.

A single tear rolled down her cheek as Callie sang the concluding bars of the song and Tanner walked out the door.

The roar of applause was deafening as she made her way back to a smiling Digby.

"That was beautiful, Miss Callie."

Callie smiled her thanks as she reached his side. Suddenly grateful for the safe haven he offered, she slipped her arm through his and whispered, "You're a fine man, do you know that, Digby Jones?"

"I am if you say so, ma'am."

"I am looking for Senor Tanner."

Annabelle Chapin appraised Manuelo coolly as he stood on the boardinghouse doorstep. He felt silently resentful under her scrutiny. He had experienced such scrutiny before. It was in the eyes of many when they looked upon him; but never in the eyes of Senora Brown, who had looked upon him with kindness from the first day she saw him.

For that reason he had worshiped her.

For that same reason, he despised this woman as she responded, "What made you think you'd find Tanner McBride in my boardinghouse?"

Manuelo attempted a smile. "It has not been difficult to discover where Senor Tanner's interests lie while he passes time in town. I was told Senorita Winslow has taken a room here."

"That's right, but Tanner hasn't, and I allow no fraternizing in the rooms."

227

"Senor Tanner is a very resourceful person."

"He's not here."

"Perhaps if you could check Senorita Winslow's room."

Her expression tightening, Annabelle Chapin pointed to a window above them that overlooked the street. "See that window up there? That's her room, and it's dark. She's not there, and neither is Tanner. If you want to find either one of them, I'd suggest you try the Roundup. I understand it's the place to be since Miss Winslow came to town."

"*Lo siento*, Senorita Chapin. I did not mean to offend. Senor Jeb sent me out to collect the horse Miss Winslow borrowed. He needs it to—"

"Don't bother to explain. It's not my business."

"*Sí. Muchas gracias.*"

Annabelle closed the door, and Manuelo turned down the boardwalk with silent satisfaction. The room overlooking the street . . .

Bill Hanes's office was small, sparsely furnished, and meticulously neat. His neatness had been the quality that had impressed Tanner most strongly about the eloquent attorney while he was growing up. Hanes had never arrived at the house to conduct business without being fastidiously groomed. The legal affairs he was to discuss were always completely organized, with all the paper work ready to be neatly signed and witnessed. Along with that memory, however, came the sharp recollection of the lack of commentary or advice he offered to Ma, who had watched in silence as everything went Pa's way.

Those memories brought a scowl as Tanner turned toward Bill Hanes. Hanes closed the office door behind them and walked briskly toward the desk. Withdrawing a sheet of paper from a drawer, he glanced at it, then said, "Your sister asked that I not tell your father she had written until she made her decision whether or not to return. I don't believe she meant to include her siblings in that request, and since you and Lauren were so close, I thought you'd like to see her letter."

Hanes extended it toward Tanner. "Here, read it for yourself."

Tanner hesitated as Lauren's image returned vividly to mind. Lauren . . . all red hair and freckles, a tomboy too stubborn to cry when Pa ignored her, and too angry to forgive her favorite brother the day he left her behind.

Tanner accepted the sheet and started to read.

. . . since I have established a full and busy life apart from the Circle M . . .

Tanner's throat grew tight. So Lauren had

made a good life for herself. He was glad.

. . . Stone left the ranch after I did, leaving the Circle M to my father and his new bride, as my father apparently wished . . .

She still faced the truth head on.

. . . Recalling the bitterness with which Tanner departed the Circle M . . .

Tanner felt a pang of familiar anguish.

. . . I have not heard from either of my brothers in several years . . .

His letters had gone unanswered.

. . . You need not include any reference to Clare Brown McBride . . .

Her anger remained.

. . . whether I would eventually choose to return to the Circle M . . .

If she chose to come.

Tanner was silent for long moments when he finished reading the letter. Then he forced aside the painful memories it had stirred to inquire abruptly, "Are you going to tell Pa about Lauren's letter?"

"Lauren asked me not to."

"That's not an answer."

Struggling with obvious annoyance, Hanes responded, "I'm not your enemy, Tanner. And I'm not Lauren's enemy, either. There's no conflict of interest here." His irritation fading, Hanes sighed. "No, I'm not going to tell your pa unless he asks me directly if she responded to my letter."

Tanner placed the sheet back on the desk, his expression sober. "I appreciate that. And . . . thanks for letting me read the letter."

"You don't have to thank me, Tanner."

"Yes, I do."

Tanner extended his hand, and Bill Hanes shook it firmly.

Countless memories assaulted Tanner as he pulled the office door closed behind him and started back in the direction of the Roundup. Lauren's plaintive plea sounded again in his ears.

You're my best friend, Tanner. Don't leave me!

He had had no choice.

I hate you. Tanner. I hate you more than I ever loved you, and I never want to see you again!

The familiar torment he felt at Lauren's words knotted tight inside him as the Roundup came into view.

The smoke and heat of the crowded saloon assaulted him when he pushed open the doors and surveyed the room. He caught sight of Callie conversing with several wranglers at the end of the bar. She laughed aloud at something one of them said, and the sound trilled through him. He started toward them, his stride hard and deliberate.

Joey, Neil, Wayne . . . Callie smiled at the wranglers who had edged up beside her at the bar. She liked them and their easy ways. She had grown up working alongside men just like them, and she was comfortable with their joking banter. They made her laugh when she hadn't thought she had a laugh left in her. She was grateful for that, and for Digby who had stood aside when the younger men engaged her in conversation, but who remained nearby.

The fellows were laughing, taking turns relating a story about a night they had spent on the trail, easily sharing a part of themselves with her in a way that Tanner refused to do. Neil concluded the tale, eliciting loud guffaws from the men in their group.

"Callie . . ."

Callie's laughter froze in her throat. Turning toward Tanner, she was about to give a haughty reply when his expression stopped her cold. Something—an aching misery in his eyes—reached out to her, leaving her powerless to resist when he drew her a few feet from the others without explanation, then whispered, "I don't want to argue with you anymore."

Callie's throat tightened.

The translucent power of his gaze held hers for long moments before Tanner looked up at the wranglers, who were looking at him with cool speculation. Allowing no room for debate, he stated flatly, "We'll see you later, boys."

Feeling the weight of their stares, Callie forced a smile and a wink as she added, "Thank you, boys. You've been fine company." She managed a special smile for Digby as Tanner's arm slid around her.

The noise of the saloon faded from Callie's ears when Tanner looked down again at her, his eyes conveying an ardent message as clear as the spoken word.

The message was, *You're mine.*

He had waited several hours. The saloons along Sidewinder's main street still blazed with light and noise, but the townsfolk had long since retired to their beds.

Slipping silently through the alleyway beside the boardinghouse, Manuelo approached the rear entrance. The door was unlocked to accommodate the late return of roomers. It was not difficult to enter unseen.

Once inside, Manuelo walked silently down the hallway toward the rear staircase. All was quiet. Everyone slept.

When he arrived at the doorway of the room that overlooked the street, he removed a metal file from his pocket and slipped it into the lock. It opened easily. Within seconds he was inside.

Manuelo lit the lamp, his confidence building. He went through the dresser drawers quickly, obtaining little satisfaction from the limited assortment of feminine articles inside. His dark skin creasing into deep, frowning lines, he turned toward the bed and sank to his knees. Yes, a suitcase was underneath. He opened it quickly.

He saw the gun. It was small and deadly. He smiled at its presence. Beneath it lay a Wanted notice bearing the name and likeness of a man named Terry Malone. Noting a bulge in a side pocket, he reached inside and withdrew a folded sheet of newspaper. He attempted to read it, but was frustrated by his poor skills. Refusing to abandon his attempt, he continued to search the fine print until a familiar name jumped out at him. His eyes widened. The name was Tanner McBride.

Exultation fired his face with heat as Manuelo folded the paper carefully and put it in his pocket.

Careful to replace the suitcase as he had found it, Manuelo stood up and looked carefully around the room to make certain no trace of his entry was visible. He turned down the lamp and with a cautious glance out into the hall, drew the door closed and locked it behind him.

Senora Clare's beautiful face flashed before him as he rode out of town minutes later, and Manuelo smiled. Senora Clare wanted Senor Tanner. Manuelo would do what he must, as he always had, to make her every wish come true.

Weary beyond bearing, Callie breathed a sigh of relief as the Roundup's doors were finally closed for the night. Tanner had followed the last stragglers out through the doors with a promise in his eyes that had not needed voicing. Aware of Ace's scrutiny as she tipped Barney a salute and headed for the door, Callie felt a surge of true regret. She had deliberately maintained her distance from Ace throughout the evening in an effort to avoid any conflict that might arise. A backward glance revealed that Angie had walked up to his side. Callie smiled, confident that Ace's concern would fade when Angie's willing flesh met his. She knew that was the way it should be, and she was glad.

One step out onto the boardwalk and Tanner's arm slipped around her. His mouth met hers for a brief, searching kiss that left her breathless before he pulled back and drew her along with him.

They had walked several steps when Callie said, "The boardinghouse is the other way."

"It's too late to make the trip back to the Circle M. I took a room at the hotel for tonight."

"I'm going back to the boardinghouse."

"Annabelle was clear enough about there being no fraternizing in the rooms."

"I know."

"Stay with me, Callie."

"No."

"Callie . . ."

Callie pulled herself free, only to feel Tanner's hand grip her arm, holding her immobile as she attempted to walk away.

"Let me go."

"What are you afraid of, Callie?"

"I'm not afraid of anything."

"Are you afraid of me?" Tanner's clear eyes searched her face.

"No."

"You're afraid of yourself, then."

Callie blurted, "This isn't the way I intended things to be!"

"What do you mean?"

"I thought . . ." Callie bit down on her lip and closed her eyes.

"You thought it could be light and easy between us, is that it?"

Callie avoided his gaze, and Tanner cupped her chin and tilted her face up toward his as he whispered, "Answer me, Callie."

"I thought . . ." Unable to control her trembling, Callie forced herself to continue. "I thought it could be good between us if I got to know you."

"It is good between us."

"But Ace was right."

"I don't want to talk about Ace."

"He said I don't really know you."

"You know me, Callie." Tanner paused, his strong features softening as he whispered, "You took one look at me tonight after I came back to the Roundup and you knew what I was feeling."

"Yes, but—"

"It doesn't take words to get to know someone as well as that. It doesn't take words to show you care about someone, either. You showed it to me when you walked away from those cowpokes tonight without needing an explanation from me."

"You never make explanations." Callie shook her head. "You left while I was singing. I didn't know where you were going or if you were coming back."

"You weren't sure I was coming back?"

"You didn't come back the last time you left unexpectedly."

Tanner hesitated, then said, "I went with my father's lawyer to his office. He wanted to show me something."

"Something?"

Tanner hesitated. "My sister wrote him a letter." Callie heard the pain in his voice as he said, "Her name is Lauren."

"Is she coming back to be with your pa?"

"I don't know."

"She wrote to the lawyer, but she didn't write to you?"

"The last time I was with her, she said she never wanted to see me again."

"Oh."

"You wanted to know more about me. There's nothing good to tell, Callie."

"I don't believe that."

"If you don't, you're the only one who doesn't."

"Tanner . . ." His pain seemed to reach out to close the distance between them. "I'm sorry," Callie whispered. "I'm so sorry."

"I don't want your pity, Callie."

Hardly aware of her intention, Callie went to him in a quick, short step. Slipping her arms around his neck, she pressed her mouth warmly to his. She felt the shudder that shook his strong frame the moment before his arms closed around her to crush her close.

Her breathing uneven when he released her at last, Callie whispered, "I need to hear you say something, Tanner." She took a shaky breath. "I need to hear you say you need me tonight. *Me*, not just any woman."

"Callie—"

"Say it, Tanner. Say it, or I'm going back to the boardinghouse."

"You know how I feel."

"No, I don't!" In the throes of an emotion she could not combat, Callie said "I didn't plan on things going this way between us. I thought . . ." She took a breath. "The whole town was talking about you when I arrived. Everybody said you and that woman your pa married . . ." She paused again. "They were wrong. I knew that as soon as that woman said your name. But I don't know what else is true or untrue."

"We don't need words."

"Tanner . . ."

"Come with me now."

A look, a touch, a moment of silent longing.

Callie slipped into his arms. Tanner was right. At that moment, words were not needed at all.

Callie struggled awake. She was in a strange bed in the darkness of an unfamiliar room.

Tanner's arms tightened instinctively around her in his sleep, drawing her closer. Her momentary fear slipped away as his muscular length warmed her body. Their lovemaking had been swift and passionate, then tantalizingly slow and fulfilling. Her body ached from Tanner's loving . . . and it ached for more.

Callie's throat choked tight with incredulity. Tanner McBride, who had made such tender love to her . . . the same man who had Matt's blood on his hands.

"What's wrong, Callie?" Tanner had awakened. "You're shaking."

"Nothing's wrong."

"Tell me."

"No."

"All right, then," Tanner whispered against her lips. "Whatever's tormenting you, just close your eyes and forget it. Here and now, this is where you belong . . . in my arms."

Callie could not reply.

"Everything that's gone wrong seems right again when we're together. Isn't that enough?"

"I wish—"

"It's right for us to be together, Callie. Nothing could be more right. Nothing else matters."

A familiar lethargy took hold when Tanner's

mouth touched hers, and Callie closed her eyes. No, nothing else mattered. Not now . . . and not for a little while longer, as the loving began anew.

Chapter Seven

"It's almost morning and Tanner hasn't come home yet, Manuelo!"

"*Sí*, senora, I know."

"So you know! What good does that do me?"

Clare moved a shaky hand to her brow, then strode across the darkened kitchen toward the window where first light was breaking across the night sky. Day would soon dawn, bright and clear, but the day would not be bright for her. She had known it would not after she had risen from her solitary bed and gone to Tanner's room to discover that he was not there.

A frenzy of rage had swept over her as she pictured Tanner and that woman together in clear detail. She had stormed downstairs to Manuelo's room behind the kitchen and awakened him to vent her fury.

Still in its throes, she breathed heavily, her slender body shaking with frustrated passion.

"Senora Clare . . ."

Rounding on Manuelo with unrestrained rage, Clare hissed, "Don't even speak to me if you have nothing to offer but platitudes!"

"Do not despair, senora. You sent me to town to learn what I could about the woman, but you had already retired when I returned and I did not want to wake you."

Clare went suddenly still. "Did you find out something?"

"The woman is new in town. She is employed at the Roundup Saloon."

"A saloon!"

"She was hired to entertain—to sing. Senor Tanner met her the first night she was there. He fought a man called Billy Joe Thompson who sought to replace him at her side. It was a vicious encounter that stirred much talk. Senor Thompson has not come back to the Roundup since."

"Tanner fought a man for her—for a saloon woman?"

"Sí. The woman is well liked in the saloon."

"I'm not interested in how well liked she is! What else do you know?"

"The woman speaks vaguely of her past, claiming that she moves often."

"Is that it?" Clare's fair complexion flushed. "Is that all you've learned?"

"No, senora." Manuelo held out a folded sheet of newspaper. "I searched the woman's room and found this hidden in a suitcase under her bed."

Snatching the sheet from him, Clare unfolded it with shaking hands. She scanned the newspaper her frustration mounting.

"At the bottom . . . Senor Tanner's name . . ."

Her gaze narrowing on the portion Manuelo indicated, Clare read:

LOCAL MAN KILLED
IN BANK ROBBERY

April 9, 1886—Matthew Logan, 31, local rancher, was shot and killed during a robbery of the Foster State Bank. Three men escaped with the contents of the bank vault. The leader was identified as Terry Malone, a drifter who was seen in town the previous night. The other two men were unidentified. Arrested by Sheriff Ira Glennan for a suspected part in the robbery was a fourth man identified as Tanner McBride of Sidewinder, Texas, who was subsequently released when witnesses could not positively identify him as being present in the bank at the time of the robbery.

Matthew Logan is survived by a sister, Caldwell Logan. His funeral was attended by Miss Logan and local ranchers and citizens who deeply grieve the death of this popular rancher.

Clare looked up from the paper. "You found this in the woman's room?"

"*Sí.*"

"Does she know you were in there?"

"No. No one saw me."

"You're certain?"

"*Sí.*"

Clare nodded. This woman's meeting with Tanner was no accident. She was up to something . . . something of which Tanner obviously wasn't aware.

Clare pondered the situation a moment longer. Tom would be livid if he knew his son had been involved in a bank robbery in which a man was killed. He would consider it another of Tanner's fiascos. It would be yet another blow to his pride from the son who had disappointed him in everything he did. He might even *disinherit* Tanner.

246

Clare smiled, her spirits lifting. This was a card she had the option to play if she so chose.

Her smile dimming, Clare raised her chin with new resolution. She needed to know more first— what the woman intended—and there was only one way she would find out.

"Manuelo . . ." Casting a cautious glance around them, Clare continued in a whisper, "This is what I want you to do."

"Wake up, Callie."

Callie stirred, then went still again.

"Callie . . . wake up." Crouched beside the bed, Tanner brushed a wayward strand of hair from her cheek. Her skin was smooth and clear . . . soft, the softest he had ever touched. It felt like velvet under his lips. As he watched, her thickly fringed eyelids fluttered, then opened into narrow slits that allowed a glimpse of honey gold as she whispered, "It's still dark outside."

"It'll be light soon. I have to go back to the ranch. I don't want to leave you here."

"W-what?"

Callie's brows drew into a confused frown. She had not fully awakened. He longed to strip off the clothes he had just donned and lie down beside her, against the warm, welcoming flesh now concealed by a light coverlet. But he needed to get back to the Circle M. His nights were his to spend as he wished, but he had determined before making the journey home that for as long as he remained at the Circle M, he would pull his weight on the ranch. He had no illusions that his efforts would be appreciated by his father. Instead, his efforts were a silent tribute to his mother, who had loved and lost; and who, in death, was in danger of losing her legacy to the woman who had replaced her.

Callie had rolled onto her back, inadvertently exposing a rounded breast as her eyes again closed. The coverlet slipped low. The pink crest beckoned him and he brushed it with his lips. He saw her shudder and he drew back as a corresponding heat jolted directly to his groin. Callie was flushed and warm . . . and vulnerable . . . so vulnerable that he wanted to gather her into his arms to protect her from a world that was unkind, and from tongues that would judge her harshly for her association with him.

He tried again.

"You have to get up . . . Callie. It'll be light soon. You have to get dressed if you want to return to the boardinghouse before everyone there wakes up."

"Oh . . . yes." Callie sat up, then snatched up the coverlet to cover her naked breasts. She swept his fully clothed figure with a glance, then looked at the chair where her clothes had been hastily abandoned. Unexpected tenderness filled him at her belated modesty. Tanner covered her mouth with his, his kiss lingering until the coverlet slipped from her fingers and her arms wound around his neck. Refusing to give in to the emotions threatening again to assume control, Tanner drew back, then swung Callie to her feet, saying hoarsely, "You'd better get dressed . . . before it's too late for both of us."

Out on the street at last, Tanner was silently amused as they walked back toward the boardinghouse. The brilliant red of Callie's dress appeared to glow in the gray light before dawn, making a farce of their effort to go unnoticed. Reaching the boardinghouse at last, Callie reached for the knob on the front door, but Tanner grasped her hand, holding it back. To her silent inquiry he replied, "You can use the back entrance. Annabelle always leaves it open for her guests."

Callie's lips were tight when they reached the back door, and Tanner added by way of explanation, "If you're wondering how I know about this door, I grew up in Sidewinder, remember?"

Callie glanced away. "You didn't need to explain."

Turning her back to face him, Tanner whispered, "Yes, I did . . . and no, you aren't another in a long line of women I've brought back to their rooms here at dawn. Don't think that for a minute, Callie. I don't want to tarnish what we have together. I needed to make that clear to you, just like I need to tell you that I'll be back tonight."

"You don't owe me anything, Tanner. If you come back, it'll be because you want to, not because . . ."

Perplexed by the change that had come over her, Tanner asked, "What's wrong? Don't you want to see me tonight?"

"Yes . . . no, I mean—"

"Callie, listen to me. I need to go back to the ranch. I didn't come home to get free room and board from my pa. I came home to settle some things that have gone unsettled for too long, but that's not going to happen until the rest of my family comes back—*if* they decide to come back. In the meantime, I'm going to earn my keep while I'm on the Circle M."

"But the Circle M's your home."

"It was."

"Your pa's wife—"

"Is that what's wrong?" Tanner searched her disturbed expression. "That's the only thing

Clare ever was or ever will be to me—my pa's wife."

"Tanner, it's just that . . ." Halting abruptly, Callie shook her head. "Never mind."

Callie turned to leave, but Tanner caught her arm and brought her back toward him. His response to her uncertainty came from the bottom of his heart. "Callie . . . darlin', I know this is still strange for you with everything happening so fast, but the truth is, it couldn't have been any different between us, no matter how or when we met. I was never more sure of anything than I am of that . . . and you'll be sure soon, too."

Folding her into his embrace, Tanner held her warm and close against him. Her body fit his as if she were born to be in his arms, and as his mouth grazed hers, he suddenly knew that she was. Separating himself from her at last, he ordered gruffly, "Go inside. I'll see you tonight."

Waiting until the door closed behind her, Tanner turned toward the street.

Shaken by the myriad emotions that had rocked her on leaving Tanner's arms, Callie approached the door to her room unsteadily. She heard a sound behind her and turned with a gasp to see Annabelle Chapin standing in the hallway shadows.

"Oh, it's you! You scared me!" Callie raised a hand to her hair, well aware that her carefully upswept coiffure of the previous evening hung in tangled disarray on her shoulders, and that the hasty donning of her gown was more obvious than she would have liked.

Standing silent for long moments, her tawny hair lying smoothly against the shoulders of her simple, floor-length robe, Annabelle responded softly, "I heard voices at the rear door. My boarders are usually in by this time."

Callie averted her gaze, then turned toward her door without replying. She was in no mood for another of this woman's lectures.

"Wait . . . Callie, please."

Callie? Intrigued by a note in Annabelle's voice that she hadn't heard before, Callie turned, enabling Annabelle to continue, "I know you think this is none of my business . . . and it isn't. It's just that I was pretty curt the last time I talked to you, and I've regretted it." Appearing momentarily at a loss, Annabelle went on slowly, "I've been unfair to you, Callie. I judged you harshly when I first saw you. When you took up with Tanner, it seemed to me that I was right. I suppose it was sometime during the middle of this past night when I suddenly got a glimpse of myself and the way I've acted, and I didn't like what I saw. I don't know when I started setting myself up as judge and jury about people, but I figure it's time for me to stop."

When Callie started to speak, Annabelle shook her head and said, "Wait, please let me finish." She continued, "But what I've just said doesn't change the truth of the past, and the truth is that the McBride men have damaged too many women's lives for me *not* to give you fair warning. Tanner's handsome, and he's a charmer when he wants to be. All the McBride men are. It's their gift . . . being able to turn women's heads without even trying, but I've never known a woman who didn't end up regretting it when she let a McBride into her life."

Anxious to bring the encounter to an end, Callie responded, "I suppose you mean well, but I'm not interested in anything anyone has to say about Tanner. I can make my own judgments and I know what I'm doing."

"All right." Annabelle shrugged. "I can't argue with that. I just wanted you to know that if . . . if things got difficult and you ended up needing somebody to talk to, I'd be here to help."

Turning to depart without waiting for Callie's reply, Annabelle looked back to add with obvious sincerity, "Tanner was right in one thing he said. He and I were friends, once. For that reason, and for your sake as well as Tanner's, I hope I'm wrong." Unlocking her door with a shaking hand, Callie walked inside and pressed the door closed behind her. She leaned back against it and fought to restrain the emotions threatening to overwhelm her.

As if she needed someone else to warn her against Tanner . . .

Callie reached for the lamp, still struggling for control. Never more aware that she needed to rein in her runaway emotions, she heard Tanner's voice again in her mind.

This is where you belong, Callie . . . in my arms.

Everything that's gone wrong seems right again when we're together. Isn't that enough?

It's right for us to be together, Callie. Nothing could ever be more right. Nothing else matters.

No, she wouldn't listen!

The *last* place she should be was in Tanner's arms.

Everything that had gone wrong *did* seem right again when they were together, but afterwards . . .

And it did matter! Matt's blood was on Tanner's hands. Nothing could ever be more *wrong* than that.

Her heart aching, Callie raised her hand to her brow. It did matter . . . so very much.

* * *

"Wait up a minute, Tanner."

The soft summons echoed eerily in the early morning silence of the livery stable. Preparing to mount, Tanner turned toward Doc Pierce as he strode through the rear door. "Going back to the Circle M?" Doc asked.

Impatient to get started, Tanner responded gruffly, "That's right."

"You spent the night in town?"

"That's right."

"A man of few words." Doc Pierce chuckled. "Well, if you don't mind waiting until I get my horse saddled, I'll ride out with you so I can check on your pa."

Tanner frowned. "All right."

Doc raised his wiry brows as he approached the rear stall. "Looks to me like you're anxious to get back. Have a tiff with your lady friend?"

The clear blue of Tanner's eyes turned icy.

"All right, I get the message. Talking about her is off limits."

"Look, Doc—" Tanner snatched the saddle blanket off the rail and threw it across Doc's horse—"The truth is, I'm late. The boys will be riding out soon, and I want to be with them when they go."

"Is that your pa's idea, or yours?"

"The Circle M isn't my home anymore, Doc. I was invited, but I'm not exactly a welcome guest there."

"So you're paying your way."

"That's right, and I don't have time for conversation." Swinging the saddle onto the horse's back, Tanner tightened the cinch, then said, "Are you ready?"

Mounted, they emerged from the stable minutes later. They had traveled some distance in silence when Doc said, "I hear your sister wrote to Bill Hanes."

Tanner's head jerked toward him.

"Bill Hanes and I have been consulting on this case for months—almost a year since your pa first got sick. It isn't a breach of client confidentiality, you know. We've been kinda needing to lean on each other to decide what's the best route to take with your pa as a client and a patient."

"You mean Pa gave you a choice?"

"In a way. Your pa's got a lot of things he's wanting to settle before his time is up."

Tanner did not respond.

Doc shook his head. "You're not going to give him an inch, are you?"

His dark brows knitting into a sober line, Tanner said, "You were there that day . . . when Ma was killed. You heard him. He didn't give me an inch, either."

"He was grieving, Tanner."

"No, he wasn't!" A familiar outrage twisted Tanner's lips as the emotions of that day returned with vivid intensity. "My pa didn't waste a minute in grieving. Ma was dead, and all he could talk about was that wheel—the wheel he had told me to fix, and the fact that he supposedly thought I hadn't obeyed his orders."

"*Supposedly . . . ?*"

Tanner did not reply.

"Things haven't been going any better with Clare?"

Tanner's silence spoke volumes.

Doc shrugged. "I'm glad to see that you found somebody to take the edge off your anger. Talk is, that Callie Winslow's something special. From what I hear, there're a whole lot of fellas in town wishin' they were you."

"They don't stand a chance."

"Is that right?"

"That's right. . . . as right as it'll ever be." Tanner paused, then added unexpectedly, "In case I haven't mentioned it, I want to thank you for taking care of Pa like you've been doing."

Doc scrutinized Tanner silently as he continued, "My pa's a bastard. He doesn't give a damn about anybody but Clare, and she knows it. It gives her a special power over him. I need time to straighten some things out with him, once and for all, and I appreciate that you're helping to give me the time to do it—because I know Clare would do otherwise if she had her say."

"I suspect there might be some truth in what you say about Clare, but as for the rest, I don't know."

"Meaning?"

"No matter what he's done, Tom McBride's your father."

"No matter what he's done?" Tanner's strong features tightened. "We'll see."

Apparently unwilling to pursue that topic any further, Doc followed silently behind as Tanner nudged his mount into a lope.

"All right, boys, get a move on. The sun's comin' up, Tiny has breakfast ready, and we've got a full day's work ahead of us."

His angular face creased in an uncommon frown, Jeb watched as the ranch hands filed toward the door of the bunkhouse. He followed them, his scowl deepening. He had a funny feeling stuck tight in his craw. He'd had it since the previous night, when Butch Cotter's snoring had gotten the best of him and he decided a walk outside the bunkhouse might be better than stuffing a sock in Butch's mouth.

It had been a real surprise to see Manuelo come riding up the road toward the ranch house in the moonlight. It occurred to him that he might not have given the fella a second thought, except for the way Manuelo had slowed his pace when he neared, then walked his horse toward the barn so there would be less chance of his being heard. Jeb had liked it even less when Manuelo emerged minutes later and slipped furtively through the shadows to disappear into the house.

Jeb gave a disapproving grunt. That fella had come sneaking home to the ranch like he had something to hide, and the thought had stayed on his mind, leaving him more wakeful than he would have liked. It had pried him from his bunk at the break of dawn. He had emerged from the bunkhouse before the other men had awakened and had seen Manuelo sneaking back out of the house with what looked like a fully packed saddlebag in his hand. Leading his horse out of the barn minutes later, Manuelo had mounted some distance from the house where the sound of his departure would not be easily heard, and then had ridden out of sight.

It was stranger than strange. Jeb knew for a fact that Manuelo had no life of his own—that he lived to please Clare. In the five years since Manuelo had arrived at the Circle M with Clare, Jeb couldn't remember a single time when the shifty-eyed fella had strayed from her side of his own accord.

Hardly conscious of the tantalizing breakfast smells emanating from the kitchen, Jeb took his place at the table. Tanner wasn't there, but somehow he wasn't surprised. It was his thought that if he were in Tanner's place and had that female vulture picking at him day and night, he'd stay as far away from her as he could, too.

Clare appeared unexpectedly in the dining room doorway, and a smile tugged at Jeb's lips. Speak of the devil . . .

"Tiny . . ."

The round-shouldered mute did not look up when Clare addressed him.

"Tiny!"

Jeb withheld his smile. Tiny had a way of turning Clare inside out with irritation.

"I'm talking to you, Tiny!"

Turning toward her without expression, Tiny waited as Clare ordered, "I want a tray readied for my room. You may rest assured Mr. McBride will hear about it if it isn't delivered to me immediately."

Taking his opportunity, Jeb asked, "I was

wonderin' where Manuelo is, ma'am. Seems to me we haven't seen as much of him as usual these past few days."

Clare responded with a glance as black as night. "Manuelo is my personal servant. Where he goes and what he does aren't your concern."

"Yes, ma'am. I just thought he might be sick or somethin'."

Not bothering to reply, Clare addressed Tiny again. "I expect my tray to be delivered promptly, do you understand?"

Tiny turned deliberately back to the kitchen without acknowledgment, and Clare's face flamed. Jeb looked down at his plate, aware that the other ranch hands followed suit with poorly concealed amusement.

Jeb was luxuriating in the silent satisfaction of that moment when the sound of approaching hooves turned all in the room toward the dining room window.

Dressed in the split skirt and shirtwaist she had worn the previous day, Callie was absorbed in her thoughts as she walked briskly down Sidewinder's main street. Morning traffic moved easily down the rutted thoroughfare, but she gave little thought to the delivery wagons making their appointed stops, to early risers facing the new day with a determined step, or to the few nighttime revelers who staggered unsteadily homeward. Her head ached and her appetite was nil. She knew she could blame both those complaints on the fact that she had had little sleep the previous night, but she knew she would only be fooling herself.

Callie raised her chin, silently facing a sober truth. She'd had little sleep because she'd had little desire to sleep while in Tanner's arms. She'd had little sleep in the time since he'd left her at the boardinghouse door because her guilty conscience had refused to allow it.

Hours of silent self-recrimination as dawn yielded to a bright morning had increased her distress. The need she had glimpsed in Tanner's eyes had awakened a response in her that she could neither account for nor deny. The earnestness in his deep voice when he spoke tender endearments had set her heart racing, and the memory of his arms around her . . . his body pressed tightly to her . . . set her quaking anew.

Callie raised her chin. The undeniable truth was that she was at a loss to combat Tanner's appeal.

She needed help.

Her gaze intent on an office at the end of the street, Callie took a stabilizing breath and increased her pace. Her plan had been so simple: to ingratiate herself with Tanner so he would speak freely, so he would reveal where his accomplices were hiding. What she had not taken into account was Tanner himself. Sometime in the middle of the previous night—as she had struggled to catch her breath in the midst of Tanner's lovemaking—she had abandoned her plan as a failure.

Crossing the street at a stride just short of a run, Callie stepped up onto the boardwalk and pushed open the door to the telegraph office. She forced a smile for the thin, owl-eyed fellow who looked at her with a raised brow, then reached for the telegraph blank on the counter. She wrote quickly, then handed the operator the sheet. She slapped down the required fee, turned back toward the door, and was out on the street again before she had time to change her mind.

Yes, she needed help.

And there was only one place where she could get it.

Tanner breathed a sigh of relief as the ranch yard came into view and he recognized Jeb's mount milling with several others in the corral beside the barn. The men hadn't left for work yet. As his stomach growled in loud complaint, he wondered if he might even have time for breakfast before they left.

Tanner's mouth lifted into a half smile. He was tired, but he wouldn't have given up one moment with Callie for more sleep. It had been damned hard leaving her, and the truth was that the day ahead of him stretched out in a seemingly endless progression of hours until he could be with her again.

Breaking into his thoughts, Doc commented, "There's Jeb by the door. It looks like he's waiting for us."

Reining up at the house, Tanner greeted Jeb with a frown as the foreman said conversationally, "Howdy, Doc," then added, "Good to see you back, Tanner. I figured you took my advice when you didn't come back to the ranch last night, but I didn't expect to see you come back frownin'."

Doc interrupted, questioning, "How's the boss doing?"

"Same as yesterday, as far as I know."

"Where's Clare?"

"Upstairs. She don't usually eat with the help unless she's got a reason."

A twitch of his nose his only response, Doc pushed open the door and headed for the stairs.

His expression sobering, Jeb halted Tanner

when he attempted to follow Doc into the house. To Tanner's silent inquiry, he replied, "Clare's in a mood this mornin'. There's somethin' goin' on. I don't know what it is yet, but since things ain't goin' Clare's way, I figure you need fair warnin' that she's schemin'."

Tanner glanced at the staircase.

"You'd be wastin' your time goin' up there. There ain't a chance in the world that Clare will let you in the room while Doc's there. And like I told Doc, as far as I know, there's no change in your pa's condition." Jeb paused. "On the other hand, you're lookin' mighty tired this mornin'; and the fact is, if you're intendin' to ride out with me and the boys and are expectin' to get some breakfast, too, you'd better tell Tiny to pack up somethin' for you and make fast work of it, because we're leavin' in a few minutes.

Nodding, Tanner started past Jeb. He halted as Jeb inquired unexpectedly, "Tired as you are, boy, would you say the trip into town last night was worth it?"

Tanner hesitated. Searching the foreman's craggy face for silent moments, he then replied, "I'd say it was worth every minute."

Leaning casually against a shadowed storefront, Manuelo watched as Callie walked up the street toward the boardinghouse. She walked briskly, her gaze straightforward, ignoring the glances of those she passed. She was upset.

Anticipation tightened within Manuelo as he straightened up and, walking slowly, followed the woman at a distance. He had arrived in town a short time earlier and had gone directly to the boardinghouse to keep watch on the woman as Senora Clare had instructed. Ignoring the discomfort of hunger, he had waited until the woman had emerged from the boardinghouse and had started rapidly up the street. He had seen the panicky look on her face. When she entered the telegraph office, he had known what he needed to do.

The woman disappeared through the doorway of the boardinghouse and Manuelo paused. He was confident she would remain there for a while, until her emotions were under better control. He would take this opportunity and make good use of it.

Manuelo walked back toward the telegraph office, his mind working feverishly as he maintained a deliberately casual pace. Senora Clare had said the woman was up to something, that she would betray herself sooner or later, and that he must be there when she did. He had not expected that the time would come so soon.

Pausing outside the office, Manuelo peered cautiously through the window. The telegraph clerk was alone as he worked at the telegraph key tapping out the message. It was the woman's message, he was sure. As he watched, the clerk listened intently to the tapping reply, then, appearing satisfied, discarded a handwritten message sheet into a basket beside his desk.

Manuelo smiled. The discarded sheet would soon be in his hands.

"What are you doing here, Doctor?" Clare's expression was frigid as she met Doc Pierce at the door of her husband's room. Effectively blocking his entrance, she continued, "If I had felt you were needed, I would've sent for you."

"I know you would have, but my Hippocratic oath nags at me sometimes." Dismissing Clare's greeting with those words, Doc brushed past her. At Tom McBride's bedside, he scrutinized his patient briefly with a professional eye. His question was perfunctory when he asked, "How're you feelin', Tom?"

"The same."

Doc doubted that. It had taken only one glance to see that Tom McBride's color had worsened since he had last seen him, that his breathing was labored, and that his voice had weakened.

Tom was deteriorating more rapidly than Doc had anticipated. He could not quite account for that, considering Tom's formerly robust constitution.

Removing his stethoscope from his bag, Doc shifted his fragile patient carefully, not bothering to comment as he pressed the instrument to his patient's chest and back. He listened intently to the uneven throbbing that vibrated in his ear. Nine months. He was beginning to doubt his own prognosis.

"Have you been eating well, Tom?" Doc placed his palm against his patient's forehead. "Have you been drinking enough water?"

"He hasn't been hungry, and . . . well—" Doc did not miss the pained expression Clare so expertly allowed her husband to glimpse—"if he drinks too much water, he has trouble with his . . . his control."

Doc touched the dry skin on Tom's skeletal hand. Anger elevated his tone as he snapped, "Control or no control, this man is dehydrating, Clare!"

"I can't make him drink if he doesn't want to, Doctor."

"Yes, you can."

"It isn't her fault, Doc." Tom glanced anxiously at Clare. "She's doing her best."

"It seems to me that her best isn't good enough right now."

"Don't you dare attack me!" Clare responded with unexpected shrillness. "You're the doctor! You're the one who's supposed to be able to help Tom, but you're failing miserably!"

"Calm down, Clare."

"Calm down—when you practically accuse me of neglecting my husband? Calm down—when you're no better than the rest of the people who treat me so shabbily?"

"Clare . . ." Noting that Tom's breathing was growing increasingly labored, Doc urged softly, "You aren't doing Tom any good acting this way."

"The way *I'm* acting? Are you suggesting that I'd behave in any way that might hurt my husband?"

"Clare . . ."

"You're like everyone else! You don't believe that I love my husband . . . that I *live* for him! You've been talking to Tanner, haven't you? Did he tell you more of his lies? Did you believe him?"

"Please, Clare . . ."

"I love my husband, and he's . . . he's slipping away from me! What will I do if he dies? Who will care for me the way he's cared for me? I'll be all alone. Tell me, what will I do?" Clare gripped Doc's arm. "Answer me!"

Aware that to respond would only add fuel to the scene Clare was enacting, Doc reached for his bag. He turned back sharply as harsh, choking sounds came from the bed behind him.

"Tom can't breathe, Doctor!" Clare's piercing cry reverberated in the room. Slipping in front of Doc unexpectedly, Clare laid herself against Tom's body, hindering Doc's access to his patient as she clung resolutely to her husband with gulping sobs.

"Get out of my way, Clare!"

Grasping Clare by the arms when she refused to budge, Doc was stunned by the woman's unexpected strength when he attempted to move her. He was still struggling to dislodge her clinging hands when Tiny burst through the doorway behind them and jerked Clare away from the bed without visible effort. Clare's vociferous protests reverberated behind him as Tiny held her immobile and Doc worked frenetically over his patient.

Noting Tom McBride's increased agitation when Clare began a new round of shrieking, Doc ordered, "Get her out of here and keep her out!"

Doc turned back to his patient, his fury barely subdued. Tom McBride's skin was turning blue.

His eyes were rolling back in his head.

Tom McBride would never last nine months.

This day had become one of the longest days of her life.

That thought trailed through Callie's mind as she approached the telegraph office for the third time that day. She had sent the telegram that morning. She had expected a prompt response, and when it did not come, each disappointment had been deeper than the last.

The owl-eyed clerk looked up when she entered, and Callie's heart began an anxious pounding. His expression joyless, he replied to her unspoken inquiry, "It just came. I was going to have one of the local boys deliver it to the boardinghouse, but you saved me the trouble."

Her hand shaking, Callie accepted the sheet. Refusing to read it under the clerk's curious scrutiny, Callie left the office with mumbled words of thanks. She waited only until out of the clerk's line of vision before reading:

TO CALLIE LOGAN
SIDEWINDER, TEXAS
HAPPY TO REPORT ONE MEMBER OF THE GANG APPREHENDED AND STO-LEN MONEY RECOVERED. TERRY MA-

LONE AND ACCOMPLICE BLACKIE SHERWOOD STILL AT LARGE. TEXAS RANGERS HAVE TAKEN OVER CASE. HAVE NO FURTHER INFORMATION AT THIS TIME.

SHERIFF IRA GLENNAN

Callie clutched the missive, her disappointment keen. She had wanted to hear that *all* the bank robbers had been caught. She had told herself that if they had, the truth about Tanner's part in the robbery would be revealed and there would be no further need for the deception she presently maintained.

Suddenly ashamed of her weakness, Callie raised her chin and started unsteadily back in the direction from which she had come. But she had not received the response she had hoped for. Nothing had really changed. Matt's killers were still free, and because they were free, she was not.

Back in her room, Callie discarded the wrinkled telegram. Soberly she readied her red dress for the evening to come.

This day had become one of the longest days of his life.

The sun was dropping rapidly into the horizon

when the Circle M ranch house came into view. Riding steadily beside Jeb in the lead as the ranch hands trailed behind, Tanner was silently grateful that the seemingly endless work of repairing fences—hard work in weather that was unseasonably hot—had been completed. He was hungry and weary to the bone, but his thoughts swept past the long ride back to town to the moment when he would hold Callie in his arms again.

Almost amused at the effect Callie had on him, Tanner resisted a smile. Somehow the pain of old frustrations, guilt, and suspicion dulled when she was near. For the first time in many years, he was able to imagine a future that was not clouded in darkness—and if he still ached at the estrangement between his siblings and himself, if he was still haunted by his uncertainty about his mother's death, he was somehow able to believe for the first time that life would go on, whatever truth was finally revealed . . .

Because of Callie.

These thoughts were struck from his mind when he caught sight of Tiny standing in the doorway of the house. A sixth sense sent a chill down his spine. There was something about Tiny's stance . . .

Kicking his mount into a gallop, Tanner slid

to a halt in front of the ranch house and ran to Tiny's side. Breathing hard, he watched the rapid movement of Tiny's hands. His heart stilled.

"Pa's had another attack?"

Tiny gestured again.

"It's a bad one and Doc's still with him?"

Tiny's nod of acknowledgment sent Tanner racing through the doorway and up the stairs. He halted abruptly when Doc stepped out of his father's bedroom and pulled the door closed behind him. He waited for Doc to speak.

"Your pa's been taken real bad, Tanner." Doc's tone was grave. "He might not make it."

Doc's statement struck Tanner with the force of a blow, knocking him a step backward as Doc continued, "He's sleeping now and holding his own. If he lasts for another twenty-four hours, I figure he might make his way through this."

"He can't die yet, Doc." Tanner heard himself speak as if from a distance. "I have to talk to him first. There are some things I have to know."

"Not now, Tanner."

"If he dies—"

"If you go in there right now and excite him, you might put an end to him on the spot."

"Doc—"

"Listen to me, Tanner. Whatever you want to

talk about has probably already waited for more years than you care to count. Another few days won't make that much difference."

"Doc—"

"Don't bother asking to see your father! Doc won't let you!"

Turning toward Clare, who stepped into sight in the hallway behind them, Doc ordered, "Keep your voice down, Clare."

"This is *my* house, not yours, Doctor!"

"If you don't keep your voice down, I'll have Tiny come and remove you again."

Turning toward Tanner abruptly, Clare rasped, "Are you going to let him get away with this, Tanner? Are you going to let him keep you out of your own father's room, like he's keeping me out? He has no right!"

Tanner responded coldly. "Keep your voice down, Clare."

"What are you, a parrot? Or are you merely a coward, quivering under this man's authority?"

"I want my father to live long enough to answer some questions that need answering, and I'll do what I must to make that happen." Tanner's McBride blue eyes pinned her. "I'd think you'd feel the same . . . *if* you wanted him to survive this attack."

"Of course I want Tom to live! I love him!"

Interrupting their exchange, Doc interjected, "If that's what you both want, I suggest you move away from this door. Tom's life is hanging in the balance right now."

"So you say, but I know better." Clare was livid. "Tom wants me in there! He wants to feel my presence beside him!"

"Clare . . ." Doc looked at her intently over his glasses. "You've proved to me that you can't be trusted to be with Tom right now. You're too . . . emotional. Your *deep feelings* for your husband . . ." Doc paused, then continued resolutely, ". . . they seem to confuse your judgment."

"I don't know what you mean."

Doc's eyes narrowed. "You are aware that your interference earlier today when Tom had his attack almost cost your husband his life, aren't you?"

"That's not true!"

"If Tiny hadn't dragged you out of my way—"

"You're lying!" Clare turned toward Tanner, her eyes bright with tears. "Don't believe him, Tanner. He's trying to turn you and everyone else against me."

"Clare." Drawing her attention back to him, Doc continued, "I'm not your enemy."

"You're behaving as if you are."

"I'm trying to make you see that however good your intentions, you're doing your husband harm in your present state."

"All right!" Her delicate features taut, Clare took a stiff step in retreat. "But you may rest assured that I'll have much to say to my husband when he recovers."

Turning abruptly on her heel, Clare stomped back down the hall and slammed her bedroom door behind her.

The sound was still reverberating when Tanner turned to Doc's weary expression and said, "Her *deep feelings* for my father?"

Doc sighed. "I'm doing the best I can, Tanner. Go back downstairs and have your supper. I'll call you if there's any change." Tanner had taken two steps toward the stairs when Doc added, "But I wouldn't go beyond shouting distance if I were you, not if you want to be sure you'll be here if your pa's time should come."

Rounding on him in sudden anger, Tanner grated, "You said he had nine months!"

"Yes, I did, but the trouble is, it's starting to look like the Man upstairs might have something else in mind."

Silent for a long moment, Tanner started back toward the first floor.

* * *

Damn that ornery old man! Doc Pierce hadn't heard the last of this!

Standing in the silence of her room as the sound of Tanner's footsteps faded, Clare seethed. Her acting had been supreme when she had thrown herself on Tom's bed, calling his name as he struggled for breath, but it was obvious that the old practitioner hadn't been fooled for a minute. Had it not been for the twist of fate that had brought him out to the ranch on that particular day, Tom would surely be dead, and she would be free. She would never forgive Doc Pierce for that, or for having her forcibly removed from the room. Most of all, she would never forgive him for saying all those things he had said in front of Tanner. She'd pay him back for that if it was the last thing she ever did!

Stomping to the window, Clare stared out at the winding road that led to town. If Manuelo had been at the ranch, no one—Tiny included—would have been able to keep her out of Tom's room.

Manuelo . . . he was her only true hope, now. She was depending on him, as she had depended on him so many times before. If he brought her the information she needed about that conniving tart who had captured Tanner's fancy, she would be able to redeem herself in Tanner's eyes.

Clare struggled against frustrated tears. But she wouldn't wait forever. She was tired of waiting—for Tom to die, and for Tanner to be hers at last.

Clare unconsciously shook her head. No . . . she wouldn't wait much longer.

The din of the Roundup numbed Callie's mind. She turned toward the loud shriek of laughter that came from the bar. Was it her imagination, or was the smoke thicker than usual, the music from Charlie's piano more deafening, the room so crowded that it was almost suffocating?

Unable to resist, Callie glanced at the saloon entrance as she had countless times in the past few hours. Tanner had not come. Somehow, throughout the long day of conflicting emotions, it had not occurred to her for a minute that he wouldn't.

I've never met a woman who didn't regret it when she let a McBride into her life.

Annabelle's words haunted her.

"Say, Callie, are you listenin'?"

Callie came back to the present with a jolt. She looked at the fair-haired cowboy standing beside her, a smile of true regret on her lips as she said, "I'm sorry, Mitchell. My head's aching and I'm having trouble keeping my thoughts straight tonight. I'm afraid I'm not very good company."

"You're fine company." Mitchell smiled, his freckled skin flushing as he said, "And I figure I'm a lucky man. I wasn't expectin' you'd have any time for me at all tonight, bein's how popular you've been since you came to town."

Callie forced a smile. "You're a nice fella, Mitchell."

"But he's not as nice as I am."

The deep-voiced interjection turned Callie toward Ace. Taking her arm, Ace faced the surprised cowboy and said, "You'll have to excuse Callie for a little while. We have some business to discuss."

"Damn, Ace!" Mitchell smacked the bar with the flat of his hand. "That ain't fair!"

"Business comes first, you know."

"Says who?"

Ace smiled. "I do."

Following stiffly as Ace led her to a table, Callie allowed him to seat her before she asked flatly, "Are you going to fire me?"

"Hell, no! Whatever gave you that idea?"

She almost wished he would.

"Callie, honey," Ace took her hand in his familiar way. "Look, you're keeping your distance from me for your own reasons, but I still consider us friends . . . and the truth is, I'm worried about you."

Ace's warm, brown-eyed gaze held hers, and Callie's throat was suddenly tight. She responded hoarsely, "How many times do I have to tell you that I can take care of myself?"

"I don't believe that now any more than I did the first time you said it."

"You should."

Ace ignored her response. "He's not here, is he?"

"Who?"

"Don't play games with me, Callie."

Callie raised her chin. "No, Tanner isn't here."

"He said he would be, didn't he?"

Callie did not reply.

"You don't have to answer me. The way you've been watching the door all night, you don't have to."

"He'll come . . . eventually."

"And you'll take him back with open arms, if *eventually* means a day, a week, or a month, is that it?"

Callie's jaw was tight. "Yes."

"Why?"

"I have my reasons."

"Whatever they are, they aren't good enough! Callie . . ." Ace squeezed her hands tightly in his. "I've seen his type a hundred times before. Hell, I *was* Tanner McBride for more years than I

want to admit; and the truth is, seeing myself
again in Tanner McBride isn't pleasant." Ace
paused. "You're hurting already. I can see it in
your eyes, and I've seen that look so many times
before. Forget about him. There're any number
of fellas in here mooning over you tonight who'll
treat you better. You'd have your choice."

"I've made my choice."

"You made a mistake! Take a good look
around you and start over."

Loud introductory chords snapped Ace's attention toward the piano, and he cursed. Ignoring the shrill whistles sounding from the crowd
when Callie stood up, Ace snapped, "Ignore
them. You're with the boss. You can sing later."

"Don't worry about me." Callie's forced smile
dimmed. "I told you once before that I'm not
really the person you think I am."

"Yes, you are—whether you think you are or
not."

Choosing not to respond, Callie started toward the piano.

Tanner awakened with a start. Momentarily dis-
oriented, he glanced around the living room,
frowning as memory returned. Pa's condition
was unstable. Doc had warned him to stay near,
in case the end came rapidly. He had sat down

in the living room chair and leaned his head back for just a minute.

Tanner glanced at the clock. It was past twelve. Callie was probably wondering where he was. She'd be angry, or worried, or both. He'd get into town as soon as he could and explain.

"Tanner . . ."

At Doc's appearance on the stairs, Tanner stood up abruptly, his heart suddenly pounding.

"You didn't get to bed yet?"

Tanner took a breath, then asked, "How is he, Doc?"

"I can't really say." Doc shook his head. "Your pa seems to be holding his own, but I don't see much improvement." He paused. "It could still go either way."

Forcibly rejecting the unexpected sadness Doc's words evoked, Tanner said, "I have to talk to him."

"Not yet."

"Doc . . . it's important."

"It won't do any good to talk to him if he can't answer."

"Is he conscious? In pain?"

"He's semiconscious, and he has pain, but I'm doing my best to spare him." Pausing, Doc said, "Go to bed. You'll only be down the hall if I need to call you."

Tanner nodded. He was eye level with Doc on

the stairs when he forced himself to ask, "Did Pa ask for me?"

"No."

"But he asked for Clare, right?"

Doc did not respond.

Tanner walked into his bedroom and closed the door behind him, then stood stock still. What had made him ask those questions when he knew what the responses would be? He supposed the reason was that he had needed to be sure he hadn't misjudged his pa, that his pa really didn't give a damn about him, or anybody else . . . except Clare.

He had known what the answers would be . . . so why did he feel so damned bad?

It was past midnight, but Sidewinder's main street was still brightly lit. With a last glance through the window of the Roundup, where he had maintained silent surveillance for many hours, Manuelo turned in the direction of the boardinghouse. His feelings were mixed as he walked unnoticed along the active street. It had always been that way with him. It was as if he were invisible, except for those times when he was regarded with suspicion or distaste by passersby. He had only come into true existence upon meeting his dear Senora Brown, who had depended on him and had given him a reason for living. Now it was Senora Clare who depended on him, and who would be very happy with the information he already had to bring her.

Manuelo smiled, crooked, yellowed teeth briefly flashing. But he was determined to bring her more.

Arriving in front of the boardinghouse, Manuelo surveyed it briefly. All the windows were dark. Everyone slept. He made his way to the rear entrance and slipped through the doorway, then up the stairs as he had done once before. Inside the woman's room in seconds, he needed only the light streaming through the window from the street to find the suitcase underneath the bed, where he was certain the telegraph sheet would be concealed. It was there, wrinkled and casually discarded.

Replacing the case underneath the bed, Manuelo moved to the window to scrutinize the words on the printed sheet. His illiteracy did not bar him from recognizing the words he hoped to see.

Elated, Manuelo folded the sheet carefully and placed it in his pocket. Back on the street he approached the livery stable with a measured pace calculated not to attract attention. He reclaimed his horse, then wasted no time leaving the town behind him.

*   *   *

Tiny snapped awake with the realization that he had been dozing. Seated on a chair inside Tom McBride's room, he saw the bedridden man twitch in sleep, but he saw no additional distress. He then listened for sounds of movement beyond the bedroom door. There were none.

He stood, aware that it was still a few hours until dawn. Doc Pierce was old. He had needed to retire to a spare bedroom for some sleep. Doc had left him to watch over his patient, knowing he could be trusted.

Uncertain what had awakened him, Tiny opened the bedroom door and looked out into the hallway. Satisfied that it was empty, he closed the door and resumed his seat. Doc Pierce had said the next few hours would tell the tale whether Tom McBride would live or die, but Tiny already knew what the outcome would be. Tom McBride had come close to death, but he would survive this most recent attack, just as he had survived the others. Tiny was certain of that, because Tom McBride had told him that he was determined to survive for the nine months he needed.

Alerted to another sound beyond the bedroom doorway, Tiny jumped to his feet and jerked the door open. The hallway was empty.

Frowning, Tiny closed the door again and resumed his vigil.

"What are you doing here at this time of night?"

Clare stared at Manuelo, who stood just inside her bedroom doorway. Securing her robe, she glanced at the darkness beyond her window and continued, "It's hours until dawn. If anyone should see you—"

"I have come to bring you the information you asked for. It is information of great importance."

The sudden pounding of her heart erased the last trace of sleep from Clare's mind. "About the woman?" At Manuelo's nod, she demanded, "What is it?"

"The woman was distressed when I arrived in town. It was visible in her manner when she emerged from her room this morning and walked directly to the telegraph office. I waited until the clerk sent her message and discarded the sheet on which she wrote. I then entered the office and offered to clean it for a sum that was too meager for the man to refuse. In that manner I obtained the written copy of the woman's message. I secured the reply that she received by going to her room when she was working and—"

"I'm not interested in *how* you obtained the information. Just give it to me!"

Snatching the wrinkled sheets Manuelo withdrew from his pocket, Clare walked to the lamp and turned it higher. She read the contents, then read them again.

Clare looked up, her eyes bright. "Just as I thought! Her name isn't Callie Winslow. She's *Caldwell Logan*, the sister of the fellow who was killed in the bank robbery. It's no coincidence that she came to Sidewinder. She followed Tanner and threw herself at him, with some convoluted plan in mind to make him pay for her brother's death, no doubt!"

Smothering her jubilant laughter with the flat of her hand, Clare took a staggering backward step. "Oh, this is too fine to be believed! She pretended to be a saloon woman and took Tanner in completely with her charade. She had him eating out of her hand. She made him believe she wanted him, while all she really wanted was revenge for her brother's murder!"

Aching with the laughter she forcibly subdued, Clare allowed her enjoyment full rein. Then she gripped Manuelo's arm to say, "Mama would be proud of the way you've helped me in this. She had faith that you would never let me down, and you haven't betrayed that faith."

His dark eyes filling with moisture, Manuelo grated, "*Muchas gracias*, senora."

"But your work isn't done. Tom's had another attack. Tiny's on guard in his room, and I don't want him to know you've been in here to talk to me. You must go down the rear staircase quietly . . . without a sound. I'll take care of the rest."

"*Sí*, senora."

Manuelo slipped back out into the hallway and drew the door closed behind him, but the servant's stealthy departure was already dismissed from her mind as Clare walked to her mirror and picked up her brush.

Tanner moved restlessly in his sleep. Myriad images haunted his dreams. He saw himself lying on the hallway floor, his jaw throbbing as Pa stood healthy, strong, and angry, leaning over him. He spied Clare standing behind his pa, her smile victorious. He glimpsed again the accusation in Stone's eyes. He saw Lauren with tears streaking her cheeks . . . and his heart wept as well.

Then he saw Callie, and everything changed. Warmth filled him as she approached. She was smiling, her skin smooth and clear, her eyes like warm honey, her mouth so sweet. He reached for her, wanting to know again the merging of body and spirit when their flesh was joined.

289

She was in his arms again. Her body was pressed to his, and he clutched her tight against him. But—her body felt strangely foreign against his. Her warmth felt cold even as she pulled him closer, as she pressed her mouth to his. His ardor became distaste as she sought to deepen her kiss. Repulsed, he pushed her away and awakened abruptly to the darkness of his bedroom.

Tanner looked at the bed beside him. Revulsion swept his senses as he spat, "Clare . . . damn it! What are you doing here?"

"You seemed only too eager to welcome me a few minutes ago."

On his feet in a moment, Tanner reached for his trousers. Aware of the nakedness Clare made no attempt to hide, he grated, "You're mistaken."

"Am I, Tanner? I don't think so."

"Either you're going to leave or I will."

"No, Tanner! We need each other tonight!" Sitting up, her delicate features composed in an earnest plea, Clare whispered, "I came to you for consolation, a consolation you need as much as I do."

"Consolation!" Tanner swept her with a look of disgust. "Is that what you call it?"

"Why do you fight me, Tanner? You know it's

inevitable that we'll be together. Tom's sick. He can't last much longer."

"This is your husband you're talking about—the man you love and have 'deep feelings' for."

"He's sick. He's been sick a long time. He's not the man I married anymore."

"He'd be glad to hear you say that, I'm sure."

"But you'll never tell him, will you, Tanner?"

Rising to her feet, the fair skin of her naked body glowing in the semidarkness of his room, Clare moved sinuously toward him. "It's all right to give in, you know. You've protested and resisted long enough. You've done everything a good son should. It's time to do what you want now . . . to *have* what you want."

Clare attempted to press herself against him, to draw his mouth to hers, but Tanner pushed her away. His clear eyes as cold as his voice, he grated, "You sicken me."

"I sicken you?" Clare's slender frame grew rigid. "I make you sick, but *Callie* doesn't."

"That's right."

"Callie Winslow . . ." Clare reached for the robe that lay discarded on the floor. She slipped it on, her smile stiff. "But her name isn't really Callie Winslow. It's Callie Logan. You didn't know that, did you?"

"Logan . . ."

"The name sounds familiar to you, doesn't it? It should. Matthew Logan is the fellow you *killed* during a bank robbery only a few weeks before you came home to visit your dying father."

"You're crazy!"

"It's true, every word." Clare's eyes glowed with triumph. "I know it's true because it comes straight from your dear Callie herself."

"Callie told you . . ."

"Fool! Of course she didn't tell me, but she might just as well have. She sent a telegram to her hometown today. The telegram was addressed to Sheriff Ira Glennan, Foster, Texas."

"Sheriff Glennan . . ."

"You should recognize his name, I'm sure. You were locked in his jail long enough before you were released—before Caldwell Logan returned to town to find her brother had been killed."

"I don't believe any of this!"

"Don't you?" Pulling crumpled sheets of paper from the pocket of her robe, Clare waved them in front of his eyes, then threw them on the bed. "Here's the proof. It's all yours! Read it. Keep it. Burn it. Do whatever you want with it! I won't need proof when I tell your father how you've disgraced him, how you allowed a woman to make a fool of you, how you've shamed the McBride name again!"

Tying her robe tightly around her, taking a moment to smooth the fair hair that lay unbound against her shoulders, Clare added, "On second thought, perhaps you'd better save it— to keep you company during the long, *empty* nights to come."

Clare covered the distance to the bedroom door in a few delicate strides. Her hand on the knob, she turned back to add, "Oh, thank you for so generously donating your portion of the Circle M to the bequest that will be mine. That's what you've done tonight, you know. And, Tanner . . ." Clare's eyes were like sharp daggers. "Fool that you are, you don't know what you've missed."

The door clicked closed behind Clare. The sound was still resounding in his ears when Tanner reached for the papers she had thrown on the bed.

Another morning.

Callie opened her eyes, squinting at the slender rays of sunlight filtering through her bedroom window. She glanced at the clock on the dresser. It was early, too early, considering the hour when she had gotten to bed, and the restless night that had followed.

Pulling herself to a seated position, Callie brushed a wayward strand of hair from her cheek. Where did she go from here? Somehow, after having lain flesh to flesh with Tanner, after having looked into his eyes as he whispered tender endearments, she had not believed that she would awaken this morning in her lonely bed.

Lonely . . .

Callie closed her eyes. Try as she might, she could not deny that she was lonely for Tanner . . . that the previous evening had dragged past with each minute stretching into an eternity as she waited for him to appear in the saloon doorway. She had thought of countless excuses for Tanner's failure to come, despising her weakness with each new addition to the list. She had ended the night by forcing herself to admit that the Tanner who had held her in his arms and spoken those tender words was only a small part of the total man—a total man who obviously gave no more thought to breaking a promise than to the taking of a life.

Cutting deepest of all, however, was her knowledge that she would accept any excuse Tanner offered—not merely because she must in order to bring Matt's killers to justice—but because she *wanted* to.

Unable to bear her disturbing thoughts another moment, Callie stood up and reached for her clothes. She turned toward the door at the sound of loud voices in the hallway. She recognized Tanner's voice at the same moment that a heavy pounding sounded on her door. She opened the door to see Tanner, with Annabelle standing angrily two steps behind him.

One glance between them, and Annabelle turned away without another word.

One glance at Tanner's face, and Callie's heart stilled.

Callie made no protest when Tanner moved her backwards into the room and thrust the door closed behind them.

"Who are you?"

"What do you mean, who am I?"

Tanner stared at Callie's pale face. The features were the same. The honey-gold eyes returning his stare still touched a hidden core of him with their heat. Her smooth skin still drew his touch. Her full lips still raised a familiar yearning. But the heat in her eyes was suddenly tempered by caution. Her smooth skin had lost its color, and as he watched, she bit down on her lip to still its trembling.

"What's your name, Callie?"

"My name? You know my name."

"Callie Winslow."

"Yes."

"Or is it Callie *Logan*?"

Tanner saw the jolt that shook her. "It is, isn't it? You're Matt Logan's sister."

The warm gold of Callie's eyes went suddenly cold. "That's right."

Tanner gripped Callie's arms, holding her motionless under his quiet rage as he spat, "You came to Sidewinder to find me, didn't you? Why? What were you expecting to gain?"

"My brother's dead and his killers are free."

"His killers—am I supposed to be included in that group?"

"Aren't you?"

Tanner snatched back his hands as if they'd been burned. He shook his head, "Strangely enough, I walked away from you that first night because I thought I'd add too many complications to your life. I should've realized when you came looking for me the next day that something was wrong. The trouble is, one look at you and I was done for. I wanted to believe you. I wanted to think that you felt the same way about me that I felt about you. I made it easy for you. Hell, I played right into your hands, but it was all pretense on your part, wasn't it?"

"My brother's dead! I swore I wouldn't let his killers go unpunished!"

"What did you expect to get from me? The names of the bank robbers? Where they were hiding? Maybe recover the money they stole? Maybe you thought you'd get it all if you waited around long enough . . . if you *tried* hard enough."

Callie did not respond.

"You can't make yourself deny it, can you?" Tanner took a hard breath. "Well, you can congratulate yourself. You wanted to make me trust you, and you succeeded. I wouldn't have believed any of this could be true if I hadn't read those telegrams with my own eyes."

"What telegrams?"

"You underestimated Clare. She's much better at this game than you are." Callie's eyes widened as he withdrew the clipping and the crumpled sheets from his pocket, then threw them on the dresser, continuing, "And you didn't even realize they were gone."

His gaze frigid, Tanner added, "Just so you know, I underestimated Clare, too, but, that's all right. I never make the same mistake twice."

The expanding ache within him was almost more than he could bear. "Sorry," Tanner rasped. "You wasted your time, but you shouldn't be too surprised at that. Everybody told you you'd be wasting your time if you took up with me."

Callie remained silent, and Tanner quizzed, "No excuses? Nothing to say?"

"I'd like an answer."

"An answer?"

"My brother's killers—are you included in that group?"

The last spark of hope within him flickered, then died in the long moment before Tanner walked out the door.

Chapter Eight

"How are you feeling, darling?" Clare leaned over Tom's bed, her flawless countenance angelic. She held her smile firmly in place as Tom raised an unsteady hand to grasp a lock of her pale hair. Concealing her revulsion, she waited for his reply.

"Better. I feel stronger today."

"I'm so glad." She reached toward the half-empty plate on the nightstand. "Would you like to eat a little more?"

"No."

"You're certain?"

"I'm fine, Clare. You can tell Tiny to take it away."

Clare nodded. She would have liked to tell the

odious mute more than that, but now was not the time. The severity of Tom's attack two weeks previously had altered her position. Doc Pierce now checked his patient more regularly. He paid more attention to the care Tom was given. There was no longer any opportunity for the scant meals she had ordered, or for the meager intake of liquids she had insisted upon. Doc Pierce had made his position clear, and any contradiction of the treatment he had ordered for Tom would be looked upon with suspicion.

Clare forced her smile to brighten as Tom stroked her hair. She could not afford suspicion. She needed to be patient. Her patience would be rewarded in the end.

"Did you check to see if any mail came for me when you were in town, Clare?"

"Mail?" Clare paused. Mail had been the last thing on her mind when she had traveled to town with Manuelo that morning. Was he suspicious? "No. Were you expecting any?"

"Possibly from Lauren and Stone, or . . ."

"Or?"

Taking care to conceal her annoyance when Tom did not answer her, Clare responded, "No, you didn't have any mail." Forcing a note of sympathy into her tone, she added, "But there's still time, dear. Lauren and Stone may still come."

Clare did not miss the twitch of Tom's lips before he asked, "About Tanner . . . is he behaving himself?"

Clare remained silent. Tanner was behaving himself, all right. In the two weeks since she had thrown the telegrams on his bed, he hadn't missed a day riding out with the men, and he hadn't gone into town to visit that conniving tart—much to Callie Logan's dismay, Clare was sure. Of course, Tanner hadn't spoken more than three words to her during that time, either, but that was only temporary. She would wear him down.

"Clare?"

"Tanner wants to talk to you, Tom."

"I don't want to see him."

"He says it's important."

"I already told him that I don't want to talk to him until the others arrive."

"Tom . . ."

"You didn't answer me. Is he behaving himself?"

"Tanner's behaving himself as well as can be expected, I suppose."

"If he's disrespecting you in any way—"

"No . . . no." Clare rubbed Tom's bony arm consolingly. "The only disrespect he shows is by not speaking to me."

301

"Not speaking to you!"

"Not a word beyond a simple good morning or good night."

"Well, that's as much as I can expect from him, I suppose."

When she expected so much more.

The McBride blue of Tom's eyes was never clearer as he said, "This is hard on you, I know, but . . . it won't be much longer."

"What are you saying?"

"The nine months . . . they'll pass quickly, and you won't be tied to this room anymore."

"Tom!"

"I'll settle everything before that. I'll see to it that everyone is rewarded accordingly. That's a promise."

"I wish you wouldn't talk like that."

"I want you to know . . . I want you *to always remember* that I made that promise to you."

Turning toward the sound of familiar footsteps in the hallway, Clare resisted a frown. "It's Doc Pierce."

Tom shook his head. "That man's going to wear himself out riding all this way as often as he does."

"I tried to tell him it wasn't necessary, that I take good care of you."

"I suppose he's trying to make sure I don't

make a fool out of him by dying before nine months are up."

The door opened without a knock to admit Doc's stooped figure.

"Isn't that right, Doc?"

Clare forced a smile as Doc replied, while she silently cursed the man's every word.

Jeb glanced up at the cloudless sky, then lowered his gaze to scan the surrounding terrain with a practiced eye. Tanner rode beside him as Jeb turned and drawled, "I'm thinkin' we've got as many strays as we're goin' to take out of this part of the range." Lifting his hat, he wiped his forearm across his brow and said, "I'm damned glad, too, because it's mighty hot, and it's startin' to look like there's no relief in sight."

Tanner felt no need to comment.

Jeb squinted in his direction. "You haven't been doin' much talkin' lately. Haven't been smilin' much, either." When Tanner maintained his silence, Jeb added, "Come to think of it, you never did much of either. That truth aside, I figure somethin's botherin' you. If you want to talk about it . . . get it off your chest—"

"There's nothing to talk about."

"Well, if it's your pa—"

"Doc says he's getting better. He says he might

even last out the nine months, like he figured."

"You want to talk to your pa, but he still won't have none of it, is that right?"

"He gave strict orders to keep me out of his room, and Doc says not to excite him. That's not about to change."

"Is it important—what you want to talk to him about?"

"Yes."

"Anythin' I can help you with?"

"No. It's between Pa and me."

Jeb shook his head. "That's what I figured. But that ain't all that's botherin' you, is it?"

Tanner darted him a dark look.

"Don't look at me like that, boy!" Jeb's sun-darkened skin flushed a shade darker. "You may think this is none of my business—and maybe it ain't—but that's not goin' to stop me from askin' anyways." Jeb waited. When Tanner made no response, he pressed, "About that woman in town, that Callie Winslow—"

Tanner snapped, "What about her?"

"You was feelin' real good about her for a while, until your pa had that attack."

"Pa's attack has nothing to do with her."

"The ranch hands do a lot of talkin', you know. They gossip like old ladies, and they're sayin' you and that Callie were the talk of the town for a while."

Tanner's expression turned black.

"They say she's a handsome filly, with a way about her that draws fellas to her. I hear there ain't a man in town who ain't tried to take your place, but that gal ain't havin' any." Jeb paused. "What happened, boy? That woman made you happy. Ain't there no way you can settle whatever differences you two had if you just—"

"Jeb." Tanner interrupted him, his strong features grim. "I know you mean well, but things are more complicated than you realize."

"The boys are sayin' that Ace fella's been takin' her under his wing. That worries me."

"She's free to do what she wants. I don't have any ties on her."

"But does she have ties on you?"

Tanner turned his mount abruptly. "I'm going down into the wash. There're always a few strays hiding down there."

"Tanner . . ."

Tanner jammed his heels into his mount's sides, cursing softly at the image of Callie ever present before his mind. Aware that his haste was imprudent when he reached the sandy soil of the wash, he drew back on the reins and made his way cautiously along its winding route. It had been a hard two weeks since he had left Callie standing alone in the silence of her room. He had needed to remind himself over and over again that Callie wasn't really Callie, that everything between them had been a lie, and that the woman he had believed her to be didn't really exist.

Spotting a steer a distance away, Tanner rode warily toward it. He slapped his lariat at the animal's hide and drove it out into the open ahead of him—with Callie's image still haunting him. The game was over, but Callie was still in town. What was she waiting for? Did she think he wouldn't be able to stay away from her?

Tanner hesitated at that thought. *Was she right?*

The ache inside Tanner deepened. Callie had come to Sidewinder to find her brother's killers. She had looked him in the eye, believing he was one of them. He had held her in his arms. He had opened his heart to her and made love to her without holding back. She had returned his loving just as fully—but none of it had made any difference at all.

Tanner's jaw hardened. Lies . . . all of it. He ached for her, but he'd get over it. Other fellas wanted her. Well, that was fine with him. He was done with her.

Brilliant afternoon sunlight shone through the windows of Sidewinder's only dress shop, making the small store uncomfortably warm as Callie moved her hands absentmindedly through the rack of ready-made gowns. The gowns were gaily colored, contrasting sharply with her mood. The astoundingly red garment she had previously bought there was now pale and limp from repeated washings, and the heavy gold satin, her only alternative, was too suffocating to be borne another night. She had hesitated to purchase another gown, telling herself it was a frivolous expense, that she would not be remaining in Sidewinder much longer, but . . .

Callie refused to finish that thought. She had not seen Tanner since that night two weeks previous when he had tossed the clipping and telegrams on her dresser, and had ended all contact between them. She had told herself that was the end of it, but an inner part of her had not truly believed it could be true. Her emotions in sharp conflict, she had lived those two weeks with a smile fixed on her face and an ache in her heart, denying until she could deny it no longer that she missed Tanner desperately.

She had been in contact with Sheriff Glennan by wire in the time since. Her desperation had only increased when he wired back that no further progress had been made in apprehending the other members of the gang.

Her attention caught by a striking blue gown, Callie withdrew it from the rack. The shade was glorious, reminiscent of the brilliant color of Tanner's eyes. Her heart pounding and her eyes suddenly moist, she held it up against her, then folded it over her arm and started toward the proprietor.

She could not leave Sidewinder—not yet. Matt had died, cruelly, needlessly. She could not allow his death to go unpunished, whatever price she might be forced to pay.

Tanner's image appeared unexpectedly before her mind's eye, and Callie's throat tightened. Whatever price she must pay.

"You're not looking so good, Tanner."

Looking up at Doc Pierce as the elderly practitioner exited his father's room and stood waiting for him at the top of the stairs, Tanner replied caustically, "I'm not your patient, Doc. Your patient's the fella who's lying in a bed behind that door. He's the one you should be checking up on."

"And I'm doing a damned good job of it, too, if I do say so myself." His infrequent smile briefly surfacing, Doc Pierce said, "Your pa's doing better. He's asleep right now, but he's getting stronger. You, on the other hand, look worse each time I see you."

Ignoring Doc's comment, Tanner glanced around the hallway.

"If you're looking for Clare, she's downstairs. She does her best to keep out of my way these days." Doc shrugged. "I must've done something to offend her."

Tanner made no comment.

"I get the feeling she's making sure to stay out of *your* way, too, these days."

Doc was fishing for information, but Tanner was too tired to rise to the bait. After many nights of sleep made restless by Callie's image, each day on the range had begun to seem a little longer than the last. Jeb had said that the ranch hands gossiped like women, and Doc had doubtless heard them talking. Certainly, the ice between Clare and himself had been obvious the past two weeks—a situation that suited him fine. What did not suit him was his father's relentless insistence that he be barred from his bedroom, and his own suspicion that his pa had a reason for keeping him out.

"We haven't seen much of you in town of late."

"I haven't had a need to go in."

"You haven't, huh? Well, I guess you haven't had a chance to talk to Bill Hanes, then."

Tanner was instantly alert.

Doc continued, "I don't know whether you're

aware of it or not, but Clare paid Bill Hanes a visit this morning." He paused. "She wanted to see a copy of Tom's will. She said she felt it was her right as Tom's wife."

"She never asked to see the will before?"

Doc shook his head.

"Did he show it to her?"

"You know better than that. If Tom had wanted Clare to see that will, he wouldn't have gone through the trouble of having Bill write it up when she was away from the ranch."

"I bet she didn't like being turned down."

"She tried cajoling Bill into showing it to her, and when that didn't work, she ranted and raved for a while, then threatened to tell Tom that Bill wasn't respecting her as Tom's wife. That didn't work, either."

"She must have a reason for wanting to see it. Maybe Pa said something that made her uncomfortable."

"Maybe. All I know is that Bill was mighty angry after she left."

"About the will . . ."

"I don't know anything about it. I'm only Tom's doctor, and my work's done here for the day." Doc paused. "Have you seen your pa at all since his last attack?"

"No."

"Do you want to see him?"

"No."

Doc scrutinized Tanner's frozen countenance. Turning back abruptly toward his patient's bedroom door, he said, "Well, I'm going to be leaving, but I have to go back into your pa's room to get my bag. Like I said, he's asleep. I'm going to leave the bedroom door open for a few minutes to let some of the cooler air from the hallway in there. It'll give him some relief. Take care of yourself, Tanner."

Tanner watched as Doc disappeared back into the bedroom, leaving the door open behind him. His stomach knotted tight as he approached the doorway, then looked inside. Pa was sleeping, all right. He was pale and skeletal, not even a shadow of his former self, but Tanner was suddenly more acutely aware than ever before that his pa would continue to dominate the Circle M as long as there was a spark of life left in him.

Uncertain if that realization caused him comfort or pain, Tanner turned away and strode toward his room.

Bill Hanes was still fuming. Glancing toward the window, the aging solicitor saw that evening had arrived. Many hours had passed since the moment when Clare McBride had walked into his office, a butter-wouldn't-melt-in-her-mouth expression on her faultless countenance as she had asked to see her husband's will.

Bill Hanes unconsciously shook his head. The audacity of the woman was inconceivable—surpassed only by her arrogance! She had actually believed that all she had to do was smile, and he would oblige her every request.

Well, his name wasn't Tom McBride.

What had followed had been less than pleasant. He had emerged from the confrontation more uncertain than ever as to what Tom McBride saw in the woman.

Slapping his desk drawer closed, Hanes frowned. His head jerked up at the sound of a heavy knock on the door. He responded, then took a backward step as the door opened.

"Tanner . . . come on in."

Tanner hesitated, then entered the solicitor's office. The long ride into town had seemed endless.

"This is a surprise." Bill Hanes's expression confirmed the truth of his statement. "I wasn't expecting a visit from you tonight."

"I wasn't expecting to come into town tonight, either."

Bill Hanes scrutinized him for a silent mo-

ment, then said, "I know this isn't a social call,
Tanner. What's on your mind?"

Tanner returned Hanes's scrutiny. He had
spoken truthfully when he said he hadn't intended coming into town. He had been saddling
his horse, his conversation with Doc repeating
itself in his mind, before his intention was clear
even to himself.

Tanner began cautiously, "Doc was out at the
ranch today. He said Clare paid you a visit this
morning."

"Yes, she did, but what does that have to do
with you?"

Suddenly impatient, Tanner replied bluntly, "I
didn't come here to play games with you, Mr.
Hanes, so I'll say it straight out. Doc said Clare
asked to see my pa's will."

"That's right." Hanes's lips twitched revealingly. "I didn't show it to her, though."

"So Doc said."

"All I'll say about the exchange between Clare
and me is that she didn't accept my refusal
gracefully."

"According to the letter you sent to me and the
others, my pa's will leaves all the heirs equal
shares of the inheritance."

"If they meet the restrictions he stipulated—
the nine-months clause. Whoever doesn't meet

it will forfeit his or her share to Clare."

Tanner's expression tightened. "I came to ask if those are really the terms stated in the will."

The solicitor's expression was suddenly as tight as his own. "They are."

"Then why did Clare come? What does she know that we—?"

"She doesn't know anything. To be truthful, I think your pa's last attack made her start thinking. I think she was testing me—to see if she could count on me to work to her benefit if things became difficult."

Tanner waited.

"I told you, Tanner, I'm not the fool your pa is when it comes to that woman. If it's any consolation to you, I'll say it outright. I will not show Clare your father's will unless your pa tells me to."

"That isn't what I came here to find out." Tanner's gaze was direct. "I need to know something else. I need to know if my pa was truly fair in that will."

"Fair?" Bill Hanes peered at him over the rim of his glasses. "You already know the terms of the will."

"Yes, I do."

"Then?"

Tanner held the solicitor's gaze silent moments longer.

"I can't show you the will, Tanner."

"I'm not asking to see it. You know what I'm asking."

Bill Hanes searched Tanner's gaze more deeply. His voice dropped a note lower. "I suppose I do."

"A simple yes or no is all I'm asking."

Tanner saw the war that raged behind Bill Hanes's eyes when he said, "I suppose you have a right to know."

Tanner waited. An eternity passed before Bill Hanes replied, "The answer is . . . yes."

Relieved, Tanner extended his hand. His handshake was firm, his response concise and sincere when he said, "Thank you, Mr. Hanes," then left the solicitor staring after him as he walked out the door.

"Beautiful Dreamer."

Seated at his usual table in the corner of the Roundup, Ace shook his head as the last notes of Callie's song trailed away and applause swelled from the crowded saloon floor. He supposed his customers were getting tired of hearing that song, but one glance at Digby Jones, who was watching Callie with moist eyes, revealed that he was not.

When Callie returned to the bar, Digby took

her hand and raised it to his lips. The old coot was crazy about her, and it was obvious that Callie had a soft spot for the fella as well. He supposed that soft spot was what set Callie apart from the rest of his bar girls. She was young and inexperienced, despite her ease in handling the wranglers who flocked around her. The calluses hadn't hardened around her heart yet. If it were up to him, they never would.

Sitting back, Ace watched as Callie eased herself in between two wranglers who made room for her at the bar. He saw the admiration in their eyes as an easy banter began between them. How could they help but admire her? Her new blue gown aside, Callie was beautiful, and when she turned those honey-colored eyes on a man, well . . .

But he was worried about her. He had seen the change that had come over her in the past two weeks. He had seen the moments when her smile faded unexpectedly and unhappiness welled in her eyes without any apparent cause. He could not count the number of times that she glanced toward the entrance, then looked back at the crowd, her vivacity a little more forced than before. She was thinner, too, her vibrant natural color paler. And when she thought no one was watching, she looked downright sad.

It was all Tanner McBride's fault, he was sure. He knew that fella's type, and he—

"Say, Ace . . ."

Looking up, Ace saw Angie standing beside his table. Hesitating a fraction of a moment, he pushed out the chair beside him in silent invitation. Angie sat. Angie was all woman, from the top of her dark, upswept hair to the tips of her red, high-heeled shoes. She had ten years on Callie—at the least. Those ten years had matured her into a fun-loving but sincere woman who made no attempt to hide how much she loved him. He loved her, too. He supposed he might even marry her one day, but he knew instinctively that the worry lines between her dark eyes were not caused by that particular concern.

Leaning toward her, Ace pressed his mouth to Angie's. Her lips clung to his, and his heart warmed. He whispered reassuringly, "You're my woman, Angie."

Angie's expression flickered. He knew she was waiting for more—for an explanation he might never be ready to make. How could he tell her that Callie reminded him of a girl he knew a long time ago, a girl he had loved and left behind? How could he explain that, looking back from a position of maturity, he had little respect for the man he had been then, and that watching Tanner McBride was like looking at that man in the mirror.

Ace's jaw unconsciously firmed. He had been drawn to Callie the moment he saw her. His first instinct had been to protect her from the life she was about to embrace, and that instinct had grown stronger the moment he saw Tanner McBride. His decision was made before it was clearly formulated in his mind, and his goal was now clear. Callie would not end up alone in tears, like that girl long ago.

"Ace . . ." Angie's eyes sought his. He saw the torment reflected in them when she said, "You didn't have to say that, you know."

Momentarily uncertain, Ace asked, "I didn't have to say what?"

"That I'm your woman."

"You *are* my woman."

Angie raised her chin. "There are no strings attached, you know."

"Meaning?"

"Meaning, if you've got your heart set on somebody else now, I—"

Ace interrupted her. "I don't have my heart set on anybody but you, Angie." He paused, then continued, "If you're wondering about Callie . . ."

Angie's lips quivered, and Ace stood up

abruptly, then drew her to her feet beside him. He ushered her across the saloon floor and into the back room, then closed the door behind them. Alone with her at last, he was suddenly ashamed of his thoughtlessness. In trying to spare Callie the pain he had caused someone else years earlier, he had wounded the woman who loved him.

Closing his arms around Angie with murmured words of regret, Ace drew her close. She was warm in his arms, her womanly softness pressed against him as he whispered against her hair, "You're the only woman I want, Angie. Callie's important to me, that's true. She reminds me of someone I knew a long time ago. I suppose I do love her in a way. More than that, I feel responsible for her somehow, but the way I feel about her doesn't change my love for you. Don't ever doubt that, Angie."

Drawing back from him, her lips trembling, Angie cupped Ace's cheek with her hand and whispered, "I suppose that's what I needed to hear."

Angie's touch was familiar, and Ace turned to press a kiss against her palm. She offered her mouth to him, and Ace accepted it lovingly.

This was the way it was—Angie and him . . . and Callie.

*   *   *

"Howdy, Callie."

The evening revelry of the Roundup was heightening as Callie turned away from the great mahogany bar to see Boots Little standing a few feet to her rear. She returned the smiling wrangler's grin, then moved aside to allow him space beside her at the rail. "You're getting to be a regular customer here, fella." She winked. "And there's always room for regulars right beside me."

"You ain't bein' fair, Callie," Barney Gross protested as he was pushed down further along the bar. "I was here first tonight."

"That ain't so," Digby Jones piped up. He had maneuvered into his customary spot at Callie's right. "*I* was here first tonight, just like I always am. Ain't that right, Callie?"

Callie leaned toward the whiskered cowboy with true warmth. "That's right, Digby. Don't let it get around, but I'd be lost if you didn't come to see me every night."

Whistles and catcalls sounded along the bar, turning nearby customers toward them as the echo of her own words resounded in Callie's mind. The sentiment was true, but the words were as false as her smile. She was already lost. She had been lost since that night two weeks earlier when Tanner had turned his back on her and walked away.

"You're lookin' mighty good tonight, Callie. You're just about the prettiest thing I ever did see in that new blue dress."

Callie snapped back to the present, to the pale haze of smoke growing ever thicker, to the merry din growing ever louder, and to the fellows looking at her, depending on her for a smile, a laugh, and a song—while silently hoping for more. Each night was a repetition of the last, an endless parade of hours, but Boots was waiting for her reply, and she obliged him, saying, "You sure know how to flatter a lady, Boots."

"I ain't flatterin' you. I'm just sayin' the truth, that it's a real fine thing to see you lookin' back at me after a long day on the range."

More catcalls and whistles greeted that remark, but Callie was unexpectedly touched. Patting his hand, she said, "Don't you listen to those fellas. You make a lady feel special, and there's nothing nicer than that at the end of a long day, either."

The rejoinders continued unabated while glasses were emptied and refilled. Callie maintained her smile with sheer force of will, but the sadness inside her expanded almost beyond bearing. She glanced toward the door, ever hopeful, only to be disappointed again.

"... ain't that right, Callie?"

Callie looked back at the sound of her name, suddenly aware that her throat was too tight for a reply. She had no need to turn to identify the touch on her arm. It was Ace. "It's time for the lady to take a break, fellas. You're wearing her down."

"Hell, Ace, are you this lady's watchdog?"

"She just finished tellin' us she'd be lost without us."

"That ain't so!" Digby interjected proudly. "Callie said she'd be lost without *me*."

Turning Callie away from the bar, Ace stated unyieldingly, "Don't worry, I won't be keeping her long." His expression sobered when he seated her at his table. "I meant what I said, Callie. You're looking weary under that smile."

Callie responded with forced flippancy, "Just when those fellas were telling me how fine I look."

"Callie . . ."

"I'm fine."

"You can hide behind that smile with those fellas at the bar, but you can't with me."

"Look, Ace, I don't need you watching out for me."

Ace's jaw tightened. "You're torturing yourself about Tanner McBride. It's over. Put it behind you."

"I said I don't want to talk about it." Callie glanced toward the corner of the room to see Angie watching them. She frowned. "Angie's looking this way and she doesn't look happy."

"I'm not worried about Angie right now."

"You should be."

"Don't change the subject."

"You're a friend, Ace, but that doesn't give you the right to tell me what to do."

"You've said that before, but that hasn't stopped me yet. It won't, either, until you—"

Halting in mid-sentence, Ace stared at the door. Callie turned to follow the line of his gaze, and her heart seemed to stop.

Tanner.

Halting her when she attempted to stand, Ace said, "No. Let him be."

"I need to talk to him."

"Do you? Why? Explain it to me." Ace leaned toward her, his expression ardent. "What do you have to say to him that you haven't already said?"

"I need to tell him that I—"

Callie's protest trailed away as Tanner reached the bar, then leaned toward a tall, blond saloon girl and whispered into her ear. Marcy turned full against him with a broad smile, and Callie's heart squeezed tight.

Ace commented stiffly, "So now you can stop fooling yourself."

Unable to respond, Callie remained motionless as Tanner signaled for drinks. Marcy pressed closer to him and the conversation between them grew more intimate. Callie barely breathed when Tanner emptied the glass that had been placed in front of him, whispered again in Marcy's ear, then started back toward the door.

Incredulous, Callie watched as he walked out onto the street and disappeared from sight without ever glancing her way.

A shriek of laughter penetrated Callie's benumbed state, returning her to the reality of loud music, smoke-laden air, and the congestion of the crowded room. Speaking at last, her voice emotionless, Callie replied, "You're right, Ace. I can stop fooling myself now."

Standing without waiting for his reply, Callie returned to the bar.

Tom McBride's room was hot and still as Tiny entered and approached the bed. The day had been long and trying. Clare's mood had been difficult after her morning trip to town, but it had worsened immeasurably when she learned that Tanner had left the ranch before supper. The hands had disappeared into the bunkhouse immediately after eating in order to avoid her, and Tiny had created such a din while cleaning up that he had all but drummed her out of the kitchen.

Tiny's mouth lifted in a brief smile. His position in the household was unique, allowing him satisfaction that no one else was presently able to obtain with the demanding Mrs. McBride. However, he had no illusions. He would be the first person she dismissed from the Circle M when Tom died, but he didn't care. With Tom McBride would go any responsibility he had to the Circle M. With Tom McBride would also go his best and truest friend.

The lamp on the nightstand glowed brightly, illuminating the devastation wreaked on Tom McBride's formerly handsome face as Tiny approached. He heard the concern in Tom's voice as he rasped, "Where's Clare, Tiny? I called her, but she hasn't answered me."

Tiny moved his hands in broad gestures designed to relieve the sick man's anxiety.

"She's downstairs? Where, in the yard?"

Tiny signed again.

"Tell her I want to see her."

Tiny hesitated. How could he explain to this man who teetered on the edge of death that he had overheard Clare talking to Manuelo, saying she'd had enough of the stench of the sickroom for one day, and she wouldn't answer Tom McBride's summons again, even if he was calling her with his last breath?

The answer was apparent. He could not.

Tiny's hands moved in a descriptive response.

"She went for a walk?" Tom's mouth twitched. "Where? I need to know."

Tiny frowned, his hands moving briefly.

"Find her, then come back and tell me where she is." Tom's eyes drooped wearily, despite his anxiety. "You're my eyes and ears, Tiny. I'm depending on you."

Tom's words rang with a bittersweet knell in Tiny's ears. Tom was depending on him. The situation was the reverse of when they had first met. Tiny would willingly spend his life, if necessary, to repay the debt he owed.

Tiny left the room as Tom's eyes fluttered slowly, exhaustedly closed.

Callie twisted and turned in the throes of a vivid dream. She walked alone on a vast, open prairie where the wind whistled eerily and the buffalo grass undulated in rolling waves of green. Dispirited and weary as her journey stretched endlessly onward, she sank to the ground, surrendering to her exhaustion. She lay back against the damp blanket of grass, longing for an end to her quest.

She closed her eyes, a smile touching her lips as she was unexpectedly encompassed by comforting warmth. Relaxing, she allowed the warmth to caress her skin, to bathe her with its compelling heat. She reveled under a touch that thrust aside her anxiety.

Groaning, Callie reached out to capture the warmth and draw it closer. She felt its grip tighten around her. She felt its intensity deepen. She gasped an unintelligible word of encouragement, her bemusement halting abruptly at the sound of a rasping reply.

Callie awakened with a start. She was lying in her bed at the boardinghouse, and looking back at her were eyes that were clear and blue, unmistakable even in the pale light filtering through the window from the street. Recognition shuddered through her, but the name on her lips was swallowed by the warmth of a drugging kiss.

Tanner!

Elated, Callie slipped her arms around his

neck, drawing him closer. His kiss deepened, and she yielded to the sweet press of his flesh against hers, accommodating his weight. Joy soared to life within her as Tanner's loving assault intensified.

Returning kiss for kiss, caress for caress, encouraging each intimate foray with breathless ardor, she met his soaring hunger with a hunger of her own. She heard Tanner's whispered curse when he paused briefly, then thrust himself deep inside her.

For a moment, Tanner remained motionless. Callie's breathing was uneven when he stirred, slowly at first, his sensuous strokes quickening and deepening. She was lost in the rapidly escalating wonder between them when she felt Tanner throb within her. Her body responded with a spontaneous pulsing of its own, hurtling them both from the height of their mutual passion to sudden and consummate release.

Callie was still breathless, clutching Tanner tight, when she felt him draw back from her. Opening her eyes, she was startled out of the glowing aftermath of their lovemaking by his unexpectedly savage expression. She remained motionless, frozen into immobility as he stood up and reached for his clothes.

Pulling on his pants without a word, Tanner

then turned to look down at her. His heaving chest gleamed in the pale light as he grated, "Nothing to say, Callie? No questions?"

"Q . . . questions?"

"You were waiting for me to answer a question when we parted the last time."

Callie whispered, "Tanner, please . . ."

"Please what, Callie?" Crouched over her, his face only inches from hers, he whispered, "Ask me. Go ahead. We've just finished making love. Maybe I'll tell you anything you want to know. That was your plan from the beginning, wasn't it?"

"No, I—"

"What do you want to know?" When she did not respond, Tanner responded for her. *"Tell me about the bank robbery, Tanner. Tell me the names of the men who were involved. Tell me where to find them. Tell me where the money is hidden . . ."*

"Why are you doing this?" she demanded. "My brother was murdered! Why can't you understand that I won't be able to rest until his killers have been punished for what they did?"

"His killers . . ." Tanner's brief smile was devoid of mirth. "Am I a part of that group—that's another question you want answered, isn't it? Tell me, Callie . . . how far are you willing to go to find out what you want to know? If I lie down beside you now and promise to answer your questions, will you let me make love to you again?"

The shuddering within Callie erupted in a shaky plea. "Tanner, please . . ."

Tanner leaned closer still. His lips brushing hers, he whispered, "Sorry, but I didn't come to town tonight to answer your questions. The truth is, I didn't come to town to make love to you, either. It just seemed fitting somehow."

"Fitting?"

"That's right. I was on my way back to the Circle M when I suddenly realized that we had never said good-bye."

Pulling himself to his feet, Tanner turned toward the chair where the remainder of his clothing lay. He was fully dressed when he looked back at her.

Tanner swept her with a deprecating glance, then raised his hand to his forehead in an informal salute. His cold gaze was unwavering.

"Good-bye, Callie."

Silent, incredulous, Callie was not capable of speaking a word of reply when the door clicked closed behind him.

Chapter Nine

"You're sure of this?"

Shaking with anger as she clutched her robe around her, Clare faced Manuelo behind her closed bedroom door. A week had passed since Tanner had followed her morning visit to Bill Hanes by leaving for an unknown destination before supper. She had dispatched Manuelo to discover where he had gone, and the servant had reported that Tanner had gone to Bill Hanes's office, and had then stopped briefly at the Roundup—without having any contact at all with Callie Logan. Yet it had been almost dawn when Tanner returned to the Circle M.

Dissatisfied with Manuelo's inadequate report, she had not spared him her disapproval.

He had been trying to compensate ever since.

First light had barely touched her window-pane when Manuelo had knocked at her door that morning. She had known in an instant that he had something important to relate, yet she had been taken totally by surprise at what he had told her. Twitching with ire, she spat, "That skinny old witch in the post office couldn't have made a mistake?"

"The woman is old and a fool, senora," Manuelo said softly in an effort to calm her. "She is also curious and likes to gossip, but she is rarely wrong."

"Why did she tell you, and not me when I was last in town?"

"Perhaps she feared to speak to you directly." Withholding from his beloved mistress the fact that the townsfolk disliked her, that women in particular found her disagreeable, Manuelo continued carefully, "Or perhaps she thought you already knew."

Clare pushed back a lock of fine, gold hair, her delicate jaw tight as she spat, "But I didn't know. When did she say the letter was received?"

"Several weeks ago."

Clare's face flushed a shade darker, and Manuelo felt uncomfortable. He had returned to the ranch late the previous night, too late to carry this tale to his dear senora, and he had been glad. He had known that to tell her what he had discovered would only infuriate her and she would spend a restless night. Yet he had not dared to wait past the first morning light before appearing at her door to impart the information he had learned. He had been correct. Senora Clare was enraged.

Señora Clare's mounting fury was apparent as she snapped, "I'll fix him! You'll see! Damn it, I'll make him pay!"

"Get out of here now," Clare spat. "I have to get dressed, but then I'll make sure he gets what's coming to him."

Manuelo turned toward the door with a scowl of concern. His senora did not do well while in a temper.

"Manuelo."

Manuelo turned back to Clare.

"Don't go far. I may need you."

Nodding, Manuelo opened the door. He glanced into the hallway, then made his way soundlessly down the rear staircase. His heavy features were dark. Senora Clare was too angry. He had seen her this way before, and he had viewed the unfortunate results.

Manuelo nodded to himself. Yes, he would remain close by.

* * *

"He received the letter weeks ago, Tom." Kneeling beside her husband's bed as morning sunlight filtered through the window into his room, Clare forced herself to disregard the sickroom odors that so nauseated her as she composed her face in an expression of pained dismay. She continued, "Bill Hanes is your lawyer. He shouldn't be keeping secrets from you."

"You're sure about this?"

"Martha Peabody saw Lauren's return address on the envelope when Bill Hanes picked up his mail. She said he looked surprised when he saw it."

"Bill would have told me if Lauren had written to him."

"Maybe your trust in him is misplaced. It seems strange to me that Tanner and he have become such good friends lately."

"That's damned fool nonsense, and you know it!"

Clare drew back from the bed. "If you say so."

Frowning, Tom scrutinized his wife's flushed face. He reached for her hand. When she snatched it back, avoiding his gaze, his frown darkened.

"Are you mad at me, Clare?"

"No."

334

"You are, aren't you?"

"I think you're being foolish!" Turning heavily laden eyes toward him, Clare said soberly, "If Lauren wrote to Bill Hanes, you should know about it. It's not as if . . . as if . . ."

"As if I have much time left, is that what you want to say?"

Clare brushed away a tear that trailed down her cheek and took Tom's hand. "Yes, darling, that is what I hesitated to say. I know how much you want to settle things."

"Don't upset yourself." Tom patted her hand. "I'll get to the bottom of this."

"What can I do to help you, Tom?" Clare leaned against the sickbed, her expression anguished. "I'll do anything."

Hesitating briefly, Tom said, "Tell Tanner I want to see him."

Clare's lips separated with surprise. "Tanner?"

"That's what I said."

Clare stood up abruptly. "I think that would be a mistake. Bill Hanes is the one who—"

"Tell Tanner I want to see him, Clare."

Clare nodded stiffly at her husband's tone and left the room.

"Angie . . . wait a minute."

Quickening her step, Callie walked toward the

tall brunette standing in the doorway of the general store. Having missed breakfast at the boardinghouse for the third time that week, Callie had started out for Sidewinder's only restaurant. She was surprised to see Angie already on the street.

Callie hastened her step. The week that had passed since Tanner's visit to her room in the middle of the night had been long and torturous. After he left, she had been temporarily uncertain if the intimate moments had all been a painful dream—but Tanner's scent had been too fresh in her nostrils, and the taste of his mouth too sweet on her lips for it not to be true.

She had finally accepted the awful truth. Tanner hated her. She had seen it in his eyes and had heard it in his voice when he said good-bye. He would not be back. Yet she had remained in town, knowing that while everything between Tanner and her had changed, her ultimate goal remained the same. She needed to find Matt's killers, just as she needed to know, once and for all, if Tanner was one of them.

No, she couldn't leave Sidewinder. Not yet.

But the days had gotten longer and had become increasingly difficult to endure. She wasn't popular with the women at the Roundup. Lola was the only one who had made any attempt to break the wall of silence that the other women maintained. As appreciative as she was of the petite blonde's effort, she had not pressed for a closer friendship for fear of turning the other women against Lola. Her popularity with the male customers had filled the long evenings, and she had consoled herself that it didn't matter if the other women disliked her, because her position there was only temporary.

But Angie was different. Ace had assured her that Angie understood the boundaries of their friendship. She knew *he* believed that was true, yet . . .

Hesitating when she reached Angie's side, Callie attempted a smile, then said, "I wanted to take this chance to talk to you—about Ace."

Angie's chin rose. It occurred to Callie that without the heavy evening makeup of her trade, Angie was younger and prettier than she had realized, with a vulnerability about her that had been concealed by her professional smile. She recognized also, with a feeling of dismay, a torment in Angie's dark eyes that was not unlike her own.

Compassion and regret merged, almost overwhelming her. "Ace and I are friends, Angie," she said simply. "I'd like us to be friends, too."

There was an uncomfortable silence before Angie replied with unexpected candor, "That might not be easy . . . but I'm willing to give it a try."

Angie's expression did not change as she offered Callie her hand.

"Wait a minute, Tanner!"

Tanner paused beside the corral gate. He turned toward Clare as she approached across the yard. He glanced at Jeb, who had halted beside him, his expression dark. It had been a damned long week since Tanner had turned his back on Callie and walked out her bedroom door. He had slept poorly in the time since. His body ached with fatigue during the day, but that fatigue did not affect his sleeplessness at night.

Thoughts of that visit to Callie's room raised painful memories. He had made a mistake going to the Roundup after his visit with Bill Hanes. One step through the swinging doors and he had been struck with a wave of jealousy. When he saw Ace and Callie sitting together in the corner, it had been all he could do not to storm over to the table and drag Callie away. A perverse side of him had forced him toward the bar where Marcy had responded to his whispered words with practiced ease. He had smiled down at Marcy as she pressed herself against him, aware only of Callie. It had taken all his remaining will-power to down his drink and walk calmly back out the door without even glancing in Callie's direction. He wasn't really sure how far he had ridden on the road to the Circle M before he turned his mount back toward town.

It hadn't been difficult to get into the boardinghouse and make his way to Callie's room. He had done it before. Whatever his intentions had been when he entered her room, all had been forgotten when he saw Callie asleep in her bed.

Damn it all, lying down beside her and taking her into his arms had seemed so natural! She had responded to him instinctively in her sleep, and when her eyes opened, fool that he was, he had almost believed he had seen joy reflected there.

But she had still wanted an answer to her question and everything between them had again been exposed as a lie.

Despite it all, it had been damned hard to leave her.

Despite it all, it had been damned hard to stay away.

Clare reached his side, thrusting everything else from his mind. The breakfast he had just consumed turned to a lead weight in his stomach as he looked down at her, barely concealing his distaste. The fine sheen of perspiration bead-ing on her forehead somehow only succeeded in adding a glow to her perfect features. He realized more clearly than ever before that he was facing beauty and evil in one deceiving package.

Clare dismissed Jeb with a glance, ignoring the foreman as he walked away. "You knew about this all along, didn't you, Tanner?" she hissed.

Tanner regarded her coldly. "I don't know what you're talking about."

"About the letter Bill Hanes received from Lauren a few weeks ago."

"From Lauren . . ."

Clare's lips were tight. "Don't insult me with a denial! Manuelo went to town last night to pick up the mail. Martha Peabody in the post office mentioned that Bill Hanes received a letter with Lauren McBride's return address on it a few weeks ago."

"So?"

"You went to town to talk to Bill Hanes last week, the same day that I did."

"What if I did?"

Her control obviously waning, Clare rasped, "Bill Hanes wouldn't tell me anything I wanted to know, but he told you, didn't he?"

"What are you trying to say?"

"You can't get away with your lies, Tanner!

Tom knows about the letter. He wants to talk to you."

"He wants to talk to me?"

"He sent me out to get you."

Tanner remained motionless.

"He wants to talk to you *now*, Tanner!" When Tanner still did not respond, Clare pressed with mounting ire, "What are you waiting for?"

Tanner smiled.

"Are you laughing at me, Tanner? If you're intent on making an enemy of me, you're making a mistake."

Her agitation no longer amusing him, Tanner sobered. "I'm not trying to make an enemy of you, Clare. The truth is, I want as little as possible to do with you."

"I'll never believe that!"

"I'm tired of arguing with you."

"That's right, save your energy. You'll need it when you face Tom. He knows you've been plotting with Bill Hanes against him."

"What?"

"He knows you've both been keeping secrets from him."

"That's loco!"

"Ask him, then. He's waiting." Clare paused, her smile hard. "Or are you afraid to face him? You are, aren't you? You're afraid of your weak, dying father!"

"You seem to forget, Clare. I haven't been avoiding my father. He's been avoiding me."

She sneered, "Are you trembling, Tanner?"

His clear eyes holding hers, Tanner whispered, "I don't think I fully realized—until this moment—how great a fool my father really is."

"Bastard . . . you'll be sorry you said that!"

"No, I won't."

Turning on his heel, Tanner started toward the house with Clare's voice ringing behind him.

"Mark my words, Tanner. You *will* be sorry."

"You wanted to see me, Pa?"

Tanner stood at his father's bedside. Close up, his pa's deterioration was so obvious—his face so gaunt, his color so poor, and his body so feeble—that Tanner was swept with pity. But pity was thrust from his mind in the next second when Tom's clear eyes pinned him, and his voice emerged with unexpected strength. "All right, Tanner. What's this all about?"

He'd never change.

Tanner responded, "Maybe you should tell me."

"Playing dumb never worked with me before. It won't work with me now."

"Playing dumb . . ." Tanner shook his head. "Maybe that's what you call it. It might help if you'd tell me what you think I've done."

"Clare says Bill Hanes received a letter from Lauren a few weeks ago. What do you know about it?" When Tanner did not respond, Tom McBride raised himself from his pillow and spat, "Damn it, tell me the truth!"

"You're asking the wrong man, Pa." Tanner frowned as his pa dropped back weakly against the pillow. Watching the rapid rise and fall of his father's bony chest, he continued, "You should be talking to Bill Hanes, not me."

Tom McBride stared at him, his gaze steady despite his weakened state. "You're making a mistake, Tanner."

"Any mistakes I've made since I came home have nothing to do with you."

"Don't get involved in things that don't concern you."

"I think you're forgetting something, Pa. You're the one who wanted me to come back."

"That's right, but you came of your own free will. It looks like you're going to have to wait awhile until the others return, so I'm telling you again. Whatever's going on—stay out of it. And stay away from Clare."

"Clare again."

"That's right—Clare! If you know what's good for you, you'll listen to me. If you don't, you'll end up paying for it in the end."

"Is that all you brought me in here for?"

"Isn't that enough?"

"Not for me. I have something to say, too."

"I don't want to hear it. I'm done talking. Get out of here."

"I'm not plotting against you, Pa. I've never done anything behind your back, and anything I've had to say, I've always said to your face. That hasn't changed."

"It's time for you to leave, Tanner."

"But you never believed me before, and you don't believe me now."

"I said it's time for you to leave."

"What are you afraid of, Pa? Why won't you listen to what I have to say? Is it because you think that I—"

"I said get out . . . and I meant it."

Silent for a long moment, Tanner nodded. "All right, if that's the way you want it."

Frustrated beyond measure, Tanner left the room without another word and started toward the stairs. He stopped abruptly when Clare stepped into his path. Her smile was victorious as she whispered, "You can't win, Tanner . . . not without me."

"Not without *you*?" Tanner laughed harshly. "You can't seem to understand that you're wasting your wiles on me, so I guess I'll have to explain things to you more clearly. You see, I'm the man whose pa was seduced by a scheming whore—a whore who convinced my pa to dishonor the grave of the wife who had loved him all her life. That same whore made him turn against his own flesh and blood and force his children out of their home. My pa's dying now, and he still can't see that scheming whore for what she is." His gaze intent, Tanner concluded, "I've made some damned fool mistakes in my life—mistakes that I regret—but there's one thing I know for sure. I'll never . . . ever . . . be fool enough to fall into the same trap my pa fell into. So . . . that said, just get out of my way."

Leaving Clare behind in stunned silence, Tanner did not spare her another glance as he walked down the stairs and out the door.

A whore, was she?

Enraged, Clare stood in the hallway where Tanner had left her.

He'd never be fool enough to fall into her trap, would he?

Clare's dainty hands clenched into fists.

"Clare . . . are you out there?"

Clare jerked toward the sound of Tom Mc-Bride's voice. Tanner was blind! It wasn't his father who was trapped. It was *she* who was

trapped, by a feeble invalid confined to his bed—
a man who clung to life *and to her* with unre-
mitting tenacity!

Why didn't he die?

"Clare . . ."

Die, damn it! Die!

"Clare?"

Clare closed her eyes, forcing herself under
control. With a fixed smile on her lips, she
walked slowly toward her husband's room. She
paused briefly out of sight, then stepped into
view in the doorway, her light eyes never more
sincere when she asked, "Tom, dear . . . did you
call me?"

Concealed in the shadows of the hallway, Manuelo felt true hatred churn within him. He had
heard it all! He had heard Senor Tanner call his
beloved mistress a whore. He had seen Senora
Clare's beautiful face flush hotly, and then go as
white as chalk. He had watched her compose
herself so she could respond to the invalid's
summons.

He would make sure Senor Tanner regretted
his offensive words. He would not fail his beloved Senora Clare.

Hardly conscious of the wranglers who walked
their mounts cautiously across the sunlit pas-

ture behind him, Tanner glanced up at the cloudless sky. It was almost noon, and the disagreeable task of moving aggressive bulls to different pastures was almost completed. Hours had passed since he had left the ranch house behind him, but he could not stop mulling over the scene between Clare and him that morning.

Tom McBride's face flashed before him, and Tanner frowned. If he were a more charitable person, he might actually pity his pa for sacrificing his wife, family, and the respect of others for a woman who claimed to love him but whose only true love was for herself.

Tanner hesitated, frowning at that thought. He, too, had allowed a woman to use him for her own purposes. Like his father, he was somehow unable to free himself from wanting her. But the similarities ended there. Unlike his father, he was determined not to—

A loud bellow and spontaneous shouts from the wranglers around him startled Tanner from his thoughts. Suddenly aware that he had wandered between two challenging bulls, he wheeled his mount sharply, barely avoiding the older bull's rush toward him. His heart pounding, he put enough distance between the two animals to soothe the charging bull's ire, then looked down, cursing under his breath at the sight of the bloody gash on his mount's foreleg.

"Damned right! You should be cursin'!" Reining up beside him, Jeb shook his head with disgust. "What happened to your common sense? You know better than to take your eyes off a mean critter like that bull. Hell, you knew better than that when you was just a boy!"

Dismounting when the bulls were driven a safe distance away, Tanner inspected the seeping wound on his mount's leg as the horse snorted with pain. Beside him, Jeb grunted, "You're lucky. Them horns just grazed him. He'll be healed inside of a week, but neither one of you might be as lucky next time." Squinting against the bright sunlight, Jeb continued, "You can't go on this way, boy."

Tanner glanced up at him, and Jeb's mouth flattened into a straight line. "It wasn't your pa this time, was it? It was that damned Clare." When Tanner neither confirmed nor denied his guess, Jeb snapped, "Don't let her get to you, boy! You keep this up and you'll end up six feet under, with her collectin' your share of the inheritance."

"It's not the inheritance that's eating at me. That isn't the real reason I came back. I came back to settle some things with my pa, but he's not going to let that happen until he's good and ready."

"Your pa does things his way."

"I'm not going to wait much longer, Jeb. The way Pa looks, I've got my doubts that he's going to last nine months, and I'll be damned if I'll let him die before I can settle things with him."

"Like I said, your pa does things his own way."

"Maybe not." Tanner shook his head. "Clare's smart. Sometimes I think she's too smart for him. She's trying to turn him against Bill Hanes. If she does, Pa's in trouble."

"Don't underestimate your pa. He may be dyin', but I've seen the look on that woman's face when he calls her name. He's still in control and she knows it. She's not goin' to chance doin' anythin' that might make her lose any part of what's comin' to her in his will."

"She's got a surprise coming. Pa didn't tell her everything about that will."

Jeb paused, then prompted, "You had a talk with Bill Hanes?"

Tanner nodded.

"Are you sayin' what I think you're sayin'?"

Tanner nodded again.

Satisfaction lit Jeb's small eyes. "I didn't think your pa had it in him."

Tanner's mount gave a snort of pain, turning them both toward the restless animal and the cut that still oozed on its foreleg.

Jeb sobered. "You'd better get that animal's leg fixed up before there's any more damage."

"He's all right. He'll last until we finish driving those bulls."

"Most of that work's done. You're better off takin' care of that horse. I'd take it easy ridin' back, too. You don't want to split that cut any wider."

Tanner hesitated.

"I'm still foreman here, so get movin' . . . and if you feel like takin' the rest of the day off and maybe goin' to town—"

"I'll come back as soon as I get a fresh mount."

"Tanner—"

"I said I'll be back."

But Jeb was no longer listening. The foreman was looking at a point in the distance behind him, and Tanner turned to follow his gaze.

A lone rider was approaching. That big buckskin gelding . . . it couldn't be anybody else.

His jaw hardening, Tanner waited for the rider to draw up beside him. Big, brawny, his blond hair glinting under the broad brim of his hat, and a familiar smile on his lips, Terry Malone dismounted and offered him his hand. Ignoring it, Tanner grated, "What're you doing here?"

Dropping his hand back to his side, Terry

laughed aloud. "Anybody'd think you ain't happy to see me, Tanner."

Hardly aware that Jeb had mounted and ridden off to rejoin the men, Tanner pressed, "I asked you what you're doing here."

"Hell, you invited me—when we was drinkin' that last evenin'! You showed me a letter from some lawyer fella and said I should come home with you to share your inheritance. That's how I knew where to find you—but I'm thinkin' you don't remember that, do you? As a matter of fact, I don't suppose you remember much at all about the last time we met."

"I remember enough . . . too much."

"You're talkin' about the bank robbery."

"That's what I'm talking about, all right."

Terry's smile faded with startling abruptness. "That was a mistake from beginnin' to end. I got talked into it by them other two fellas."

"That wasn't the way it looked to me. You were the man giving the orders when you rode off and left me in that alley for the sheriff to find."

"Don't blame that on me. It wasn't my fault if you was still too drunk from the night before to know what was goin' on."

"That's the point. I *was* too drunk to know what was going on when you told me to hold on to the horses until you and the boys got back. I started snapping out of it a little too late—when I heard the gunshots and saw you and the others come rushing out of the bank with money bags in your hands."

"Yeah, two full sacks." Terry paused, his expression darkening. "Is that what you're thinkin' about—that you should've gotten a share of the money?—'Cause if you are, you're too late. Texas Rangers caught up with us where we was holed up a couple of weeks back. They caught Slim. Blackie and me got away by the skin of our teeth. We split up. I don't know where he ended up, but it don't make a damned bit of difference, because them rangers got the money."

"I'm not talking about the money."

"It was that damned fool Blackie's fault! I told him to keep an eye out in case somebody sneaked up on the cabin, but he was too interested in watchin' me divide the loot to follow orders."

"I said I'm not talking about the money."

"What are you talkin' about, then?"

"A man got killed in that bank—a rancher named Matt Logan."

"Oh, that." Terry shook his head. "That never should've happened. I told them boys there shouldn't be no shootin', but Blackie got nervous, and when that rancher moved, he shot him."

"Blackie again—"

"Yeah, Blackie!" Terry's eyes darkened, briefly challenging him. "Right or wrong, it don't do no good talkin' about it now. You can't bring back the dead."

Callie's face flashed before him as Tanner stared at Terry with disbelief. There was not a trace of remorse in Terry's eyes, either for the man who had been killed or for the family he had left behind. It came to Tanner with unexpected suddenness that the person he had once been, who had traveled with Terry Malone and joined in his escapades without a second thought, no longer existed. The man he now was, could only make one response.

"You made a mistake coming here, Terry. You'd better leave."

"I ain't leavin'." Terry's face tightened into an unexpected snarl. "The law's after me. I ain't got a cent to my name, and I need a place to hide."

"This isn't the place."

"It sure is." Terry took an aggressive step forward. "I need a place to stay, and you owe it to me."

"I don't owe you anything."

"You've got a convenient memory, ain't you?

I remember a time when I put my life on the line for you. If I hadn't taken the chance of crossin' that swollen river to get you a doc, you wouldn't be here today."

Tanner remembered that night. It had been raining for days, and the thunder was deafening as he lay alone on a narrow cot, shivering with fever. Terry had left the cabin hours earlier, and he was so sick that he thought he'd soon be breathing his last. He remembered the relief he felt when Terry walked back through the door of that deserted cabin with a doc behind him.

Tanner was suddenly saddened. Terry had risked his life that night to save him. Where had that fellow gone?

"Well?" His broad smile absent, Terry was waiting.

Terry was right. Tanner did owe him.

"All right." Relief flashed across Terry's face as Tanner continued, "The Circle M line shack isn't much to look at, but it's on the northwest corner of the property. Nobody will know you're there."

Terry frowned. "I don't have to go hidin' out in no line shack. Nobody knows me around here. You can take me on as one of the hands."

Panic nudged Tanner's mind. He knew Terry. Terry would go into town the first chance he got.

Callie had probably seen the Wanted notices. She knew what he looked like. She'd recognize him immediately.

Tanner shook his head. "That's too dangerous. The law here knows I was mixed up in that bank robbery somehow. If talk gets back to town about me hiring another hand when everybody knows the situation between my pa and me, the sheriff might decide to look into it."

Terry mumbled a curse.

"I'll take you to the shack. There are some supplies there. I'll bring you more as soon as I can. As far as I'm concerned, you can hole up there as long as you want—but if you go anywhere near town, you're on your own."

Holding his breath until Terry reluctantly agreed, Tanner mounted up and headed his injured horse toward the line shack.

Concealed in a forested patch nearby, Manuelo drew back so he would not be seen as the two men came dangerously close to his position.

Manuelo smiled as he watched them disappear from sight. Senor Tanner was unaware that he had been following him most of the morning. He had cursed Senor Tanner's escape from the angry bull, unaware that fate was about to thrust an even greater opportunity for vengeance into his hands. Senor Tanner had not seen him hide in the foliage when the stranger approached. Nor had Senor Tanner seen him creep closer as the two men conversed.

So no one would ever know that Senor Tanner's friend was hidden in the line shack on the northwestern corner of the Circle M property?

Manuelo suppressed the urge to laugh aloud as he mounted his horse and turned back toward the Circle M ranch house.

"He called the man Terry."

Exhilaration brightened Clare's eyes, eyes that had been red-rimmed from furious tears when Manuelo returned to the house.

Clare glanced around the rear yard where Manuelo had found her, making certain Tiny was nowhere near to overhear as she said, "That man was Terry Malone . . . it had to be! So Tanner's going to hide him from the law." She laughed aloud. "That is so choice! Tanner—hiding the man who killed his lover's brother!"

"Senor Malone claimed another man bears the blame—"

"I don't care what he *claimed!* Terry Malone was the leader of the gang. He was responsible for that killing. What do you suppose that little tart would do if she discovered where Terry Malone was hiding?"

Manuelo's lips parted in a smile.

Clare's expression sobered. "You said she had a gun in her case?"

"*Sí.* A small gun, in very good condition."

"She probably thinks she knows how to use it."

"So it would appear, senora."

Clare considered that thought. "She doesn't intend to use it on Tanner. She would have done that already if she did. No, she's looking for Terry Malone." Enjoying herself, Clare continued, "This is your chance to do a good deed, Manuelo. That woman came all the way to Sidewinder to avenge her brother's death. It's your duty to tell her what you know."

Uncertain, Manuelo regarded her in silence.

Clare continued, "You must tell her that you accidentally overheard Tanner and Terry Malone talking, and that you are concerned your dear Senora Clare is in danger because a killer is being hidden on the Circle M. You must tell her that you could not tell anyone on the ranch because they are all Tanner's friends, and that you didn't want to go to the sheriff because you haven't been treated fairly by the law in the past. You must tell her that everyone on the ranch knows her real name and her real reason for coming to Sidewinder, and you thought she would know what to do about Terry Malone."

"*Sí*, senora."

Clare warned, "You must be convincing, Manuelo. Everything depends on whether that tart believes you went to her because you felt you could go to no one else."

"She will believe me."

"I'm depending on you."

"I will not fail you."

The fine line of Clare's lips tightened. "Tanner made a mistake this morning when he called me a whore. He'll regret it, Manuelo. We'll both see to that."

Speaking with the fervor of a vow, Manuelo replied, "*Sí*, senora. We will."

"Damn it all, I need a drink!"

Terry Malone's angry growl reverberated in the small, dank cabin. Running his hand across the corner shelf, he swept the assorted cans and bottles to the floor with an angry thrust, then turned to survey the one-room structure where Tanner had left him a short time earlier. A filthy bunk in the corner . . . a three-legged table with two mismatched chairs . . . a fireplace housing several generations of bats, to judge from the droppings littering the stones—but not a single drop of red-eye to be found.

Terry scowled. He didn't like it. He didn't like it at all.

Cursing again, Terry kicked the nearest chair and sent it flying across the room. He deserved better than this. He had saved Tanner McBride's life, damn it! He had treated that fella like a brother, going so far as to bring him in on that bank robbery when he really wasn't no help at all.

Terry paused at that thought. If the truth be known, he'd had it in for Tanner since the day years earlier when Tanner had walked out on their friendship. He hadn't liked the way Tanner had said he wouldn't stand for any more of the shenanigans they had been getting into. He had told himself then that the day would come when he'd prove that Tanner was no better than he was.

In the time since, he had faced some hard truths. He was thirty-one years old. His youth was passing real quick, and he didn't have anything to show for the years that had slipped away. He had been determined to line his pockets with enough cash to last him through the dry spells, and he had known there was only one way to get money easy and fast. He had met Blackie and Slim along the way, and he and those fellas had formed a real good partnership.

Their plans for the bank robbery had been firmly in place when he had met Tanner that night.

Terry's scowl deepened. Tanner had been drunk. He had waved that letter from his pa's lawyer under his nose—a letter about his inheritance. He had said he didn't want anything to do with his pa, and they had drunk to that more times than he could count. But Tanner had had a head start on him, and when he finally passed out in that alleyway beside the bank, Terry had let him sleep it off there. He had awakened him only in time to shove the reins of their horses into his hand and tell him that he and the boys would be right back.

A smile twitched at Terry's lips at the memory of Tanner's expression when Blackie, Slim, and he came running out into that alleyway with money bags in their hands and gunshots sounding behind them. He had laughed aloud when he looked back to see Tanner attempting to mount up, only to have the sheriff drag him down from his horse.

Terry snickered. So much for Tanner McBride thinking he was better than Terry Malone.

Terry's scowl returned. As for the rancher who had gotten himself killed in the bank, that wasn't his fault. He had warned everybody not to move. That fella hadn't listened, and he had shot him dead—but he hadn't been about to admit that to Tanner. Blaming Blackie for the deed had been instinctive. Blackie had never hesitated to use his gun. Blackie hadn't blinked an eye when he shot that Texas Ranger during their escape from the cabin. Like him with that rancher, Blackie probably hadn't given it a thought since. As he had said to Tanner, there wasn't any point to it. Dead was dead. You couldn't change it even if you cared.

Terry gave a disgusted snort. But the law had almost caught up with him, and here he was now, stuck in a rat's nest without a bottle to his name.

Terry kicked the second chair across the room. He might be stuck in this damned cabin for a while, but he wasn't about to stay without something to keep him company. As for Tanner's threat about turning him out on his own if he went into town, that was just a bluff. Tanner couldn't afford to let the law catch up with him on his pa's ranch. And if, by chance, Tanner thought he could drive him off, just let him try.

Hurrying outside, Terry mounted and kicked his horse into motion. Sidewinder was the name of the town, and that was where he was heading.

Tanner plodded steadily forward as the Circle M ranch house finally came into view. He glanced back at his mount, which limped badly behind him. Jeb had been right. The gash on his leg needed attention. He had pressed the gelding beyond his limits. He had ridden only a short distance from the line shack when the animal began favoring the wounded leg, and he had been forced to dismount and lead him. He had been walking ever since.

Terry Malone returned to his mind, and Tanner felt a familiar agitation. He had brought Terry to the line shack as promised, but the look on Terry's face had said it all. Terry didn't like it there, and he knew Terry well enough to know that he wouldn't stay there very long. Tanner had to work fast.

Callie's face flashed before his eyes, and Tanner's stomach tightened. He had to find a way to make Callie go home. It would not be easy, he knew. She had come to Sidewinder to find her brother's killers, and she had sacrificed much toward that end. She had even pretended to love him.

That thought deepened the ever-present ache within him, and Tanner walked faster. But first he needed to settle Terry in, to make him comfortable enough in that cabin so he'd stay holed up there until he could figure out a way to convince Callie to—

Tanner's thoughts halted abruptly as a mounted figure emerged from the Circle M barn and started riding toward him. The rider's frantic pace sent apprehension jolting through Tanner. His fears were confirmed when Tiny drew up beside him, leaped from his horse, and started signing.

His heart pounding, Tanner watched Tiny's frantic motions.

"Clare sent Manuelo to town?"

Tiny signed again.

"Trouble . . . you overheard them talking."

Tiny's motions became more rapid, and Tanner gripped his hands.

"Wait. Slow down."

Tiny nodded and motioned again.

"Manuelo spoke of a stranger who had come to the ranch. A bad man." Tanner stilled. "Was the man's name Terry Malone?"

Tiny nodded, and Tanner fought for composure. "She sent Manuelo to town? Why?"

A few more motions.

"She sent him to talk to the woman." Tanner drew back. "Was the woman Callie Logan?"

At Tiny's nod, Tanner cursed aloud.

"What did Clare tell him to do?"

Tanner read the rapid signing. He translated, mumbling, "She told him to tell the woman

363

about the stranger. They spoke of a gun the woman concealed in her room."

A gun.

Tiny continued to sign as Tanner asked abruptly, "How long has Manuelo been gone? An hour? Longer?" He took a deep breath at Tiny's reply. Longer.

Reaching for the gunbelt on his saddle, Tanner strapped it around his hips. Exchanging reins with the mute without a word, he mounted the able horse and turned him toward town at a gallop.

Manuelo waited in the the doorway of the saddlery. The store was closed, providing shelter from prying eyes as he maintained his unrelenting surveillance of the street. Shifting in discomfort as the late afternoon sun baked his skin, he grew suddenly still. He drew himself slowly erect as the figure he sought came into view on the boardwalk.

Manuelo waited as the woman drew closer on her way to the saloon where she worked. He assessed her closely as she neared. The woman's hair was of an uneven color liberally streaked from the sun. It was no match for his dear senora's light, lustrous hair. Her painted features were small and fine, but they were no match for his senora's delicate countenance. The woman's body was slender, but rounded in the breast in a way that did not allow her the fragile quality that his mistress had. He shook his head. Senor Tanner could not possibly prefer this Callie Logan to his dear senora.

The woman drew nearer. Manuelo awaited his opportunity, then stepped out into her path. He heard her startled intake of breath. He saw her spontaneous backward step and speculative glance. He then said the words that would draw her in.

"Senorita, I must speak to you . . . about Senor Tanner."

Callie's heart pounded more loudly with each step she took. Retracing her path back to the boardinghouse, she entered and walked stiffly up the stairs, unaware of Annabelle's curious glance.

After unlocking her door with a trembling hand, Callie thrust it closed behind her. She had been startled when the Mexican stepped into her path. There had been something about him, a look in his eyes that had raised the hackles on the back of her neck, but he had caught her attention the moment he spoke Tanner's name.

Callie stripped off the blue gown she had

donned only minutes earlier, her mind racing. Could it be true? Could Tanner truly be sheltering Terry Malone on his ranch—Terry Malone, her brother's killer? If the fellow, Manuelo, had not described Terry Malone in such detail, if his description of Terry Malone had not matched completely the description and sketch on the Wanted poster bearing his name, she might have doubted him.

The ache inside Callie deepened. She didn't want it to be true. She didn't want to believe that Tanner, who had made such tender love to her, whose confidences had touched her heart, and who was rarely absent from her mind, had played a part in Matt's death.

She had to know the truth.

Manuelo had said Tanner was allowing Terry Malone to hide from the law in a line shack on the northwestern corner of the Circle M.

Casting her gown aside, Callie reached for the shirtwaist and split skirt that hung nearby. Dressed, she pulled on her boots, then withdrew her case from underneath the bed. She lifted the lid and stared at the Wanted notice for long seconds before picking up the gun that lay beside it.

A sissy gun.

She could almost hear Matt's words—Matt,

whose sudden, contagious grin would never flash again.

Standing abruptly, Callie thrust the small gun into the pocket of her skirt, then kicked the case back under the bed and turned toward the door.

Ace glanced up at the swinging doors of the Roundup. Frowning, he looked back down at his cards.

"What's your bid, Ace?"

Ace did not respond.

"Come on, Ace. You're holdin' up the game."

Scowling, Ace slapped his cards down on the table, then stood up abruptly. He turned toward the buxom redhead standing nearby. "Take over for me, Pearl."

The woman assumed his seat with a smile and a quip that raised laughter around the table, but Ace heard none of it. Instead, he walked to the bar, caught Barney's eye, and tapped the polished surface impatiently with his forefinger. He swallowed the drink Barney put in front of him, then turned to survey the crowd with a deepening scowl. He glanced toward the light touch on his arm before turning back to stare at the swinging doors.

Angie's dark eyes studied him. "What's the matter, Ace?"

"She's late."

The scarlet line of Angie's lips twitched revealingly. "A woman has a right to be late sometimes."

"She's never late."

"I was talking to her this morning, you know."

Ace looked at Angie, immediately alert.

"I met her on the street. She said she wanted to talk to me. She said you and she were friends, and she wanted to be my friend, too."

"That's all she said? She didn't say she'd be late tonight for any reason?"

"No."

Ace shook his head and looked back toward the door. "I've got a funny feeling . . ."

"She's a grown woman, Ace. She can take care of herself."

"Something's wrong."

"Ace, look at me." Snagging his attention with the sudden sharpness of her tone, Angie asked, "I want you to tell me the truth. Is she the woman you really want?"

Ace responded impatiently, "I told you how it is between her and me."

"Yes or no?"

"I've already answered that question. I'm not going to answer it again."

"Ace . . ."

Ace turned away from her abruptly, then said over his shoulder, "I'm going in the back room for a few minutes. Tell her I want to talk to her when she comes in."

Left standing in his wake, Angie stared after Ace's retreating figure. Tears welled. The conversation between them had been brief, but it had been packed with emotion that only a discussion of Callie now seemed able to raise between them. It was almost amusing. Their exchange about the other woman had been intense and revealing, while neither of them had even mentioned her name.

The heels of Callie's boots clicked loudly against the boardwalk as she maintained her brisk pace toward the livery stable. Her customary smile absent, she walked around and between the growing number of wranglers talking in small groups.

A glance at the street revealed that traffic was thickening there as well, and Callie glanced up absentmindedly at the sky. The sun would soon be setting, but she refused to allow that to affect her plans. She had traveled in darkness lit only by the moon on many occasions. She'd find her way. If not, she'd be close enough to the northwestern corner of the Circle M to find that cabin first thing in the morning.

Callie walked into the shadowed interior of the livery stable. Incapable of returning Dan's smile as he approached, she said, "I need a horse."

"The sun's goin' down, Miss Callie. It's kinda late to be startin' out." Dan scrutinized her sober expression with a squinting gaze. "It might be a mistake gettin' caught out on the prairie alone at night."

"I need a horse *now*, Dan."

Hesitating, then seeming to realize the futility of further reasoning, Dan turned toward the rear stall. Callie walked back to the livery entrance and glanced toward the Roundup. A wagon rolled past, momentarily blocking her view as several horsemen drew up at the rapidly filling hitching rail in front of the saloon. She had been expected to report for work almost an hour earlier. Ace would be wondering where she was. She didn't like leaving town without word, but she couldn't afford to let him know her intentions. It would be better if she . . .

That last thought abruptly struck from her mind, Callie stared at the horseman tying his mount in front of the Roundup. She blinked, incredulous, as he turned fully in her direction to survey the street behind him. The image on the Wanted poster flashed before her mind, and her heart skipped a beat. No . . . it couldn't be! Terry Malone wouldn't be fool enough to ride so boldly into Sidewinder—not with Wanted posters bearing his likeness in every sheriff's office in Texas!

Callie took a backward step as the fellow's gaze turned in her direction. He was tall, blond, well built—handsome—and he was riding a buckskin gelding, just as described in the Wanted notices, yet his features were partially obscured by several weeks' growth of beard.

She couldn't be sure, but there was one way to find out.

Callie slid her hand into her pocket. Her jaw firmed with resolution when it met the cool handle of the derringer concealed there.

The fellow stepped up onto the boardwalk and slipped through the swinging doors of the Roundup, and Callie started toward the street.

"Miss Callie, your mount's ready."

Turning back toward the whiskered proprietor, Callie responded levelly, "I'm sorry, Dan. I don't think I'll be needing a horse after all."

Tanner drew back on the reins of his laboring mount as Sidewinder drew near. Slowing to navigate the crush of mounted riders and wagons entering town as evening approached, he made his way onto the crowded main street. Daylight was waning. He could not be certain how much earlier Manuelo had arrived in town, or whether the devious servant had already accomplished his mission in coming to Sidewinder.

Tanner's racing thoughts ground to an abrupt halt as the Roundup came into view where Callie stood motionless at the swinging doors before she suddenly thrust them open and walked inside.

Tension twisted tight inside him. Something was wrong. Callie's posture had been rigid, and she had been dressed for the trail, wearing riding clothes and boots instead of the frivolous gown of her adopted profession—almost as if she had been forced to change her plans at the last minute.

Tanner went suddenly cold at the sight of the big buckskin gelding tied at the Roundup rail.

Damn that Terry!

Panicking, Tanner jammed his heels into his mount's sides, forcing his mount to leap forward.

Angie rushed to the back room of the saloon. Breathless, she pushed open the door, startling Ace at his desk as she gasped, "You'd better get out front, quick. Callie just walked in. She's got a gun."

On his feet in a minute, Ace snatched up his six-gun from the holster hanging near the door and pushed past her. He entered the saloon at a run, only to halt in his tracks at the sight that met his eyes.

Hardly aware of the hush that had fallen over the noisy saloon, of the patrons who had fallen back cautiously to allow her a wide berth, Callie stood a few yards from the tall, blond stranger. Her derringer pointed levelly at his chest, she demanded, "What's your name, fella?"

She saw the stranger's lips twitch in an unsteady smile as he responded, "You don't need a gun to find out my name, darlin'. I'll be happy to tell you, as long as you point that gun in another direction."

"What's your name?" Callie was starting to tremble. Close up, there was no doubting the strong, broad features from the Wanted poster, or the peculiar intensity in the fellow's gaze that somehow belied his casual tone of voice.

Callie spat, "Your name wouldn't be Terry Malone, would it? You wouldn't happen to be the fella who robbed the Foster State Bank a while back, and left a dead rancher behind him?"

"I don't know what you're talkin' about."

"His name *is* Terry, Callie." Interrupting unexpectedly from where she had fled further down the bar, Lola added, "He told me his name when he walked in."

Lola's unanticipated interjection brought a bitter smile to Callie's lips. She addressed Terry more coldly. "You probably didn't even bother to find out the name of the man you killed that day." Not waiting for him to reply, she continued, "His name was Matt Logan. He was my brother. He went to the bank that morning to pay off the mortgage on our ranch, and you shot him dead without a second thought."

"You've got the wrong man, lady."

"No, she don't."

Turning toward Lola's insistent interjection, Terry spat, "Shut up, *puta!*"

"Callie . . ." Ace had emerged from the back room. He held a six-gun pointed at Terry as he said, "I don't know what's going on, but you can put your gun down now. This fella's not going anywhere, and if he is the Terry Malone you're talking about—"

"My name ain't Terry Malone!" The stranger turned toward Ace. Callie followed his gaze as he continued, "This woman's loco! That ain't my name, and I didn't rob no bank!"

Ignoring him, Ace urged, "Put your gun down, Callie."

About to respond, Callie missed the snaking movement of Terry's hand. She did not see the gun he withdrew from his holster until he and Ace fired simultaneously. Her mind reeling when she was struck with a flash of searing pain that knocked her backward against the table behind her, Callie could not be sure who was firing when Tanner burst through the doorway of the saloon, gun in hand; when Terry, with blood staining his chest, turned his gun on Tanner; when gunshots sounded again and Terry's body jerked with the force of the bullets that finally brought him down.

Slipping soundlessly to the floor, Callie heard heavy footsteps racing toward her. Her vision fading, she saw Tanner's face as he leaned over her and took her into his arms.

"Get Doc Pierce, damn it! Hurry up!"

Tanner was unconscious of the frantic commotion around them as he turned back to Callie and cradled her in his arms. Blood streamed from her chest, and her color had whitened.

When Callie had disappeared from sight into the Roundup, he had raced down the street and leaped from his horse, then pushed his way through the saloon doors just as the burst of gunfire erupted. He remembered the jolt that had shuddered through him when Callie was thrust backward from the force of the bullet that hit her—as Terry fired again, as his own gun blazed and Terry's body slammed back against the bar, then toppled to the floor.

"Callie. . . ." Tanner drew her closer. Panic rocked his mind. "Look at me. Don't close your eyes, darlin'. Please . . . don't close your eyes."

"Tanner." Responding to his plea, Callie struggled to focus. "Tell me," she gasped. "I have to know . . . say you weren't one of them."

"I didn't have anything to do with that robbery, Callie."

"I knew. . . . but . . . I needed to hear you say it."

"Don't try to talk." Tanner brushed her cold lips with his. The pain within him cut like a knife as he whispered, "Doc's coming. He'll take care of you. You're going to be all right."

"Tanner . . ."

Callie gasped with pain and Tanner clutched her closer. "I love you, Callie." he whispered. "You know that, don't you? I loved you from that first moment I saw you. It all seemed too perfect to be true when I held you in my arms, and then when I found out who you were and why you had come to Sidewinder, it seemed to me that everything fell into place. I told myself that you were just using me, that nothing that had happened between us was real."

His throat tight, Tanner struggled to continue. "But that's over now. I was a fool to think even for a moment that I could ever put you out of my mind. I'll make it up to you, Callie."

Her voice fading, Callie whispered, ". . . my fault . . . I shouldn't have lied. But . . . it wasn't a lie . . . not when we were together. I wish . . ."

Callie's words choked to a halt. She struggled to breathe. Her eyes widened, and her voice rattled in her throat.

"Callie?" Panicking when Callie did not reply, Tanner rasped, "Callie . . ."

Callie went silent and still. Her eyes closed, and Tanner's mind froze. Clutching her close, he pressed his lips against her hair with a frantic, fervent prayer that ended abruptly when Callie went limp in his arms.

Bright sunshine shone on the spectators lining the path to the cemetery on the hill, but the funeral procession was small. Walking in the lead, his expression solemn, Tanner paused as the procession halted at last. He watched as the coffin was lifted down from the wagon and was then lowered into the open grave. He listened, unconscious of the words as the sober-faced minister said a prayer. He remained rigidly unmoving until the last shovel of dirt fell on the coffin and was finally smoothed into place.

With one last look, Tanner walked back down the hill and left it all behind him.

Chapter Ten

The bright morning sun forecast another hot day as the Circle M ranch hands gathered in the yard, whispering with furtive glances. At a word from Jeb, they followed him into the ranch house, where they paused just inside the door, then spread out to stand awkwardly against the living room wall.

Continuing on toward the small gathering at the foot of the stairs, Jeb paused at Clare's side to ask, "Is everything ready?"

Her expression cold, Clare replied, "By that I suppose you mean, did Doc Pierce get my husband out of bed yet—despite his desperate condition?" Not bothering to wait for his reply, she shrugged. "He's making a mistake. Tom is too ill. Tom's bound to have a setback. I've already told Doc that I won't have any part in it."

"That isn't exactly what I was meanin'." Jeb glanced around him. He spotted Ace Bellamy, impeccably dressed, his solemn, dark eyes intent on the stairs. He looked at the two women who stood beside him—Angie, her hand on his arm, her bright evening dress exchanged for a simple green cotton frock; and Lola, simply clothed as well. He saw Digby Jones standing flushed and silent a few feet to their rear, and Bill Hanes, with Annabelle Chapin standing rigidly erect and intensely sober beside him.

Jeb's gaze darted to the staircase when startled mumblings sounded in the room. Tiny and Manuelo were gradually descending with a robed, gaunt, and colorless Tom McBride supported between them. Jeb glanced again at Clare to see her color heighten when the men reached the foot of the stairs and lowered Tom into a chair provided for him there. He noted her almost imperceptible hesitation before she walked to Tom McBride's side.

Ace started up the stairs, and the room stirred again. He reached the head of the staircase in time to take her arm as Callie stepped into view to a chorus of admiring gasps.

*   *   *

Callie appeared pale and fragile; but wearing a simple white gown, with flowers threaded through her upswept, sun-streaked hair, she was the most beautiful bride Tanner had ever seen—his bride, and the woman he loved.

With eyes only for Callie, Tanner entered from the dining room and walked toward the staircase with Reverend Parkins. Tanner halted at the foot of the stairs, unconscious of Jeb's approach as the foreman took his place beside him.

Tanner's heart pounded. His throat was thick. It tightened to the point of pain as Ace escorted Callie down the stairs, then handed her over to him and stepped back, allowing Annabelle to assume the position of witness at Callie's side.

Tanner met Callie's honey-gold gaze. He recalled the simple words he'd whispered to her countless times during her recuperation from the grievous wound she had suffered a month earlier.

I love you. Callie. I was a fool, and I almost lost you. But you're mine now, and the mistakes of the past are behind us. All that's left is the love, and I'll never risk losing you again.

Reverend Parkins turned to the marked page in the leather-bound Bible he carried, and Tanner tore his gaze from Callie's. He listened as the minister addressed the assemblage. He waited impatiently for the vows he was about to speak as the gray-haired clergyman began.

"We are gathered here today to join Callie Logan and Tanner McBride in holy matrimony . . ."

The familiar passage rolled on. Callie held Tanner's gaze with her own as blurred images moved across her mind. She saw Tanner beside her bed, clutching her hand, his expression anguished, his deep voice quaking with emotion as he whispered the loving words which anchored her to life. She saw her silent procession of visitors: Ace, her dear friend who had made peace with Tanner during those strained hours; Angie, all former resentment erased by those few, violent moments in the saloon; Annabelle, who had turned to Tanner with an earnest apology that annulled the discord of the past; Digby Jones— dear, earnest Digby; Doc, ever watchful, seldom leaving her side; and Clare . . . who had slipped deviously into her room, her cold gaze chilling before Tanner arrived to remove her.

She had come so close to losing her life. She had still been waging the battle to survive when Sheriff Glennan's wire was received, stating that the third man involved in the robbery of the Foster State Bank was still actively being sought, but that Terry Malone's death had brought an end to the hunt for Matt's killer. She knew, however, that Tanner's rage had been such that he had not been able to accept those words until he had seen Terry Malone's body interred beneath six feet of hard, cold earth.

It seemed that so much time had passed, and this day had been so long in coming. Filled with emotion, Callie gazed ardently at her husband-to-be.

I love you, Tanner. I was so determined to avenge Matt's death that I almost lost you. I realize now that I demanded more of myself than Matt would ever have asked of me. I know he's here with me now, and that he's smiling. And I know that as long as I live, I'll love you just as I do at this moment, with more joy and love than I thought my heart could hold.

The silence of the room grew overwhelming as Reverend Parkins paused in his recitation. Tanner's gaze dropped to her lips, and Callie felt the tumult that shuddered through him. She saw the earnest commitment in his blue eyes when he took her hand, and she heard the love—sentiments that reverberated within her as well—when Tanner repeated the familiar, precious words.

"With this ring, I thee wed."

Epilogue

"No one's seen a trace of them yet, have they?"

Clare's fragile features turned downward in an unbecoming sneer, and Manuelo prepared himself for the onslaught of another tantrum. There had been many since the day that Senor Tanner took his woman to wife a week before, and the couple had then retired to the isolated cabin on the far northwestern corner of the Circle M that Senor Tanner had worked so hard to ready for his new bride. Morning had barely dawned before Senora Clare had summoned him from his room with the same question with which she had started each day since. He had hoped the vows that had been spoken between Senor Tanner and his woman would bring an end to Senora Clare's lust for her husband's younger son, but it was obvious that they had not.

Manuelo's concern deepened as Senora Clare walked to the living room window and stared out into the brightening sunlight, then rasped, "Did you ever see such fools? They've been confined in that cabin for days—-like lovesick children who can't get enough of each other! It's revolting!"

"They will soon tire of the isolation, and they will then return."

"No, they won't!" Livid, Clare turned back toward him. "Tom told me that Tanner made several things plain to him the day when Tanner walked into his sickroom and announced he was going to marry that tart. The first was that Tom was invited to witness the ceremony, but that whether Tom attended or not, Tanner intended to marry that woman here, *in his mother's house*. His *mother's* house—as if Emily McBride ever belonged here with a husband who never really loved her!"

Clare gave an unladylike snort. "Secondly, Tanner told Tom that until the other heirs returned and everything was settled to Tom's satisfaction, he and that woman would remain on the Circle M, but they'd be living in that filthy shack he fixed up for her."

Noting that his dear senora had begun shuddering with anger, Manuelo ventured, "It is perhaps better that way, with the woman out of your sight."

"Better? Really? I doubt that! I would enjoy being in that woman's company for a while, so I could show her up for the scheming slut that she is. She doesn't fool me, you see. All that talk about her coming to Sidewinder to find her brother's killer was nonsense. It was merely a ruse to trap Tanner, in the hope that she would end up with a portion of the Circle M when Tom dies. Well, she was badly mistaken! Neither she *nor* Tanner will end up with even a foot of Circle M soil! I'll see to that!"

"Senora—"

"She'll toss Tanner aside then, you'll see." Clare's delicate features brightened. "She'll turn her back on him and return to where she came from, and Tanner will come crawling back to me. Of course"—Clare shrugged—"I'll make him suffer a bit first. He deserves it. But before I'm done with him, I'll make sure he realizes all he missed while he whiled away empty hours with that cheap tart."

Clare's smile beamed. "I will so enjoy making him suffer, Manuelo. I will make him pay a hundredfold for every hour of torment he's caused me!"

"Senora—"

"Tanner said he *loves* her—do you believe it? Love!" Clare laughed aloud. "He's such a dunce. There *is* no such thing as love—only carnal desire, and that's what will win out in the end."

"Clare?"

Jerking toward the sound of her husband's unexpectedly strong summons from the bedroom on the floor above, Clare glared in sober silence.

"Clare, where are you?"

Turning rigidly toward Manuelo, Clare snapped with unexpected viciousness, "Well, what're you standing there for? Surely you have some chores to do in the kitchen."

"Clare?"

Her jaw tight, Clare spat, "I'm going upstairs." Starting toward the staircase, she turned back to Manuelo to say, "You'll see. I'll have Tanner, yet. It's just a matter of time."

Ace pulled on his trousers and walked to the window of his room. Squinting against the bright sunlight, he looked down on a main street almost devoid of traffic. Sidewinder was quiet in the early morning hours. It was peaceful, like the quiet that had somehow settled inside him since that day a week earlier when he had escorted Callie down the stairs into Tanner's arms.

Ace swallowed against the lump that rose to his throat. He was still uncertain what it was about Callie that had revived memories he had believed forgotten.

Ace's jaw hardened. He had thought to save Callie from Tanner McBride and the same anguish he, himself, had once thoughtlessly inflicted on someone long ago. He had thought he could teach Callie a few simple truths, but he was the person who had learned a lesson instead.

Startled from his thoughts as slender arms slipped around his waist from behind and full breasts pressed warmly against his back, Ace turned around to look down at Angie as she said, "What are you thinking about, Ace?"

What was he thinking about? He was thinking that the lesson Callie had taught him was simple—that love was rare and as precious as life.

Staring moments longer into Angie's dark eyes, Ace covered her mouth with his. Angie separated her lips and his kiss deepened.

Angie.

Callie.

Ace's arms tightened around Angie, at peace at last with the knowledge that he loved them both.

* * *

Early morning sunlight filtered through the lacy cover of trees, sending golden streams of light into the dark interior of the silent cabin, and Tanner awakened. Callie's naked flesh moved against his, and he drew her instinctively closer. Her scent filled his nostrils, her warmth filled his arms, her beauty filled his heart.

Tanner's gaze lingered on Callie's motionless face. The week since they had said their vows had passed so quickly. They had loved and talked and laughed, and had loved some more. They had walked in the early morning, and had taken long rides in the sun. They had bathed in a cool stream and had lain in the warm grass to dry, and had then indulged their passions again. They had returned to the cabin with no thoughts but of the present and of each other, and with no desire to allow the outside world in on the private paradise they shared.

Tanner turned Callie toward him as she stirred. He scrutinized the healthy, sun-kissed color of her cheeks, knowing he would never tire of seeing the warm flush there as sleep lingered, or the fluttering of her heavily fringed eyelids as she awoke to the new day. The coverlet slipped lower, revealing more of her smooth flesh, and Tanner brushed her rounded breast with his lips, noting with familiar pain the freshly healed scar from the wound that had nearly taken her life. He frowned, remembering the fear that had embedded itself deep inside him during those dark, endless days while she struggled to survive.

Needing her now, Tanner drew Callie closer until they lay flesh to flesh. He trailed his lips against her neck, against the line of her jaw and the slope of her cheek. He felt her palms moving over his back, drawing him closer. Her lips parted, her eyes opening briefly as she drew his mouth down to hers. The sweetness of her, the joy as their kiss lingered . . . Love expanded within him as he lay motionless, unwilling to end the wonder of the moment.

He recalled that awful moment when Callie lay gravely wounded, then went suddenly limp in his arms. He remembered his paralyzing fear, fear that continued into the long hours after Doc removed the bullet from her chest, while Callie tottered on the brink of death. He had sunk into despair. He had reviewed every moment they had spent together, cursing the time he had wasted. He had recalled his jealousy of Ace, a jealousy that halted the moment he realized that Ace loved Callie in a way that did not infringe upon the love Callie and he shared, and that Callie's brush with death had somehow made Ace value the love Angie offered him even more.

Drawing back from Callie at last, Tanner brushed a strand of hair from her cheek. He recalled his surprise when his father directed Manuelo and Tiny to take him downstairs to be present for the wedding ceremony. Burned into his memory were the few moments afterwards when his father's gaze met his, and he almost believed he saw approval flash briefly there.

Living with that moment, however, was Tanner's realization that the question that had haunted him for five long years—the question that had truly driven him home—had not yet been answered.

Then there was Clare, for whom a challenge never died. He had seen Clare's expression when she sneaked into Callie's sickroom, and then when Callie and he first stood as man and wife. He was determined that—

"What's the matter, Tanner?"

Brought back to the present by Callie's whisper, Tanner remained silent.

"Whatever it is, we'll face it together," she said.

"It might not be that easy."

Callie searched his face. Her eyes glittered with an emotion Tanner dared not identify when she said, "If it's Clare, don't worry. I can handle her."

Tanner's smile was brief. Yes, he knew she could.

Sobering, he whispered, "I can't be sure what's ahead of us, Callie. I don't know if Lauren or Stone will come home, or what will happen if they do. When Clare discovers the surprise that's waiting for her in Pa's will—"

"None of it matters. There's only one thing that's really important. I love you, Tanner."

Simple words.

Heartfelt words.

Words that lifted shadows from the heart.

Words that Tanner momentarily could not speak in return, for the emotion that tightened his throat.

So he showed her . . . tenderly, lovingly, with all the joy in his heart. . . . He showed her.

FREE BOOK GIVEAWAY!

From the imaginations of four of today's hottest romance authors comes a sweeping saga about a family divided.

In the midst of the vast, windswept Texas plains stands a ranch wrested from the wilderness with blood, sweat and tears. It is the shining legacy of Thomas McBride to his five living heirs. But along with the fertile acres and herds of cattle, each will inherit a history of scandal, lies and hidden lust that threatens to burn out of control.

The *Secret Fires* Series

ISBN	Title	Author	On Sale
0-8439-4826-4	*The Wild One*	Elaine Barbieri	02/2001
0-8439-4853-1	*The Half-Breed*	Bobbi Smith	04/2001
0-8439-4878-7	*The Agreement*	Constance O'Banyon	06/2001
0-8439-4880-9	*The Loner*	Evelyn Rogers	08/2001

Purchase *Secret Fires: The Wild One* and receive a free book from one of the participating authors as a special thank you from Dorchester Publishing Co., Inc.

Please indicate your preference:

	ISBN	Title	Author	On Sale
___	0-8439-4469-2	*Eagle*	Elaine Barbieri	01/1999
___	0-8439-4436-6	*Half-Breed's Lady*	Bobbi Smith	10/1998
___	0-8439-4492-7	*Texas Proud*	Constance O'Banyon	03/1999
	0-8439-4403-X	*Crown of Glory*	Evelyn Rogers	07/1998

PLEASE NOTE

**You must submit a dated store receipt for *Secret Fires: The Wild One*.
U.S. residents: Please include $1.75 for shipping and handling.
All non-U.S. residents (including Canadians): Please include $3.00 for shipping and handling.**

Please mail all materials to:
Dorchester Publishing Co., Inc.
Department: Secret Fires
276 Fifth Avenue, Suite 1008
New York, NY 10001

www.dorchesterpub.com.

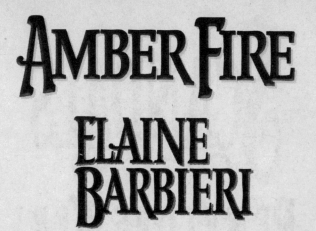

AMBER FIRE

ELAINE BARBIERI

Melanie Morganfield has grown from a precocious child to a beautiful woman in Asa Parker's lavish home. Melanie is grateful to Asa for all he has done for her, and in her devotion, she longs to make happy the final years of the man who has cared for her in every way that he could. But when she meets Stephen Hull, his dark and youthful sensuality heats her blood in a way which she can neither ignore or deny. She knows instinctively that she must not ever see Stephen again, or she will be fanning the flames which are destined to lead to amber fire.

___52290-X $5.50 US/$6.50 CAN

Dorchester Publishing Co., Inc.
P.O. Box 6640
Wayne, PA 19087-8640

Please add $1.75 for shipping and handling for the first book and $.50 for each book thereafter. NY, NYC, and PA residents, please add appropriate sales tax. No cash, stamps, or C.O.D.s. All orders shipped within 6 weeks via postal service book rate. Canadian orders require $2.00 extra postage and must be paid in U.S. dollars through a U.S. banking facility.

Name_____
Address_____
City_____ State_____ Zip_____
I have enclosed $_____ in payment for the checked book(s).
Payment <u>must</u> accompany all orders. ❑ Please send a free catalog.

SCANDALS

PENELOPE NERI

Marked by unwarranted rumor, Victoria's dance card was blank but for one handsome suitor: Steede Warring, eighth earl of Blackstone. Known behind his back as the Brute, he vows to have Victoria for his bride. Little does she suspect that Steede will uncover her body's hidden pleasures, and show her that only faith and trust can cast aside the bitter pain of scandals.

___4470-6 $5.99 US/$6.99 CAN

Dorchester Publishing Co., Inc.
P.O. Box 6640
Wayne, PA 19087-8640

Please add $1.75 for shipping and handling for the first book and $.50 for each book thereafter. NY, NYC, and PA residents, please add appropriate sales tax. No cash, stamps, or C.O.D.s. All orders shipped within 6 weeks via postal service book rate. Canadian orders require $2.00 extra postage and must be paid in U.S. dollars through a U.S. banking facility.

Name_____
Address_____
City_____ State_____ Zip_____
I have enclosed $_____ in payment for the checked book(s).
Payment <u>must</u> accompany all orders. ☐ Please send a free catalog.
CHECK OUT OUR WEBSITE! www.dorchesterpub.com

NIGHT RAVEN
Elaine Barbieri

With his fierce golden eyes, Night Raven sees a vision of the future that torments him, drives him to seek vengeance against the white man. Famed for his fearless exploits, sought after by the women of his tribe, he has sworn to show no mercy to the enemies of the Apache.

He sees her first in a dream, a woman with hair of shimmering gold and eyes of brilliant blue. Captured in battle, he is stunned when she appears to doctor his wounds, even more shocked by the traitorous longing she rouses in him. But when he manages to escape the fort, sweeping her onto his horse as hostage, he refuses to give in to his wildfire yearning. She, too, will know the torment of unfulfilled passion, he vows, for she is his enemy. But with each tender touch of her lips to his, Night Raven finds his resolve slipping, until captor becomes hostage and vengeance changes to mercy with the triumph of love.

___4723-3 $5.99 US/$6.99 CAN

Dorchester Publishing Co., Inc.
P.O. Box 6640
Wayne, PA 19087-8640

Please add $1.75 for shipping and handling for the first book and $.50 for each book thereafter. NY, NYC, and PA residents, please add appropriate sales tax. No cash, stamps, or C.O.D.s. All orders shipped within 6 weeks via postal service book rate. Canadian orders require $2.00 extra postage and must be paid in U.S. dollars through a U.S. banking facility.

Name_____
Address_____
City_____State_____Zip_____
I have enclosed $_____ in payment for the checked book(s).
Payment <u>must</u> accompany all orders. ❏ Please send a free catalog.

HAWK
Elaine Barbieri

"How can you stand to let him touch you, Eden? He's an *injun!*" Young and idealistic, Eden believes passion will overcome the obstacle of her lover's Kiowa heritage; instead, the hatred and prejudice of two cultures at war force them apart. "Her arms cling to you and your heart answers, but the woman will never by yours." Such is the shaman's prediction about the beautiful girl he once adored, but Iron Hawk refuses to believe it. Eden's betrayal might have sent him to the white man's jail, but her smooth, pale body will still be his. A hardened warrior now, he believes her capture will satisfy his need for revenge; instead, her love will heal their hearts and bring a lasting peace to their people.

___4646-6 $5.99 US/$6.99 CAN

Dorchester Publishing Co., Inc.
P.O. Box 6640
Wayne, PA 19087-8640

Please add $1.75 for shipping and handling for the first book and $.50 for each book thereafter. NY, NYC, and PA residents, please add appropriate sales tax. No cash, stamps, or C.O.D.s. All orders shipped within 6 weeks via postal service book rate. Canadian orders require $2.00 extra postage and must be paid in U.S. dollars through a U.S. banking facility.

Name_____
Address_____
City_____State_____Zip_____
I have enclosed $_____ in payment for the checked book(s).
Payment <u>must</u> accompany all orders. ☐ Please send a free catalog.
CHECK OUT OUR WEBSITE! www.dorchesterpub.com

WINGS OF A DOVE
ELAINE BARBIERI

On the harrowing train ride from the slums and tenements of New York City to the wide open farmland of Michigan, Allie Pierce and Delaney Marsh form a bond that no one can break. Traveling to find a new life of opportunity and adventure in the heartland, the two orphans uncover their hearts' only desire. From childhood to adulthood, their friendship grows into something neither have planned or expected. For without Allie, Delaney is nothing more than a street tough, striving to prove his mettle. And without Delaney, Allie is little more than a sad wisp of a girl, frightened and alone. But together, the two will be able to carve opportunity from misfortune, understanding from discord, and ultimately find a passion that will last a lifetime.

___52323-X $5.99 US/$6.99 CAN

Dorchester Publishing Co., Inc.
P.O. Box 6640
Wayne, PA 19087-8640

Please add $1.75 for shipping and handling for the first book and $.50 for each book thereafter. NY, NYC, and PA residents, please add appropriate sales tax. No cash, stamps, or C.O.D.s. All orders shipped within 6 weeks via postal service book rate. Canadian orders require $2.00 extra postage and must be paid in U.S. dollars through a U.S. banking facility.

Name_____
Address_____
City_____State_____Zip_____
I have enclosed $_____ in payment for the checked book(s).
Payment <u>must</u> accompany all orders. ❏ Please send a free catalog.
CHECK OUT OUR WEBSITE! www.dorchesterpub.com